W9-CTB-926

"Stay as long as you need to, Jess."

Chase forced himself to make the offer lightly, without any pressure. "We'll work it out tomorrow."

Funny, they spoke to each other like they were strangers. Like they'd met for the first time tonight, when in reality they'd known each other for a lifetime.

Before she could make up another excuse to refuse, Chase left, went downstairs to wait.

He needed to hear the truth from Jess, but he also feared what that truth might be. Feared that he would have to testify against her if she'd attacked Dalton for whatever reason. Justified or not, her cold-blooded father-in-law would see to it that she paid dearly, and he had the political pull and financial means to do it.

When Chase had signed up for the job, both as a soldier and deputy sheriff, he'd sworn to uphold the law. But experience had taught him that sometimes justice could be bought by the highest bidder. This was one of those situations.

Regardless, he vowed to stand by Jess, come hell or high water. After what he'd done to her all those years ago, it was the least he could do for her now.

Dear Reader,

Children are a blessing. I've learned that from being a mother for almost thirty years. Every milestone for each of my three children has been imprinted in my memories—their first steps, first words, first loves, first missteps and everything in between. Although they're well into adulthood, I still find myself worrying incessantly over their happiness. At times I wonder if I could have done a better job raising them, though I firmly believe they've turned out pretty well despite any mistakes I've made. I predict that if luck prevails, I will continue to worry about them for the next thirty years.

I believe the fierce need to protect our offspring is inherently tied to instinct, and that instinct plays a pivotal role in this book. Not only do you have a father becoming acquainted with his child, you have a mother who will do anything to protect that child, even if it means compromising her own happiness. The question is—exactly how far will she go?

You'll find the answer in *The Son He Never Knew*, and I sincerely hope you enjoy the journey.

Happy reading!

Kristi Gold

The Son He Never Knew

Kristi Gold

Harlequin®

TORONTO NEW YORK LONDON
AMSTERDAM PARIS SYDNEY HAMBURG
STOCKHOLM ATHENS TOKYO MILAN MADRID
PRAGUE WARSAW BUDAPEST AUCKLAND

If you purchased this book without a cover you should be aware that this book is stolen property. It was reported as "unsold and destroyed" to the publisher, and neither the author nor the publisher has received any payment for this "stripped book."

Recycling programs
for this product may
not exist in your area.

ISBN-13: 978-0-373-71744-6

THE SON HE NEVER KNEW

Copyright © 2011 by Kristi Goldberg

All rights reserved. Except for use in any review, the reproduction or utilization of this work in whole or in part in any form by any electronic, mechanical or other means, now known or hereafter invented, including xerography, photocopying and recording, or in any information storage or retrieval system, is forbidden without the written permission of the publisher, Harlequin Enterprises Limited, 225 Duncan Mill Road, Don Mills, Ontario, Canada M3B 3K9.

This is a work of fiction. Names, characters, places and incidents are either the product of the author's imagination or are used fictitiously, and any resemblance to actual persons, living or dead, business establishments, events or locales is entirely coincidental.

This edition published by arrangement with Harlequin Books S.A.

For questions and comments about the quality of this book please contact us at Customer_eCare@Harlequin.ca.

® and TM are trademarks of the publisher. Trademarks indicated with ® are registered in the United States Patent and Trademark Office, the Canadian Trade Marks Office and in other countries.

www.Harlequin.com

Printed in U.S.A.

ABOUT THE AUTHOR

Kristi Gold has always believed that love has remarkable healing powers and she feels very fortunate to be able to weave stories of love and commitment. As a bestselling author, a National Readers' Choice winner and a Romance Writers of America RITA® Award finalist, Kristi has learned that although accolades are wonderful, the most cherished rewards come from personal stories shared by readers and networking with other authors, both published and aspiring. You may contact Kristi through her website, www.kristigold.com, on Facebook or through snail mail at P.O. Box 24197, Waco, Texas 76702 (please include an SASE for response).

Books by Kristi Gold

To all the men and women in the armed forces
who sacrifice daily to keep the world safe.
And to those who have made the ultimate
sacrifice—giving their lives.

PROLOGUE

HE WAS THE LAST PERSON she expected to see at her dorm room doorstep.

As soon as the initial shock disappeared, Jessica Keller squealed with delight, hurled herself into Chase Reed's arms and hugged him hard. But when his frame went stiff as steel, she stepped back to assess her best friend's mood.

In the eight months since she'd seen him, he hadn't changed at all, at least when it came to his appearance. He still wore his golden hair in close-cropped military style, still wore sand-colored camouflage fatigues and heavy boots. Six-feet-three-inches of prime fourth-generation soldier, exactly what he'd always wanted to be and now was. Yet something in his brown eyes seemed different, maybe a little more intense, but definitely different. Then again, after the Towers fell three months ago, the whole world had changed forever.

"What are you doing here this time of night?" she asked when he failed to speak or smile.

"We have to talk."

Chase sounded so serious, Jess's anxiety took a major leap right behind her imagination. "Is something wrong with Mom and Dad? Your mom and dad? Or is it—"

"Calm down, Jess," he said in the reassuring tone she'd grown to expect and sometimes resent. "Everyone's fine. If you'll let me in, I'll explain." He leaned to his right and looked behind her. "Unless I'm interrupting."

She frowned at his assumption. "My roommate's already gone home for the holidays, so there's no one here but little old me."

"Are you sure you're not hiding your boyfriend in the closet?" Chase followed the query with a visual sweep down her body and back up again, much the same as she'd done to him a few minutes earlier.

A second passed before Jess realized why he might think he'd intruded on an intimate interlude. She'd answered the door wearing a tattered white terry robe, her favorite furry pink slippers and not much else.

She twisted her damp hair in a knot at her neck and sent him a dirty look. "I finished a shift at the coffee shop an hour ago and I just took a shower, so get your mind out of the sewer. Besides, the university doesn't take too kindly to boys visiting girls in their rooms after 9:00 p.m."

He looked totally skeptical. "You mean to tell me Dalton hasn't been up here after hours?"

Her long-time boyfriend happened to be a sore subject she didn't care to discuss with Chase, especially under the current circumstances. "Let's leave him out of this, okay?"

"Not a problem. He's my least favorite topic of conversation anyway. And if you're worried about breaking the rules, we can go somewhere else to talk."

"Don't be ridiculous, Chase," she said. "It's almost eleven, it's cold outside and my hair's wet. Besides, the place is pretty much cleared out. However, if you'd called me in advance, I could have saved you the trip. I planned to be back in Placid tomorrow after work."

"This couldn't wait until tomorrow."

In order to unravel the mystery, Jess stepped aside and made a sweeping gesture with one arm. "Welcome to my humble abode, heavy emphasis on *humble*."

Chase breezed past her and after Jess closed the door, she turned to find that he made her tiny room seem even tinier. She tightened the robe's sash, feeling somewhat naked even though she was sufficiently covered. "Now tell me what couldn't wait until tomorrow, Mr. Army Man."

Chase strolled between the two twin beds and picked up a photo of Dalton from the nightstand. "Where's the demon tonight?"

The "pet" name Chase had given her high school sweetheart grated on Jess's nerves. "I have no idea where he is because right now we're taking a break."

His gaze snapped to hers. "Permanent break, I hope."

She wasn't the least bit surprised by his comment. Chase and Dalton had been embroiled in one-upmanship since elementary school. "Right now I don't know what's going to happen."

His scowl returned. "So you didn't get engaged?"

Suddenly it became all too clear to her why Chase had shown up unannounced. "You've been talking to Rachel."

He set the frame down carefully though he looked as if he wanted to hurl it. "Yeah. I ran into her yesterday at the diner. She told me the Big D proposed and I figured since she's his sister, she should know."

Dalton had done more than simply propose. He'd offered to whisk her away to Vegas over the Christmas holidays for a quickie wedding. She opted to keep that little tidbit to herself. "I told him I wasn't sure I was ready to get married, and he said to let him know when I made up my mind. In the meantime, he doesn't want to see me."

Chase gave her a champion smirk. "You mean he's blackmailing you into saying yes."

Jess gritted her teeth and spoke through them. "Would you cut him some slack, Chase? We're not kids anymore and this whole competition thing between you and Dalton is getting old."

"Maybe we aren't kids, but my guess is Dalton hasn't changed, Jess. You haven't always seen the side of him that we have."

We as in him. Same song, fiftieth verse. "I know Dalton better than anyone. I also know he'd never do anything to hurt me."

He stared at the ceiling for a moment before bringing his attention back to her. "Fine. I'll drop it for now. But I need you to promise me something."

Jess hugged her arms close to her middle. "That depends on the promise."

"First, I want you to sit." He dropped down on the edge of her bed and patted the space beside him.

Jess claimed the spot and prepared for a promise she wasn't certain she wanted to hear, much less make, especially if it involved Dalton. "I'm all ears, so talk."

Chase studied the industrial tile beneath his boots. "Promise me you won't do anything stupid. I can't leave here tonight unless I know you're going to be okay."

She found his sullen attitude disturbing. "I'm not going to do anything stupid."

Finally he looked at her. "Are you sure? You've always been a jumper first and a thinker later."

She rolled her eyes at his dig over her impulsive nature. "Yes, I'm sure. If you don't believe me, then I guess you'll just have to wait and see if I have a ring on my finger Christmas morning."

His gaze slid away again. "I won't be here on Christmas."

"Let me guess. You and the guys are going on your annual hunting trip, leaving the women home for the holidays to fend for themselves. That must thrill your mother—"

"I received my orders today to head back to the base in the morning."

Jess swallowed hard to clear the fear from her throat. "Why so soon?"

He took her hands into his and shifted to face her. "I'm shipping out tomorrow night."

"To where?" She worried she already knew the answer.

"Afghanistan."

The word sounded like a gunshot in the small space and Jess felt it land straight in her heart. She yanked away from his grasp and came to her feet to face him. "You can't go, Chase. You have to find some way not to go."

"I have to go, Jess," he said. "I don't have a choice, and even if I did, I'd still go."

She was caught somewhere between panic and fury. "What are you going to do over there?"

"That's classified."

"You mean dangerous," she said as she sat on the opposite bed.

"Look, Jess, I've been training for almost three years to serve my country, just like my father and his father—"

"And your great-grandfather," she interjected. "I know the story." And she did—that story and several others pertaining to war. She recalled how her dad used to speak in an almost reverent tone about the boys who went to Vietnam and never came back. About how he'd been lucky to survive. Still, she'd never really understood the sacrifice her father and so many others had made…until now.

Chase raked a hand over his jaw and sighed. "You don't have to worry about me, Jess. I'm a damn good soldier."

Of course he was. He'd always been good at everything, from sports to school and reportedly sex—if she chose to put stock in the rumors spread over at least three counties. All that aside, when they were growing up, he'd been consumed by video games involving battles and espionage. But this wasn't a game. Not even close.

She couldn't seem to control the need to lash out. "Great. Go be a soldier. Forget about your family and all the people who love you."

"I won't forget you," he said quietly. "And I can't forget that it's my duty to keep you and my family safe."

Jess wanted to scream, to bargain, to beg him to stay. But all the pleading in the world would be futile. She couldn't change his mind and in reality, she wouldn't want him to be anything less than he was—her hero. He always had been.

As her anger began to dissolve and the sorrow set in, Jess lowered her face in her hands and sobbed from abject fear. Fear for him. Fear for herself.

Chase joined her and pulled her close to his side, holding her tightly while she dampened the front of his field jacket with her tears. They stayed that way for a time until she felt composed enough to speak. "What am I going to do while you're off battling the bad guys, Chase?"

He thumbed away a tear from her cheek. "You're going to go on with your life as usual, just like you have since I signed up for this gig after graduation."

She leaned over and grabbed a tissue from the box on the nightstand. "Just so you know, if you die, I'm going to have to kill you. You have to come back and get married and make a bunch of little Chases."

He released a cynical laugh. "You know I'm not the settling down kind, Jess."

She'd heard him say that more than once. "You might change your mind when you get over there, Chase. You might even wish you had a girlfriend back home waiting for you."

He took her right hand and laced their fingers together. "Just knowing I have your support is enough. You can send me an email every now and then."

She tried to smile but it fell flat. "I'm going to write you the old-fashioned way, with a pen and paper. I'll make sure you know all the trashy gossip from home. Heaven knows someone's bound to do something newsworthy sooner or later."

"As long as it's not you."

"I'll try not to run naked through the town square."

He grinned, flashing his to-die-for dimples that had dropped many a woman in their tracks. "I'll get you an address as soon as I have it. Feel free to send me some of your mom's oatmeal raisin cookies, too."

"I'll make the cookies."

"I thought you didn't want me to die."

She sent him her best sneer. "I take back every nice thing I've ever said about you, Chase Reed."

"You know you love me, Gertrude." He followed the use of her horrid middle name with a winning grin.

She'd forgive him anything tonight. She'd also carry the image of that smile close to her heart until he came back home again. "And you're going to miss me."

His features turned somber again. "Yeah, I am. Just don't forget me while I'm gone."

How could she ever forget him or what they'd meant to each other for most of their lives?

Chase pulled her into a bear hug and when he released her, Jess resisted the urge to cling to him. "What time does your bus leave?"

He took a glance at his watch. "6:00 a.m. sharp."

She saw an opportunity and went for it. "Do you mind staying a little while longer? Just another hour or two. We can watch some corny sitcom and make up our own lines, which no doubt will be much funnier." Anything to spend a little more time in his presence, until Jess was ready to let him go. Like she'd ever be ready to let him go.

Chase hesitated a moment. "I have to get Dad's truck back to him and I really need some sleep. Haven't had a whole lot of that lately."

Jess suspected she'd be in the same boat after he left. "You can take a nap before you head back."

"I don't know, Jess. If I fell asleep, I might not wake up in time to catch the bus."

All the more reason for him to stay. "I'll make sure you don't sleep that long. Besides, you can't march in here, announce you're about to head off to a war zone and then just leave me all by myself to deal with it."

Jess could tell by his expression she'd worn him down. She confirmed that when he said, "Okay, but only an hour or so."

"Great." She hopped onto her bed, scooted as close to the wall as she could to reserve a place for him. "Take off your shoes and stay a while, sailor."

"I'm not a sailor," he grumbled as he unlaced his boots and then toed out of them. "U.S. Army, Special Forces, and don't forget it."

Not much chance in that, thanks to the obvious reminders.

After Chase settled in beside her, Jess flipped on the TV with the remote and chose an ancient rerun. He slid his arm beneath her shoulder, she rested her cheek against his chest, like they'd done a thousand times before.

A span of silence passed before Jess said, "I wish we could go back to those summers when we used to hang out at the pond. We had some great times."

"Before you started dating the jerk," he muttered.

"He's really a good guy, Chase."

He kept his gaze fixed on the ceiling. "Being born to a father who owns half the state of Mississippi doesn't make him a good guy."

"And being rich doesn't make him bad, either."

He nailed her with a serious stare. "Are you going to marry him, Jess?"

She'd asked herself that question many times during the month she and Dalton had been apart. So far, no solid answer. "I could do worse."

"You could do better."

"He's going to take good care of me, Chase. He'll make sure I have a great life."

"Sounds to me like you've made up your mind."

Not exactly. "If I do decide to go through with it, I'll wait until you're home so you can be my man of honor."

His frown returned. "Thanks, but no thanks. I don't see myself being front and center when I believe you'll be making the biggest mistake of your life."

That stung Jess to the core. "I wish you'd give me some credit. I'm not a complete airhead."

He shifted to his side and surveyed her face. "I just want you to be happy, Jess. I want to leave here knowing you're going to have a solid future with someone who deserves you." He sounded and looked so sincere, so sweet, that Jess started to cry again.

Chase held her securely in his strong arms. "It's going to be okay," he told her in a soft, even tone.

"Nothing's okay," she said. "It won't ever be okay if you go."

He pressed a kiss on her forehead, brushed a kiss across one cheek, then the other. "I'll be back. I promise."

"You better."

As the time ticked away, they simply stared at each other, caught in a place they'd never been before. And then in one unexpected, defining moment, Chase kissed Jess on the lips. Not an innocent kiss. A deep, insistent kiss that made her head spin out of control.

In all the years they'd known each other—practically since birth—not once had they ever ventured beyond a platonic bond. Not once had Chase ever made a move on her. For years Jess had told herself she'd never wanted more from him. She'd rejected the fantasies that crept in on occasion as she wondered what it would be like to kiss him. What it would be like if he saw her as a woman, not a surrogate sister.

Chase tipped his forehead against hers. "Tell me to leave, Jess."

That was the last thing she planned to tell him. "I want you to stay." And she did, right or wrong.

He framed her face in his palms, forced her to look right into his eyes. "If I don't go, I don't know what might happen. Right now I just need…"

"To be with someone," she finished for him, knowing she risked becoming only another of his meaningless hook-ups if she let this continue. But she couldn't—wouldn't—let the chance go by, consequences be damned. "You need to feel alive, Chase, and I need that, too. Whatever happens from this point forward, nothing will change between us. We'll still be friends and no one will have to know."

"But I'll know, Jess. And I can't give you—"

Jess pressed a fingertip against his lips to silence him. "You've given me more than you know." She lifted her finger and pressed her lips against his. "Now no more talk." She took his hand and slid it beneath the robe's opening above her breasts. "Just touch."

That seemed to unleash something in Chase, some-thing uncontrolled but unbelievably sexy as he skimmed his palms down her body. Somehow she'd managed to bring them past the turn-back point, but she honestly didn't care. She only cared about the prospect of being with him completely.

Maybe this was the reason she'd held back commit-ting to Dalton. Maybe subconsciously she'd always loved Chase a little more than she'd cared to admit. More than the way he loved her as a friend.

Regardless, this could be the last opportunity to know what she'd been missing. The last chance to explore the feelings for Chase that had suddenly surfaced. Possibly the last time she ever saw him again.

She'd been caught between two men for years—the one who treated her like a queen, and the one who'd viewed her as only a best friend. The one who could give her the world, and the other who could only give her this one night.

She wanted this one night… even if it proved to be a life-altering mistake.

CHAPTER ONE

Placid, Mississippi
Ten years later

THERE HAD TO BE SOME MISTAKE.

As he pulled out of the sheriff's station parking lot, Chase Reed requested the dispatcher repeat the address one more time.

1101 Oakwood Lane.

No mistake, and no time to waste.

Chase flipped on his emergency lights and siren as he sped through downtown, concerned over what he might be facing when he arrived at his destination on the outskirts of Placid—the recently-divorced Jessica Keller Wainwright's home. He only knew that a domestic dispute call had been placed by a hysterical woman and an ambulance had been dispatched. He didn't know who had been injured or how. One thing was certain. If Dalton Wainwright had laid a finger on Jess, he'd kill him.

In the six months since he'd returned to Placid, he'd only spoken to Jess once by phone, a tense conversation that involved generalities—her new job teaching second grade, his new job as deputy sheriff and briefly about her divorce, like they were only acquaintances. Even though they'd corresponded through the years, they'd never talked about the night before he left for his first tour of duty.

He hated that he'd obviously hurt her with his careless behavior. Hated that she'd run off and married Wainwright two weeks later. Hated that he'd somehow driven her to that decision and in turn, set a course that had ultimately led to this moment.

Chase's mind continued to reel with the possibilities as he whipped into the lengthy drive leading to the massive redbrick mansion. He barely had the car stopped before he slid out of the driver's side and his feet hit the pavement. A gust of unseasonably cold, bitter wind sent a spiral of leaves across the stone walkway as he strode past the for sale sign toward the planked porch. The white holiday lights hanging from the eaves and the huge artificial Christmas tree filling the entry window gave the appearance of normalcy. But when he found the front door partially ajar, he prepared for anything but a normal situation.

Chase poised his hand on the Glock holstered at his hip as he moved into the foyer, an automatic reaction resulting from hour upon hour of military training. But in this instance, he wasn't the soldier navigating wartorn territory. He was the deputy sheriff doing his duty no matter what he might encounter.

Senses on high alert, he cocked his head to listen as he walked past the ornate staircase and down the tiled corridor. The sound of harsh sobs caused him to quicken his pace, his heart keeping an equally rapid tempo. The minute he entered the great room, he pulled up short to survey the scene.

To his left, Jess sat on the floor, her back to a white

leather sofa, hugging her knees to her chest as she rocked back and forth like a lost child. Chase instinctively started toward her until something caught his immediate attention from the corner of his eye. He turned to see a figure crumpled near the stone hearth—only to discover it was Dalton Wainwright.

When he noticed the blood pooling around Dalton's head, images of war zipped through Chase's brain. Fallen comrades, chaos and confusion. Death and destruction. A fatal error he'd made that couldn't be rectified...

Chase again forced the memories away as he walked to his long-time nemesis, crouched down, pressed his fingertips against Dalton's neck and fortunately for Jess, found a pulse.

"He's dead, isn't he?" she asked in a tone strangely absent of emotion.

"He's alive but unconscious," he assured her, although right then he wasn't sure of anything.

When he heard the wail of sirens, Chase immediately went to Jess, knelt and took her by the shoulders. "Are you okay?" he asked, even though he could tell she wasn't from the undeniable shock in her eyes.

"It was an accident," she muttered as her gaze slid away. "No one's fault."

Chase couldn't imagine Jess would intentionally injure her ex-husband, but he wasn't fool enough to deny anything was possible when it came to volatile relationships. "Look at me, Jess." Once he finally had her attention, he added, "When the paramedics get here, don't say anything about what happened."

"But I didn't mean—"

"Don't talk about it," he cautioned again. "You have to remember who you're dealing with here, even if it was an accident."

Realization dawned in her expression. "Edwin," she said in a whisper.

"Yeah. Your ex-father-in-law could make this tough on you. And anything you tell me could be used against you in court if it comes to that."

Her eyes went wide with terror. "Court?"

Before Chase had a chance to reassure her, the sound of gurney wheels echoing through the foyer interrupted his train of thought. He straightened and met the EMTs as soon as they entered the room. "He's still alive," he told a fifty-something paramedic named Joe. "But it looks like he has a pretty serious head injury."

"We'll take it from here," Joe said before he and his partner went to work on Dalton.

Chase helped Jess to her feet and guided her down the hall to the formal dining room he found nearby. After he had her seated in a chair at the polished mahogany table, he asked, "Where's your son?"

"Upstairs."

Chase wondered exactly what the boy had witnessed during the last few minutes. "I want you to stay right here while I go check on him."

She nodded like she needed complete guidance. Chase understood that all too well.

He strode back into the great room in time to find the crew loading Dalton onto the stretcher, but he didn't stop to check on his status. Instead, he took the stairs two at a time. When he reached the top landing, he discovered Danny Wainwright, dressed in a pair of race-car pajamas, standing against the wall with his gaze focused on the hardwood floor.

After Danny finally looked up, Chase was amazed over how much he resembled Jess, with the exception of his blond hair. Fortunately he couldn't see a scrap of Dalton in him, but he did see the same vacant stare his mother had exhibited a few moments ago.

More recollections of another time, another foreign place and another child intruded into Chase's thoughts. He had to get a grip on the present and stay out of the past for both Jess and her son's sake.

Chase swept his cowboy hat from his head and kept a safe distance. "Hey, Danny. I'm Deputy Reed, a friend of your mom's."

The boy blinked but remained silent.

He decided tackling Danny's immediate worry might help. "The paramedics are taking your dad to the hospital, so he's in good hands."

Still no response, and Chase wasn't real sure how to proceed. "Do you want to go see your mom?"

This time Danny shook his head, which fueled Chase's concerns. If the kid had witnessed Jess injuring Dalton, inadvertent or not, he could have a damn hard time forgiving his mother. He wasn't too keen on leaving the boy alone, but he didn't want to push him, either. "Why don't you wait in your room and I'll have your mother come up to talk to you."

Without any reply or hesitation, the boy headed down the hall and walked through a door to his right. Chase followed behind and entered a bedroom decked out in dark blue walls and baseball memorabilia. A typical kid's room that reminded him of his own when he'd been about Danny's age, only he'd been more inclined to collect football souvenirs.

When Danny curled up on the bed facing the wall, Chase felt the need to say something else, to offer some words of comfort, but he had no real experience dealing with childhood trauma. "I'll be back in a few minutes with your mom, okay?"

Danny didn't respond, didn't even shrug his shoulders to acknowledge the suggestion. With any luck, reuniting him with Jess would be the key to his comfort. Then again, maybe not, but Chase felt he had no choice in the matter.

As he sprinted back down the stairs, Chase heard the sound of an all-too-familiar voice coming from somewhere in the house. A booming voice that belonged to his father, the sheriff. No surprise that Buck would have been summoned, considering the nature of the crime. Correction. Accident. Chase refused to believe anything else until proof landed in front of his nose. Even then he'd have a hard time buying Jess flying into a homicidal rage.

He made his way back to the dining room where he'd left Jess and arrived just in time to hear his dad say, "You're going to have to give me more details than that."

Furious over Buck's tone, Chase stepped inside the opening, hands fisted at his sides. "Can I have a word with you?"

Buck turned to him and scowled. "I'm taking Jess's statement, son, so you'll need to wait a minute."

Chase was tempted to remind his father that he should call him by his proper name, not *son*. "It's important."

Buck forked his fingers through his silver hair and

sighed. "Fine," he said before turning to Jess. "Don't go anywhere."

As soon as Buck joined him at the front door out of Jess's earshot, Chase turned his fury on his father. "What in the hell are you doing?"

"My job, exactly what you should be doing, too. She told me you hadn't questioned her about Dalton's injuries."

"She said it was an accident and that's all I needed to know."

Buck hooked his thumbs in his pockets and stared him down like he was thirteen, not thirty-one. "Doesn't matter what she said, boy. You have to get all the facts to put into the report."

Chase pointed in the direction of the dining room. "That's Jess in there, Dad. The same girl who used to come with her folks to our house for Sunday dinner and dominoes."

"Yeah, and you're too close to the situation. That's why I called in Barkley to assist me. He should be here in about five minutes."

That only increased Chase's wrath. "Barkley can't find his way out of a feed sack. He'll arrest Jess first and ask questions later."

Buck raised a brow. "Any reason why you think Jess should be arrested?"

He reflected on Danny's reaction and decided to keep his mouth shut for now. "Like I said, she claims it was an accident, and I have no reason to believe it wasn't."

"You know the procedure," Buck said. "I still have to take an official statement."

"Then do it in the morning after she's had some time to recover."

"That's not the way it works, son."

"Make it work, Dad. Right now she needs to rest."

"She can't stay here, Chase. We'll need to gather evidence in case Dalton dies during the night."

On one hand, he didn't give a rat's ass if Dalton died. On the other, he had to consider what that might mean for Jess. "She can stay with me tonight and I'll have her at the department first thing in the morning."

"She can get a room at the motel."

He had no intention of sticking Jess in some seedy, pay-by-the-hour dive on the outskirts of town. "She's in shock and so is her kid. She needs to be in a place where she's comfortable."

Chase could see Buck's frustration beginning to build. "And you think that's with you? Best I recall, she hasn't come around once since you've been home."

Understandable why they'd been avoiding each other, but he'd be damned if he let his father in on a ten-year-old secret. "She's been busy getting rid of Dalton."

Chase realized how questionable that sounded when Buck said, "Maybe that's what she did tonight, got rid of him once and for all."

He couldn't quite understand why his father was bent on treating Jess like some black widow lying in wait to off her former husband. Buck might be one of the good guys, but he could be an obsessed hard-ass when it came to the job. If serving as sheriff for thirty some odd years did that to a man, Chase wanted no part of it, even if that's exactly what was expected of him.

"Tell you what, Sheriff," he said. "If you'll stop jumping to conclusions, then I'll have Jess to you bright and early. But if you're not going to stick to the innocent until proven guilty clause, then I'll be damned if I'm going to continue to work for you."

Chase could see the cogs spinning fast in Buck's head. Placid had suffered a deputy shortage for years, and there sure as hell wasn't a long line waiting to sign on. If he up and resigned, he'd leave his dad high and dry and working longer hours again, which sure wouldn't set well with the missus.

Buck took on a look of reluctant submission. "Okay, you bring her home and have her in my office no later than 8:00 a.m. And have her boy there, too. Maybe between the two of them, we can shed some light on this thing."

As far as Chase was concerned, having Danny put through the wringer was entirely up to Jess, at least for now. "Fine. You can go. I'll handle it from here."

"I'll go outside to wait for Barkley until you leave with Jess." Buck turned toward the door then stopped and pointed at Chase. "8:00 a.m. sharp or I'll come down to the cabin and get her myself."

"I'll have her there, Sheriff." And he would, right on time. He didn't sleep much these days anyway. Too much on his mind. Too many nightmares to count.

After his dad had finally left the immediate premises, Chase made his way to the dining room, only to find it deserted. Jess would've had to walk past him to go up the stairs, which made him wonder if she'd headed out the back door. With that major dilemma in mind, he strode to the back of the house and came upon a rear staircase adjacent to the top-of-the-line kitchen. Hopefully that had been her escape route, if in fact she felt the need to escape.

He opted to give Jess the benefit of the doubt and headed to the second floor. As suspected, he discovered her in Danny's room, perched on the edge of the bed, sifting her hands through her son's hair.

Chase paused a moment to take in the subtle alterations in Jess's appearance. She'd cut her long auburn hair to her shoulders and she wore the kind of loose-fitting clothes designed to hide her figure. At five-foot-three, she'd always been small in stature but tough as barbwire. But the most noticeable change could be found in her light amber eyes when she leveled her gaze on him. The former outgoing cheerleader, who could talk the bark off a tree, looked lost and defeated. He damned Dalton Wainwright for that. Damned him for sucking the life out of Jess. Damned himself for staying away from her because of his own guilt.

Chase remained in the doorway and in a low tone said, "Pack a bag for you and your son. You're going to stay with me for a few days."

"Why?"

"According to procedure, you have to leave the premises until you give your statement. And even if you could stay, do you really think that's a good idea?" He nodded toward Danny.

"No," she said, her voice barely above a whisper. "But I don't want to put you out, Chase. I can call around and find somewhere to stay. Maybe with Sam and Savannah or Matt and Rachel."

He prepared to shoot down her protest with logic. "First of all, Savannah and Sam are in Hawaii and won't be back for a couple of days. Secondly, I figure Rachel's on her way to the hospital to see about Dalton by now." Blood ties trumped friendship any day of the week, even if Rachel and Jess had been friends for years and Rachel's brother was about as sorry as they came.

"As far as the rest of the town goes," he continued, "do you want this getting out any sooner than it has to?"

She shook her head. "No, I don't."

"Then it's settled," he said. "I'll wait downstairs while you get your things together."

She twisted the ruby ring that once belonged to her grandmother round and round her right ring finger, a habit she'd developed long ago. "I appreciate your hospitality, but we'll only stay until I can make other arrangements."

Funny, they spoke to each other like they were strangers. Like they'd met for the first time tonight when in reality they'd known each other for a lifetime. "You're welcome to stay as long as you need to, but we'll work it out tomorrow."

Before she could make up another excuse to refuse the offer, Chase walked out of the room and went back downstairs to wait.

He needed to hear the truth from Jess, but he also feared what that truth might be. Feared that he would have to testify against her if she'd attacked Dalton for whatever reason. Justified or not, her cold-blooded father-in-law would see to it that she paid dearly, and he had the political pull and financial means to do it.

When Chase had signed up for the job, both as a soldier and deputy sheriff, he'd sworn to uphold the law. But experience had taught him sometimes justice could be bought by the highest bidder. This was one of those situations.

Regardless, he vowed to stand by Jess, come hell or high water. After what he'd done to her all those years ago, it was the least he could do for her now.

ALONE WITH HER CHILD in Chase's sparsely furnished guestroom, Jess claimed a space next to Danny on the twin bed. She pulled the covers over his thin shoulders and whisked a kiss across his cheek. And when he turned away from her, she felt her heart shatter one painful fissure at a time.

Still, she rested her face on the pillow, hoping that he found a measure of comfort in her presence. But since the moment they'd arrived at Chase's house, he'd refused to look at her, refused to speak a word. She couldn't really blame him after what he'd endured, both tonight and throughout his nine years on earth.

She smiled at the slight curl at the nape of his neck, remembered how she'd been terrified to hold him after he was born and then soon found it hard to put him down. She recalled his baby-soft smell, how little time it had taken to bond with him. He'd been such a joy from the beginning, the brightest part of her day.

Jess's life had been littered with what-ifs and regrets, of foolish decisions she'd wished she could take back, but having her son had never been one of them. She should have left Dalton a long time ago, when Danny had been too young to understand the ongoing battle between his mother and father. Before Dalton had begun to demean both son and wife.

Her precious baby, who'd been quick with a grin and

fast on his feet, had become withdrawn and doubted himself, just as she had since the day she'd married Dalton Wainwright. Yet over the past two months since the divorce, he'd begun to smile more often, talk more freely and even his grades had improved. Now this horrible, horrible incident could scar him beyond repair.

Jess leaned over to see if Danny was sleeping, only to determine he still seemed wide awake. "Do you want some water?" she asked.

He shook his head no.

"Do you want me to stay in here with you tonight?"

Again, another negative response.

She couldn't blame him for his anger. After all, what had happened tonight had been entirely her fault, and he was going to suffer the brunt of her decisions for years, if not forever. Mothers were supposed to protect their children, and she'd failed miserably.

Jess was torn between staying a little longer with Danny and having a serious talk with Chase. She didn't dare discuss all the details with him. She wouldn't involve him more than she already had. But she could attempt to reestablish their friendship that had been damaged a decade ago, thanks to another error in judgment. That could be asking too much, but she had to try. Like it or not, she needed Chase's support more than she ever had before.

She pressed a kiss against his cheek. "It's going to be all right, honey. Everything's going to be fine. I'll take care of you."

If only she could believe her assertions. As it now stood, if Dalton didn't survive his injuries, nothing would ever be fine again. Danny might never be fine again.

But for now, it might be best if Danny wasn't talking, at least until Jess could come up with a plan. Otherwise, her beloved son's words could destroy them both.

CHAPTER TWO

SEATED AT THE SMALL DINING TABLE, Chase glanced up from the mug of coffee when he heard the sound of footsteps. Jess approached him slowly, and considering the way her shoulders sagged, the fatigue in her eyes, she looked liked she'd been ambushed.

He shoved the chair across from him with his boot. "Sit before you drop in your tracks."

After she slid onto the seat, Jess crossed her arms around her middle like she was cold. He'd made a point to turn up the heat soon after they'd walked in the door even though he'd felt like his skin had caught fire.

Chase lifted his mug. "Want a cup?"

"No, thank you." She eyed his gun resting on the table where he'd unloaded it a few moments before.

He hooked a thumb over his shoulder toward the guest room. "How's he doing?"

"As well as can be expected, I guess. He's not saying much but I'm sure he's still in shock. I know I am."

Chase really wanted to ask Jess how Dalton's injuries had come about. She could either clear things up, or incriminate herself. He wasn't willing to take that chance because he'd be damned if he'd speak one word against her.

"You look like you could use some sleep," he said when she yawned.

Jess folded her hands together and rested them on top of the pine table. "I'm not sure I could sleep if I wanted to. Every time I close my eyes, I see these awful images."

Chase could seriously relate to that scenario. He couldn't remember a time in the past few years when he drifted peacefully off to sleep. Couldn't remember the last time he had any real peace.

"If you decide to try and rest, you can take my room. I'll sleep on the couch."

She brought her attention back to him. "I'm not going to put you out of your bed. I'll sleep on the sofa."

No point in arguing with Jess. He'd learned that a long time ago. But he'd also learned how to skirt her objections. "You sure you don't want some coffee? Maybe a beer? I'm fresh out of whiskey but I could sneak into the main house and see if Dad still has that seventy-year-old-bottle that belonged to my great-grandpa."

Jess shuddered. "I can't even stand the smell of whiskey, much less drink it. I have Dalton to thank for that."

"He always did like his booze." And women. Chase had heard from friends that the demon had been scouring the bars and cheating on Jess for years.

When Jess continued to stare blankly across the room, Chase scraped his mind for some way to lift her spirits as much as possible. "Do you want to call your folks?"

Her gaze snapped to his. "No. They just left two days ago on a cruise with Gary, Becca and the kids for the holidays. I don't see any reason to bother them while they're on their first real vacation in years."

Chase could think of one reason—giving her family advance notice in case Jess wound up in jail. "Fine. Is there anyone else I can call for you?"

She drummed her fingertips on the table, a purely nervous gesture. "Yes. I need you to call the hospital and find out how Dalton's doing."

He'd like to think she wanted to know because of Danny, but he wondered if there might be more to it. Either she still cared for the jerk, or she felt responsible for his wounds. Maybe both. "I could call but I won't get anywhere. The hospital won't release any information unless you're a family member or the family gives permission. I doubt that holds true for either of us."

She rubbed her temples like she had one hell of a headache. "You're right. I'd just hate to read about it in the paper if something happens to him."

More than likely the event would be front page news no matter what the outcome. "I have Rachel's cell number. I can try to reach her."

Jess didn't look too keen on that idea. "I wouldn't want to disturb her."

He fished the phone from his pocket and hit the speed dial. "She's probably on her way to Jackson, if she'd not already there."

After two rings, Rachel answered with a harried "Hello."

"Hey, Rachel, it's Chase. Are you at the hospital?"

"Yes. How did you know?"

At least she didn't sound too distraught, a good thing. "I answered the call."

"Of course you did. I keep forgetting you're a deputy now."

Sometimes Chase wished he wasn't. Tonight happened to be one of those times. "How's your brother doing?" He tried to sound concerned but his tone was noticeably dry.

"He's undergoing tests right now and he's still unconscious," Rachel said. "Do you have any idea what happened?"

He had a few, but none he cared to share. "Jess says it was an accident, but that's all I know."

"Where is Jess now? I tried to call the home number and her cell but I didn't get any answer."

"She's here with me. Do you want to speak with her?"

"I'd like that. I'm worried about her."

Jess waved him away when he tried to hand her the phone. "Just talk to her for a minute," he said. "She's one of your best friends and she's concerned."

After a brief hesitation, Jess reluctantly took the cell and murmured a soft "Hello."

Chase waited and watched while Jess spoke with Rachel. She sounded meek, very un-Jess-like, but he could understand why she might. While he put away his gun in the locked cabinet in the corner, he listened as Jess repeated the accident scenario without any details. And after a few brief questions about Dalton's condition, she ended the conversation.

"At least he's still alive," she said as she handed him back the phone.

He could tell she found little relief in Dalton's status. "If he makes it through the night, he'll probably be okay."

"And if that's not the case?" she asked. "What happens then?"

Nothing good. He leaned back against the counter

and crossed his arms. "Let's just worry about that if and when the time comes. Right now you need some sleep."

"I've already told you I can't sleep." Her irritable tone said otherwise.

"You can try." He pushed away from the cabinet and returned to the table. "I'll show you to my room."

"I told you I'll sleep on the couch."

"You'll be closer to Danny if you're in my room."

That seemed to get her attention. "I guess that would probably be better."

Jess took her time coming to her feet while he picked up her bag from the floor in the den. She slowly and silently followed behind him as he made his way down the hall and paused outside the guestroom.

"Do you think I can hear Danny if he calls me?" she asked.

"You'll be right next door," he said as he pointed out his bedroom.

After a slight hesitation, she entered the area and looked around before her gaze settled on the king-size bed.

He nodded toward the closed door to his right. "The bathroom's through there. After you're done, I need to take a quick shower."

She took the bag from him and clutched it like a lifeline. "Is this the only bathroom?"

"The only one with a shower," he said. "There's a half-bath next to the laundry room. I've just started framing out two more bedrooms and another bath at the back of the house."

"Why?" she asked, catching him off guard.

"Why not?" he answered back.

"I don't see why you'd need four bedrooms unless you plan on having a family," she said. "And since you're not a settling down kind of guy, well…"

Exactly what he'd told her all those years ago. "Extra bedrooms add to resale value."

"Are you going to move after you're finished with the renovations?" Her tone held an edge of alarm, like she worried he might desert her.

"I hadn't planned on it, but it doesn't hurt to prepare for the future."

She lowered her eyes. "Sometimes you can't prepare for what life throws your way."

He hated she couldn't look at him straight on, that she'd obviously lost her confidence, unlike the girl he used to know. But then her bastard of an ex-husband had played a huge role in that.

"We all make errors in judgment, Jess." He'd made more than his fair share, one that had been particularly serious. Two if he counted what had happened in her dorm room a decade ago.

She took a few steps back and pointed behind her. "I'm going to wash up now."

"Fine. I'll be right here."

"I won't be long," she said as she turned, hurried into the bath and closed the door behind her.

Chase sat on the edge of the bed and streaked both hands over his face. He should be dog-tired, but he wasn't. He should be convinced of Jess's innocence, but he had his doubts. He should disregard duty and demand the truth, but he couldn't… and not only because of job.

The truth could very well be more than he could handle.

AFTER CHECKING ON DANNY one more time, Jess climbed into the king-size bed, pulled the sheets up to her chin and surveyed the area cast in overhead light. The room had been painted neutral beige and the accessories were patently masculine, from the leather chair in the corner to the heavy pine furniture. Funny, this place had barely been four rickety walls and rough-hewn wood floors when they used to play here as kids. She smiled as she recalled their childhood games and her ongoing argument with Chase—she refused to play damsel-in-distress to his superhero just because she was a girl. Over and over she'd insisted she was quite capable of using her pretend powers to save him. But with a flash of his dimples and a few well-chosen words, he'd won the battle.

These days, he rarely smiled. These days, she had barely been able to save herself. Especially tonight.

As Jess settled deeper into the feather pillow, she absorbed the fresh, clean scent of cotton and a hint of Chase's favorite soap. She allowed the memories to take her back to a better time when she'd given him some fancy, manly shower gel one Christmas—which he'd promptly given back and said, "No offense, but no, thanks." She'd known all along he'd been a bar soap kind of guy but she'd reasoned that he could change. She should have known better.

People didn't change, at least not for the better. She'd learned that hard lesson from her ex-husband.

In response to a sudden, strong chill, Jess chafed her arms with her palms and felt the tender spot right above her elbow. She shuddered at the sudden surge of recent recollections. Horrible recollections of what had transpired only a few hours before.

The sound of the opening door startled Jess and thankfully thrust her back into the here and now. Chase came out of the bathroom wearing a pair of navy pajama bottoms and a seen-better-days gray T-shirt.

As she scooted up against the headboard, he headed to the closet, where he placed his boots beneath the neat row of jeans and shirts hanging on the rack.

"Nice place," she said, grasping for a topic other than why she had landed in his house.

"It's fairly simple."

"You have a whirlpool tub and granite countertops, Chase. I don't think that qualifies as simple."

He tossed a glance over his shoulder. "I had some help decorating."

Jess imagined he did. Female help, and she doubted his mom had contributed. Missy Reed was as country as country came. "I'm sure the county girls stood in line to help you out."

"Just Savannah," he said as he pulled out a khaki uniform shirt and hung it on a wall hook next to the closet. "She and Sam are redoing the farmhouse so she volunteered."

She experienced a little bite of guilt over jumping to conclusions. But considering Chase's legendary ladiesman reputation, who could blame her? "That was nice of her to help. I'm sorry to say I haven't seen much of her since she moved back from Chicago." She hadn't seen much of anyone for that matter.

Chase pulled some bedding from the top of the closet, closed the door and finally faced her. "You might want to give her a call when she's back in town."

Jess immediately understood the motive behind his suggestion. "Do you think I need an attorney?"

"I don't know, but it couldn't hurt."

A rock of nausea settled in Jess's belly. "I'll wait and see what happens tomorrow." If Dalton didn't survive, she'd definitely make that call. Or if the statement didn't go well, she might then, too.

Chase returned to the bathroom and only partially closed the door, allowing enough light to escape to keep the room from total darkness. Jess wasn't the least bit surprised by the gesture. He'd always been considerate and thoughtful, at least when it came to her needs.

"It's late," he said as he crossed the room. "Let me know if you need anything."

"I do need something," she blurted, driven by an overwhelming blast of anxiety.

He paused with his hand poised on the light switch and faced her again. "Ask away."

"I need you to stay with me tonight."

His gaze slid away. "Not a good idea."

She knew the root of his concerns—what happened the last time they'd been in bed together ten years ago. "I'm not going to touch you or ask anything more of you than your company. I just don't want to be alone tonight. I promise I'll stay on my side of the bed. And it's a big bed—"

"I tend to toss and turn these days. You probably won't get any sleep at all."

"We'll be restless together." Jess despised the desperation in her voice, but then she was desperate. Desperate not to be left alone with her horrible memories.

"Please, Chase. Only for a while." The same plea from their past.

He released a sigh. "Okay."

While Jess silently celebrated her minor victory, Chase replaced the bedding in the closet and closed the door. After he turned off the light, he sat on the edge of the mattress and kept his back to her, motionless as if preparing to join her. Or reconsidering.

Jess recalled the last time he'd done that very thing—right after he'd told her they'd made a huge mistake sleeping together and it would never happen again. Since then, nothing had been quite the same.

They'd exchanged letters often during his time away, but not once had they ever talked about that one memorable night. Not once had she asked him if he'd regretted it, because in reality, she hadn't. She only regretted that she'd disregarded his advice and jumped into a marriage that was doomed from the beginning. At the time, she felt she'd had no choice.

A few minutes passed before he slid onto his back, his hands laced together atop his abdomen, his body as rigid as a steel beam.

"Thank you," Jess said. "For everything. I don't know what I would've done if you hadn't been there to help me. I appreciate it more than you know."

"No problem."

The razor-sharp edge in his tone told Jess everything she'd asked of him was a problem, and suspected he had more on his mind than he'd let on. She should probably drop it, but some soul-deep need to clear the air drove her to turn on the bedside lamp and gain his complete attention. "Go ahead, Chase, say it."

"Say what?" he muttered as he flipped onto his belly, his face turned toward the opposite wall.

She rolled to her side toward him. "Tell me I'm a fool again just like you did after I told you I'd married Dalton."

He turned his head and stared at her straight on. "I never said you were a fool. I said Dalton had you fooled."

"You're right, but I can't take back my mistakes." Oh, that she could. "But I do want to make it right between you and me. We've never discussed that night in my dorm—"

"Not now, Jess."

She rose up on one elbow and supported her jaw with her palm. "When Chase? We've skirted that topic for ten years and—"

"I said not now." He turned his head again, making it all too clear that he was done with the conversation. Maybe even done with her.

Feeling weary and emotionally drained, Jess turned off the light and rolled away from Chase. Years ago, he would have held her close and reassured her. He would have been more than willing to provide a leaning shoulder. A swell of sadness overcame her as she silently mourned the loss of her best friend. She chastised herself for all the ways in which she'd ruined her life. Perhaps even her son's life.

Worse still, she might find herself without a job. The good citizens of Placid could be judgmental, and if any parent in town even suspected she'd intentionally harmed her ex-husband, they'd kick her to the curb without a second thought. Not to mention, her former father-in-law served on the school board. No job meant no way to support her child other than the money Dalton grudgingly gave her.

Everything seemed so hopeless and that only fed her remorse.

As the tears began to fall, she buried her face in the pillow, tried hard not to let Chase know that she was an emotional wreck. And just when she'd begun to honestly believe they would never be able to repair their relationship, she felt the mattress bend and Chase's strong hand engulfing hers.

"You're going to be okay," he whispered. "Danny's going to be okay, too."

Jess couldn't respond but she didn't need to. And although he only held her hand for a few moments, it seemed enough to get her through, at least tonight. Tomorrow would be another story.

THE SHRILL BUZZER JARRED JESS out of sleep and her eyes snapped open. Confused, she took a few moments to survey the room in order to acclimate to the surroundings. As she finally recalled exactly where she was, and why, she resisted the urge to pull the covers back over her head and hide away from the world. She reached out and felt the space beside her only to discover that Chase had apparently left the bed before the annoying alarm sounded. How he could be up so early was beyond her. He'd thrashed about most of the night, taking the blanket with him and rousing her from sleep that had come in fits and starts. During those awake times, she'd checked on Danny twice and with great relief, had found him soundly sleeping. If only she could say the same for herself.

Recognizing what awaited her in a matter of hours—
a trip to the sheriff's department to present her written
statement—Jess decided to get up and get it over with as
quickly as possible. She climbed from the bed, grabbed a
robe and slipped it on as she made her way to the guestroom to tell Danny good morning. When she came upon
only an empty bed, a swell of dread weighted her chest
and robbed her breath.

Panic sent her on a fast clip into the kitchen where she
thankfully found the missing deputy and her son. They
sat at the breakfast table, both bent over a bowl of ce-
real—the kind with the fruity marshmallows that made
her queasy just thinking about them. Neither seemed
to notice her presence as she watched the pair for a few
more minutes. She'd envisioned this scene many times
throughout the years—her one-time best friend and her
precious boy getting to know each other. Yet the picture-
perfect scene was only an illusion. Her entire life to this
point had been an illusion, and that wouldn't end today.

Jess approached her son from behind and ruffled his
tousled blond hair. "Time for you to get a trim, Danny."

He didn't bother to look up from the bowl or offer a
response. She sent Chase a forlorn look before checking the clock on the wall. "What time are we supposed
to do this?"

He took a drink of coffee before pushing the cup
aside. "I figure in an hour or so we'll head down to the
department for the interviews."

"Interviews" meaning both she and her child. Not if
she could help it.

Jess touched Danny's shoulder to garner his attention. "Why don't you go wash up and get dressed?"

He sent her only a fast glance before scooting back from the table and carrying his empty bowl to the sink. Funny, she usually had to ride him to clean up after meals. Then again, he didn't seem at all himself, and rightfully so.

Once Danny had left the area, Jess poured a cup of coffee from the pot on the counter and claimed the chair that her son had just left. "Did he say anything at all to you?"

Chase shook his head. "Not a word. I found him sitting in here staring off into space when I got up about an hour ago."

She closed her eyes and pinched the bridge of her nose with her fingertips. "I pray he'll come around in a few days."

"I think that depends on what he saw last night."

The long pause told Jess he wanted her to fill in the blanks despite his warning last night to keep her confessions to herself. "I don't think he saw anything except that Dalton had been injured." Lie number one. "That's why I don't see any reason for Danny to have to endure a lot of questions that will only upset him."

Chase inclined his head and fixed his gaze on Jess, causing her to look away. "Are you sure he didn't see it happen?"

"As sure as I can be." Lie number two.

"That might explain his silence," Chase said.

"As I told you last night, it was an accident. Dalton came to pick up Danny three hours late, he'd been drinking, and when I refused to let him take Danny, he grabbed my arm and I yanked it away. I guess he lost his balance but I'm not sure. It's all a blur."

Lie number three. She remembered every last detail, sickening sights and sounds included. She recalled Dalton's insistence they get back together, her refusal, his threats to take her son away from her permanently if she didn't do his bidding. His accusations. And then...

Feeling the need to escape, Jess downed the rest of her coffee and stood. "I'm going to get dressed now, unless you want to go first."

He leaned back in the chair and made a sweeping gesture toward the hall. "You go ahead."

"Okay. And after I've finished making my statement, I need to get my car and a few things from the house."

"I'll have to escort you until Buck clears the place as a possible crime scene."

Great. Nothing like being considered a hardened criminal. But then she had been guilty of more than her fair share of crimes, the first entailed marrying the wrong man. The second—not leaving him years ago. "Fine, but I want to find a place to rent today if at all possible. If I do, I'll need more than a duffle bag and one change of clothes."

"You're welcome to stay here as long as you like," he said without much conviction. "Once Dalton verifies your account of the events, you'll be free to move back into your house."

"It's not my house," she answered with more force than necessary. "Dalton made all the decisions when we had it built so I never considered it mine. During the divorce, he agreed to sell it and split the proceeds but unfortunately, people around here can't afford it. And Dalton's too damn stubborn to just buy out my half so he can move back in."

"He still wants to control you," Chase said, his tone etched with anger.

"You're right, but I refuse to let him control me anymore." Easier said than done. Even lying in a hospital bed, he was still controlling her life. If heaven forbid he died, that control still wouldn't end. "Do you happen to know of any place I can rent? Since we're on the holiday break, I'd have time to get settled before school resumes after the first of the year."

He released a cynical laugh. "Most of the rentals around here are owned by your father-in-law."

Jess hadn't stopped to consider that. "Surely there's some property available somewhere that Edwin doesn't have his hands on."

Chase kicked back in his chair and stretched his arms above his head. "I'll ask around. In the meantime, you can stay here."

She didn't see that as a viable option, especially after his obvious discomfort last night. "Thanks for the offer, but I can always go to the motel if I have to."

Chase shrugged. "Suit yourself, but you're pride isn't going to benefit you or your son. Forcing him to live in a rat-hole motel won't help matters."

As usual, he was right, but that didn't make living in his house more appealing. "I'll just wait and see what happens today."

She had one more question to ask him, one she'd been purposely avoiding to this point. "Have you heard anything on Dalton's condition?"

"I called Rachel a little while ago. He's still in ICU but he's stable."

Jess experienced some measure of relief that she

wouldn't be facing a murder charge—yet. "Then, he's going to be okay?"

"Looks like it. He's also awake."

Her relief dissolved into dread. "Did he say anything about last night?"

"He said he doesn't remember what happened. But that could only be temporary. They won't know for a few days."

"I'm glad his condition has improved," she added without a shred of sincerity.

Chase studied her as if he could see right through her deception. "I guess it probably is a good thing. Unless it's going to cause more problems for you in the long run."

Somehow Chase knew she was withholding information, but he could never know what really happened last night. No one would know if she could help it. Jess could only hope that Dalton's memory loss was permanent, saving both her and her son. If not, she'd deal with the fallout later. Right now she had to move on to the matter at hand.

"I'm going to check on Danny and then dress." As she started toward the bedroom, Chase called her name. She faced him and attempted a smile that fell short. "Yes?"

His gaze didn't waver from hers. "When you give your statement, don't forget all the misery Dalton's caused you and Danny. Consider what's best for you and not what's right."

Comprehension dawned slowly before Jess realized Chase had been telling her to cover her tracks. To do what she had to do to skirt any legal issues. Basically, to lie.

Without offering a response, Jess left the kitchen to seek out her child. She discovered the guestroom door partially ajar and pushed it open to find Danny seated on the edge of the bed, tying his sneakers. He glanced up at her with that same vacant look in his eyes, sending a pang of regret coursing through her soul.

She took a seat beside him, draped her arm around his thin shoulders and locked into his gaze. "Danny, when we get to the station, Sheriff Reed's going to ask you some questions."

A flicker of fear called out from his brown eyes, yet he didn't respond, leading Jess to continue. "It was an accident. That's all you have to say. Or you don't have to say anything at all. In fact, it might be better if you didn't say anything."

When fear turned into confusion in Danny's expression, Jess felt as if she was falling into a black hole of deceit and dragging her son down with her. Still, she saw no way around asking him to lie, if only by omission.

She tipped her head against his and whispered, "I promise you I'm going to take care of this. Nothing bad's going to happen if you'll trust me, sweetie."

He looked as if he didn't quite believe her, but he did nod his head in acknowledgment.

Jess kissed his forehead and came to her feet. "Try not to worry, Danny. It will all be over soon."

If only she sincerely believed that. If only she could convince her child of that when she wasn't convinced herself.

For the time being, Jess decided to follow Chase's advice and only disclose what she needed to get by, skirting the truth and in turn, shattering everything she'd been taught during her childhood. Everything she'd taught her only child about honesty.

Even if she continued her cover-up, she ran the risk that eventually her secrets would be revealed. Two very important secrets. The first she'd kept for over ten years, the second less than twenty-four-hours. Both were closely intertwined. That ten-year-old secret could drive an irreparable wedge between her and Chase as well as complicate her current problems.

But the second could cost her everything…including her son.

CHAPTER THREE

"You look like hell, Deputy Reed."

Chase leaned over the counter and sent Sue Ellen Parker—the sixty-something Crowley County dispatcher—his best grin. "You look mighty pretty today."

A serious blush spread across the woman's plump cheeks. "I thought you outgrew that silver-tongued devil tactic years ago. Just goes to show, once a bad boy, always a bad boy. And I'm thinkin' your bad boy ways may be the cause of your fatigue."

He wouldn't argue that point. Having Jess in his bed had prevented him from getting much rest. Sometime during the night, she'd curled up against him and it had taken all his strength not to take up where they'd left off all those years ago. Repeating past mistakes never turned out well. And if he knew what was good for him, he'd scour the county and find her a place to live before he screwed up again.

He couldn't think of a better resource for rental property than Sue Ellen, who knew everything about everyone, just like the town gossip, Pearl Allworth. But one huge difference set the two women apart—Sue was discrete while Pearl shot rumors around town like a human AK-47.

Chase sent a glance toward the small conference room across the hall where Buck was probably bullying Jess, hoping she might break. Danny was sitting in the corridor, his legs in constant motion. He felt sorry for the kid on many levels, the first being born to a bastard like Dalton Wainwright. Now to be dragged into a mess that could land his mother in jail, that sure as hell wasn't fair. But then life wasn't always fair. He'd learned that through experience.

Chase walked around the counter and took a seat next to the dispatcher, determined to do what he could to help Jess and her boy. Keeping his back to Danny, he asked Sue, "Do you know anyone who has a house for rent besides Wainwright?"

She took a pen from behind her ear and tapped it on the desk. "Is the remodeling going down the toilet?"

He lowered his voice and said, "It's not for me. It's for Jess and Danny."

Sue raised a penciled-in brow. "What's wrong with that big old house she's been living in?"

Either Sue was playing ignorant, or she really didn't know about Dalton. "Hard to believe you haven't heard about what happened there last night."

She exchanged the pen for a paper clip that she began to straighten. "I've heard, but as soon as she's cleared, she should be able to move back in, right?"

If she was cleared. Chase hoped that would be the case for both her and Danny's sake. "She doesn't want to live there, and I can't say that I blame her."

Sue leaned forward and in a hushed voice asked, "Do you think she did something to him?"

Chase refused to take the bait. "Now, Sue, you know I can't talk about an ongoing investigation." He wouldn't even if he could, especially not with Jess involved.

She patted her tightly-curled salt-and-pepper hair. "Sorry, but I can't help but wonder if he drove her to it. Not that anyone in this town who knows that sorry sapsucker would ever judge Jess if she did take matters into her own hands. Why, just the other day when I was driving downtown, I saw Dalton coming out of the general store and it was all I could do not to hit the accelerator and jump the curb in my Jeep."

Chase tried not to smile but couldn't stop himself. "I wouldn't repeat that around here. Buck might start questioning you."

Sue rolled her eyes. "Your daddy doesn't scare me, Chase. If he gives me grief, I'll pour a little salt in his coffee and he knows it."

Back to the matter at hand. "So do you know any places for rent?"

Sue tapped one temple like she was trying to dislodge a thought. "I know of a few on wheels that I wouldn't recommend to my worst enemy. But the Wooley's old farmhouse on the outskirts of town is vacant. I'm not sure Gabe has done much to it since his mama went into the nursing home about a year ago, so it might not be livable."

Chase knew the place well, and if it wasn't too rundown, it would be perfect. The house sat well off the road, giving Jess privacy and Danny a lot of room to roam. "I'll call Gabe and see if he's interested in renting it out. Thanks."

She gave him a toothy grin. "You're welcome, Deputy. Anything else?"

Chase shot another look at Danny over one shoulder. "Yeah. Could you take the boy into the break room and get him a snack? He doesn't need to see his mother upset."

"Sure," she said. "Are you going to answer the phone?"

Chase leaned around her to see Barkley seated at his desk not far away. "Only if Bobby Boy gets swamped with calls, and around here, that's not likely."

Sue rolled back her chair and stood. "You never know, Chase. We've had a lot of shoplifting calls lately."

That didn't surprise him in the least. When times were tough, people got by any way they could, even if it meant stealing what they needed.

Chase watched as Sue held out her hand to Danny and after a brief pause, he took it and allowed the woman to lead him away. A few seconds later, the conference room door opened and Jess stepped out, looking like she'd been run through the mill twice. She'd always been fair-skinned, but Chase had never seen her quite so pale.

After his dad emerged wearing his patent sheriff's scowl, Chase joined them in the hallway, ready to offer support and an explanation when Jess looked around, obviously concerned over her son's absence. "Where's Danny?" she asked, a touch of alarm in her tone.

Chase pointed down the corridor. "Sue took him to the break room. Third room to the right." After Jess hurried away, Chase faced his dad. "Is she free to go now?"

"Not until I talk to the boy," Buck said. "I need to hear his version of the story because I'm not buying the bill of goods I just got from his mother."

Chase resented his dad for continuing to treat Jess like some hardened criminal. "The kid's still in shock.

Maybe you ought to wait another day or two before you harass him like you did Jess."

"I'm just following procedure, son, like I would with anyone else who's involved in a questionable incident."

And that's what irked Chase—his dad viewing Jess like someone he'd never met before, not the kid who used to call him Daddy Buck. "Did she give you any reason to think that this was anything other than an accident?"

Buck rubbed his stubbled chin. "I don't know any more about what went on than I did before the interview. I do know she's holding something back."

Chase clung to his control before he blew a verbal gasket. "You've been in this business so long everyone starts to look guilty to you. Jess is only guilty of marrying the wrong man."

"And marrying into the wrong family. But she did marry into that family and that makes me wonder if she didn't learn a thing or two along the way."

"Like what?"

"Like how to lie to cover your ass."

Fact was, Chase worried Jess might be lying. Or at least not telling the whole truth. But he had no intention of letting on that he had his suspicions, especially around his dad. "Look, giving the boy a couple of days to calm down isn't going to hurt a damn thing. Besides, Rachel called this morning and said Dalton's awake and talking."

"I know," Buck said. "And as soon as I get the go-ahead from the doctors, I'm going to have a talk with the victim about his recollections of last night."

Chase couldn't think of Dalton as a victim no matter what had transpired. "He doesn't remember what happened, and even if he did, like you said, the Wainwrights know how to cover their asses. He might just point a finger at Jess for spite."

"And that's all the more reason to question the boy," Buck added. "But I'll make a deal with you. If Dalton regains his memory and he backs up Jess's accident story, then I won't involve the kid. But if he tells a whole different tale, then I have no choice but to question Danny. He could be the key to the truth."

Chase stuck out his hand for a shake. "Deal. In the meantime, I'm going to get Jess settled in. She's going to need some of her things from the house."

"Fine, as long as you escort her." Buck inclined his head and studied him a moment. "You gonna keep her at the cabin?"

His dad's tone sounded like he planned to hold Jess hostage. "No. I'm going to find her another place to rent."

"Good. I wouldn't want folks around here thinking you're in cahoots with a suspect. That wouldn't be proper behavior for a peace officer."

Chase gritted his teeth and spoke through them. "Best I recall, we don't name a suspect unless we know a crime's taken place."

Buck hitched up his pants. "True. You still don't need to be too friendly with her, just in case."

"She is a friend, Buck, and has been for as long as I can remember." Even though that friendship had suffered in the past few years, thanks to his stupidity.

Buck gave him a condescending pat on the back. "Look, son, people change. Jess just might not be that girl you used to know."

Chase wouldn't even make an attempt at denial because he acknowledged his dad was partially right—Jess wasn't the same. Neither was he.

Without further comment, he spun around and headed toward his office to take care of some pressing arrangements. He made a quick call to Gabe Wooley, who was more than happy to have someone renting the old home place until the family decided whether they wanted to sell it.

Satisfied he'd done something constructive today, Chase made his way to the break room to find Jess and Danny sitting at the small round table in the corner, looking like they could both use a friend.

And that's what he intended to be to them both—a friend. To hell with propriety.

"Let's go," he said when Jess looked up.

"Is it Danny's turn?" she asked in a voice barely above a whisper.

"Not today."

Her shoulders sagged from obvious relief. "We can go?"

"Yeah." Chase didn't have the heart tell her it might only be a temporary reprieve.

Jess stood and pulled out Danny's chair. "Let's go, sweetie. We need to look for a place to stay."

"I've got that covered."

Jess and Danny exchanged a look before Jess asked, "Where?"

"You'll see."

JESS COULD ONLY SEE overgrown trees and knee-high, winter-dry grass as Chase maneuvered the department's SUV up the narrow road. But she'd recognized the area immediately as soon as they turned off the highway. Many times she'd accompanied her mother to the place to deliver supplies to widowed Nita Wooley, whose health had declined in recent years. The same place where Nita and Gabe Sr. had raised five children on a limited income but a lot of love.

Once Chase stopped near the front door, Jess glanced back to see Danny staring out the window with curiosity. She could only imagine the thoughts running through his mind—his mother was taking him from a custom-built, modern multilevel semi-mansion to a small, weather-worn, single-story farm house.

As far as Jess was concerned, if the place was relatively clean, furnished and warm, they would make do. At least there was plenty of privacy and enough room for Danny to play. She even spotted a tire swing tied to an ancient oak in the front yard that would provide a much-needed diversion for her child. Yes, this would definitely do, at least for the time being.

Chase slid out of the driver's side and Jess followed suit, opening the door for Danny, who refused to take her offered hand. Maybe after they'd settled in, he'd be more himself again. Maybe he'd even talk to her again.

Chase lifted the dusty welcome mat and retrieved a key that anyone with any sense could have found and helped themselves to whatever remained in the house. But in Placid, crime was low and life was simple. Most people had very few possessions that anyone would deem valuable.

The minute Jess stepped onto the scuffed hardwood floors, she was overwhelmed by the musty smell and the amount of stuff scattered about the small living room. Numerous trinkets, along with portraits of children and their children, sat out on various tables and stationary shelves lining the walls. A family's legacy proudly on display.

Chase turned and handed her the key while Danny remained at the door. "Gabe said you'll find everything you need and then some."

She tucked the key into the pocket of her jeans while she continued to survey the living room and its personal treasures. "No kidding. I feel like I'm in a museum."

"He also said Millie comes over now and then to clean the place but she hasn't been here in a while."

Jess remembered Gabe's wife, Millie, very fondly. She'd worked in the high school cafeteria to supplement Gabe's farming income and she'd always sported a smile while serving questionable fare. Unfortunately, Gabe was about as crabby as they came. "As long as we have a roof over our heads, I can deal with tidying up. How much does he want for rent?"

Chase's gaze faltered. "Nine hundred a month plus utilities. No deposit or lease required."

Highway robbery as far as Jess was concerned, especially if her job was in jeopardy. She wouldn't know for certain until after the first of the year, unless she happened to be indicted. Even if she was cleared of all wrong-doing, some would want her contract terminated immediately, namely Edwin. Then she would have no choice but to leave her hometown. "Does Gabe know I'm the prospective tenant?"

Chase brought his attention back to her. "Not yet. I told him I was asking for a friend and I'd call if we're interested after we checked the place out. But he's going to want to know who's renting the house if you decide to take it."

What choice did she have? "The price is a little steep but beggars can't be choosers. And as far as Gabe knowing I'm renting the house, I imagine everyone's going to hear about what happened last night sooner or later." More than likely sooner.

"Okay. I'll let him know and drop off the rent during my shift."

That posed another problem. "My checkbook's at the house."

"I'll take care of it."

Jess already owed him too much. "I'll pay you back as soon as I get the rest of my things. What about the utilities?"

Chase dropped down on the shabby blue sofa. "The electricity's still on but the heat runs on propane and the tank's empty. I'll call Freddie and see if he can deliver some tomorrow."

"It's not supposed to be too cold tonight. We'll manage." Jess pointed at the pot-belly stove in the corner. "Or we could use that I guess."

"I'll see if I can find some wood before I go."

Jess didn't want him to go, but she also didn't dare ask him to stay. "As long as we have blankets, we'll be okay until tomorrow. What time are you on today?"

He came to his feet. "I work eleven to eleven."

"A twelve-hour shift?"

"That's what happens when you're short on manpower."

That meant he had little time left before he had to

leave, and she probably wouldn't see him again today. "I really need some extra clothes and my car from the house."

"I'll have to accompany you and I don't have much time. If you have enough to get by until tomorrow, we can stop by first thing in the morning."

"I guess we can make do," she said, though she hated not having control over claiming her own belongings. "But we will need food."

"I'll send Sue over with some lunch as soon as I'm back at the department. She can bring you some groceries after work."

Jess didn't particularly care for that idea. "Again, I don't have any cash and I really wouldn't want to inconvenience anyone."

"Sue won't mind as long as I promise to cover the cost, which I will."

"I have my own money, Chase."

"I'm sure you do, and you can pay me back by making me dinner sometime. I could go for some mac and cheese or tuna fish sandwiches."

He still thought she was the girl who couldn't cook to save her life. Little did he know, she'd learned a lot in his absence. "Fine. But I still don't want Sue to have to come all the way out here."

Chase inclined his head and studied her a few moments. "If you're worried she'll tell someone your whereabouts, don't. You can trust her."

Jess's concerns had more to do with shame than privacy. But her growing boy needed to eat and until she had her own transportation, she'd have to rely on the kindness of others. "Okay. As long as you promise I'll have my car back by tomorrow."

"I promise," he said.

Jess noticed her son had taken a seat in the yellow-striped chair near the door, still stoic and silent. "Do you want to pick out your room, Danny?" she asked, hoping to somehow engage him.

He shook his head no and studied the toe of his sneaker.

"Well, I'm going to take a look around and you can decide later," she said. "Don't go anywhere unless you tell me." Like that would happen since he still refused to speak.

Jess crossed the room into an adjacent hallway and came to the first door to her right—a small bathroom with a claw-foot tub on the opposite wall. When she heard heavy footfalls, she glanced back to see Chase filling the doorway. "This is great," she said as she examined the tub that appeared to be clean and in decent shape except for a few nicks here and there. "Unfortunately, no shower. Is there another bathroom?"

"Nope. But I can rig you a hand-held when I come back tomorrow."

Funny, she'd gone from four fully-equipped baths to one. "I'd appreciate that." She'd also appreciate it if he stepped back to give her some space.

When he failed to move, Jess brushed past him and continued her investigation of the premises. The first bedroom housed two sets of bunk beds, the second two double beds, all reminders that a large family had once lived there. At the end of the corridor, she came upon the largest room that held a dresser and another double bed with an iron headboard that looked to be as old as the house itself.

Again she turned to find Chase with a shoulder propped against the frame. "I assume this is the master bedroom."

He sent her a half-smile. "Yep. The place where the Wooleys made all the little Wooleys."

He could have gone all day without mentioning that. "Let's hope the mattress has since been replaced. And speaking of that, I noticed all the beds have been stripped."

"Gabe said there's clean linens in the hall closet."

At least she wouldn't have to bring those from the house. "Good. What about the washer and dryer?"

"Washer but no dryer. Nita hung her clothes on the line."

Jess felt as if she'd unwittingly stepped back in time. "I suppose that's why they invented coin-operated laundries." And the nearest one happened to be five miles away.

"The washer's in a small room off the kitchen," Chase said as he stepped into the bedroom, making the adequate space seemed too cramped for Jess's comfort.

She clapped her hands together enthusiastically. "Let's go see the kitchen, shall we?" When Chase laughed, taking her by surprise, Jess asked, "What's so amusing?"

"For a minute there I saw the head cheerleader coming out in you."

She hadn't had anything to cheer about in years. "That girl went away a long time ago. If you don't believe me, take a gander at my backside."

Chase raked his gaze down her body and back up again. "You don't look all that different, Jess."

"Try telling that to Dalton." She regretted the acid comment the moment it left her mouth.

Chase scowled as he always did whenever she mentioned his archenemy's name. "You shouldn't care what that bastard thinks."

Old verbal wounds were hard to heal. "I don't care about anything but seeing the kitchen."

He stepped aside and made a sweeping gesture toward the hall. "After you."

Jess once more passed through the living room where Danny was rooted in the same spot, still wearing his gray down jacket as if he had no intention of staying. As soon as she had some alone time with him, she'd explain this was only a temporary home. Yet she wasn't certain he truly cared one way or the other. And if his demeanor didn't change in the next day or two, she'd be forced to seek professional help for him. She prayed she could wait at least until the current legal storm blew over. If not, she'd have to trust that a counselor would be bound by patient confidentiality should Danny decide to reveal the events leading up to Dalton's injuries. Right now she had to concentrate on getting her bearings so they could begin to move in.

With that in mind, she found her way into the kitchen with a small dining area housing a wooden table, benches on both sides and a chair on each end. She began opening cabinets and drawers to discover myriad pots, pans, dishes, glasses and utensils. When she heard Chase approaching, she turned and leaned back against the well-worn butcher-block counter. "There's enough equipment here to feed an army."

"That pretty much describes the Wooley family," he said as he entered the room, dropped into one chair at the table and stretched his long legs out before him.

Jess was suddenly struck by his undeniable presence and authority, from the top of his cowboy hat to the tip of his boots. He portrayed old-West lawman to a T. Oddly, everything about him kept her off balance, as if she didn't really know him at all. In many ways, that was accurate.

She moved to the massive farm sink that provided a nice view of the pasture from the window above it. "This is really a pretty place."

Before Jess even realized he'd left the table, Chase reached around her and turned on the faucet, his body flush against her back. "The well's supposed to be working, but Gabe says to check the water since we've had a fairly long dry spell. I can sure relate to that."

Jess glanced back to see his half-smile and a hint of the consummate charmer he'd always been. "I have a hard time believing that." Even if for some strange reason, she hoped it were true.

"You know how it is around here, Jess," he said. "Not a whole lot of people our age in Placid."

She returned his smile. "Poor Deputy Reed. No one to irrigate his crops."

He brushed a strand of hair from her cheek. "Don't worry your pretty head over me. I get by."

Getting by seemed to be the recent story of her life. Getting away from Chase seemed to be the better part of valor. The innuendo had begun to take its toll on her composure, especially when he remained so close she could trace a line around his lips with a fingertip with little effort. The fact that his proximity, his words, could affect her at a time like this was beyond explanation.

Right when she started to move away, Chase stopped her progress when he said, "Will you take a look at that?"

Jess turned her focus back to the window to see Danny seated on the ground, holding his hand out to a young tabby cat that stood a few feet away, back arched and tail sticking straight up. Not only had she'd not heard him leave the house, she'd inadvertently allowed him to come face-to-face with a wild animal. "Oh, heavens. That thing is probably feral and hasn't had any shots. I need—"

"To leave him be," Chase said as the kitten skittered away.

She sent him a look of sheer surprise. "Are you crazy? He could've been scratched or bitten and ended up with rabies."

"But he wasn't and he's fine. Seems to me he just needs a little time to himself."

Jess silently admitted Chase was probably right, but her motherly instincts at times commandeered her common sense.

"You know what else he needs, Jess?" Chase said.

"A friend?"

"A dog."

Another memory, sharp as shattered glass, dug into her mind. "Danny had a puppy once when he was five. A Golden Retriever named Birdie. She chewed up a pair of Dalton's Italian loafers, so Dalton gave her away to some hunter two counties over. Then he told Danny that she'd run away because he wasn't a good boy."

"That sorry son of a bitch," Chase muttered, pure venom in his voice.

Jess had called him that very thing in her mind, but she'd never said it to his face...until last night.

Shoving aside the reminders, Jess planned to go to Danny just to make sure he'd been left unscathed, at least when it came to the cat. Yet when he took a stick and began drawing in the dirt, his mouth moving as if he were speaking to an imaginary friend, fascination kept her planted where she stood. At least that confirmed he could still talk, even if not to her. He could also still smile, she realized, when he grinned as he looked to his right to see the kitten had returned. A smile that always warmed her heart whenever his precious dimples came into view, the one on the left more prominent that the one on the right.

Overcome with the need to distract Chase, she sidestepped him. "I'm going to bring Danny in before he ends up on the wrong side of the cat."

Chase checked his watch. "And I'm going to head out."

Jess realized that after he left, she had no means to communicate with the outside world. "I left my cell phone on the charger at the house."

"I'd give you mine but I need it for work. I'll see if Sue can come up with a spare until we get yours in the morning."

If Sue didn't come through, that meant she'd spend the day wondering if Dalton's condition had deteriorated. "Thanks again. For everything."

"No sweat. That's what friends are for."

At least he still considered her a friend, or he could be playing nice out of pity. Only time would tell.

They walked side by side to the door and when they stepped onto the porch, Jess resisted the urge to throw her arms around him and ask him to stay a few more minutes. "Have an exciting day."

He barked out a cynical laugh. "Sure. About the only excitement I'll see is if I have to break up a bar fight."

She shuddered at the thought of Chase throwing himself into the middle of danger, though that wasn't unfamiliar territory. She'd had to live with that reality the whole time he'd been at war. "Tell Sue not to hurry on our account."

"Sue doesn't have any other speed."

He sent her a smile, displaying his dimples to full advantage, touched the brim of his hat and said, "See you tomorrow, ma'am," before climbing into the SUV and driving away.

As Jess rounded the house to join Danny, a cool breeze blew across her face and brought with it a sudden chill that had nothing to do with the mild winter weather. She longed to be around Chase, yet she realized the possible peril in that. The more time he spent with her child, the greater the risk that he might begin to suspect what she'd suspected—and denied—for years.

She'd ignored all the signs, just as she'd ignored Dalton's many fatal flaws. Yet in her heart she'd known all along that the quiet little boy with the dimpled smile, dark pensive eyes and sandy hair, could very well be the deputy's son.

And last night, during one fateful confrontation, the

worst had come to pass when her ex-husband, who'd never been much of a father to her son, had voiced his suspicions, too.

CHAPTER FOUR

WHEN THE KNOCK SOUNDED at the door, Jess expected to see Sue Ellen standing at the threshold for the second time today, this time with groceries. But never in her wildest dreams had she predicted that Rachel Wainwright Boyd—her former sister-in-law and longtime friend—would be gracing the doorstep. Not with her brother still lying in a hospital bed and his ex-wife believed to be responsible for putting him there.

"What are you doing here?" Jess asked, painfully aware she sounded as if she didn't welcome the visit.

Rachel's smile looked somewhat self-conscious as she held up two pieces of familiar paisley luggage. "I come bearing gifts."

Jess opened the screen wide and told her, "Come in," around her surprise.

As soon as Rachel stepped inside and set the bags on the floor, Danny sprinted across the room and wrapped his arms around her waist, nearly knocking her backward. "Whoa there, my little angel of a nephew."

Though Jess appreciated Danny's enthusiasm, she couldn't quell the tiny nip of envy. He'd refused any show of affection, at least when it came to his own mother. "Be careful, Danny. Aunt Rachel's got a baby on board."

Rachel leaned down and kissed the top of his head.

"Don't worry. This baby is going to be tough as nails if he's anything like his father."

"He's been cooped up in the house all day with me and no TV," Jess said. "That's why he's so glad to see you." After she realized how that sounded, she added, "Of course he's always glad to see his favorite aunt."

Rachel ruffled Danny's hair when he stepped back and looked at her as if she'd come to save him. "I've got a few things for you out in your mom's car that should take care of some of the boredom."

Stunned over the revelation, Jess looked through the window to discover her beige hybrid sedan parked in the driveway. "How did you manage that?"

"The same way I managed this," Rachel said as she rummaged through her purse, withdrew Jess's cell phone and handed it to her. "The charger's in a bag with a few of your clothes."

At least she wouldn't be naked and since Sue hadn't brought a spare phone, she now had a way to communicate with the outside world. Provided she actually had service. "I assume you've been talking to Chase."

"He called me a few hours ago and he told me where to find you. I volunteered to retrieve a few of your things and deliver your car."

Jess couldn't believe her friend would risk entering the enemy camp. Then again, they'd never been enemies, even after she'd divorced her brother. "How did you get into the house?"

"I used my spare key. Of course, that idiot Barkley followed me around like I was up to no good. I just ignored him when he acted like I was going to steal your car after I grabbed the keys off the hook in the kitchen. Other than that, piece of cake."

Thank heavens for girlfriends to rely on through thick and thin. "I can't tell you how much I appreciate this."

"Not a problem at all," Rachel said. "Matt's at the Stanfield farm not far away, treating a mare that came down with colic. He's going to pick me up when he's done." She hoisted a bag onto the sofa, unzipped it, pulled out a pair of red designer platform heels and held them up. "I just knew you couldn't live a day longer without these."

Jess had purchased those treasured shoes during a trip with Rachel to Atlanta six months ago. The trip where her sister-in-law had told her she was pregnant, and she'd told Rachel she was leaving Dalton. "Thanks, I guess, but I don't have any immediate plans to go out dancing."

"You can wear them around the house." Rachel tossed a lock of near-black hair over a shoulder in dramatic fashion, sheer amusement calling out from her dark eyes. "I think they'll look fabulous with your outfit, don't you?"

Jess glanced down at her gray sweatshirt and faded blue yoga pants, then frowned. "Oh, right. A wonderful fashion statement while I'm scrubbing the toilet."

They shared in a laugh before Rachel turned to Danny again. "Why don't you help me get the rest of the stuff out of the car, kiddo?"

Danny nodded and clasped Rachel's offered hand while Jess followed behind them. It took two trips to retrieve the numerous bags of clothing, groceries and Danny's toys. By the time they were finished, Jess felt as if she finally had the makings for a decent home for her child.

After Danny retreated to the bedroom with the bunk beds and closed the door, Jess invited Rachel into the kitchen to put up the food.

Her friend did a visual inspection of the area and smiled her approval. "Not bad at all."

"If you like yellow," Jess said as she began to rummage through a bag. "It's not exactly my ideal abode, but I'm afraid it's going to have to do since rental property is at a premium in Placid."

"And since my father has a monopoly on most of the rentals."

A subject she didn't care to undertake. "I wasn't going to mention that, but you're right. I doubt he'd want me as a tenant."

"My father only cares about how much of the town he can purchase at a bargain."

Jess had no reasonable defense for Edwin's actions so she chose not to respond.

They remained silent for a time while Rachel placed a few items into the freezer. "Most of this came from your refrigerator and pantry," she said. "I wasn't sure how long you planned to stay here and I didn't want anything to spoil. I also looked under the tree for Christmas presents, and then I remembered you've always been a last-minute shopper."

The upcoming holidays had been the furthest thing from her mind. "Yes, I'm a procrastinator, but my son is a snoop so I don't dare buy too early, otherwise he'll find the gifts. Besides, I still have time to shop."

Rachel frowned. "Christmas is one week from tomorrow."

"I thought it fell on a Sunday."

"That's right. Today is Saturday, Jess."

Heavens, a few hours of isolation and she'd lost complete track of time along with a good deal of sanity. "You're right. I'm a little fuzzy from lack of sleep."

She sent Jess a quick glance. "Do you think you'll be here Christmas?"

Unless she found herself incarcerated. "I don't have any definite plans about the living arrangements other than I don't intend to go back to the house."

Rachel hesitated a moment before sliding a can of soup into the cabinet. "I don't blame you."

Jess wondered if her friend did in fact blame her for Dalton's current condition. And on that note she said, "Chase told me Dalton's been awake."

Disregarding her pregnant state, Rachel hoisted herself up on the kitchen counter, a habit she'd developed in their youth. "The doctors say he's going to be groggy for a few days, but they expect the skull fracture to heal on its own without any surgery."

She swallowed hard. "Skull fracture?"

Rachel looked altogether perplexed. "Didn't Chase tell you?"

Most likely he'd been trying to protect her by withholding details. She couldn't fault him for that since she was guilty of the same. "He said Dalton probably had a severe concussion."

Rachel sent her a reassuring smile. "Hey, it wasn't as bad as it could've been. The hospital staff is pretty certain he didn't suffer any serious brain injury because he's responsive. He is rather confused and sometimes doesn't make a lot of sense when he speaks. Then again, I've seen him that way after he's been to happy hour."

So had Jess on the numerous occasions he'd come home under the influence. She'd seen him that way again last night. "So he's going to make a full recovery?"

"That's my understanding, although they're not sure he'll ever be able to recall the events that led to his hospitalization." Rachel topped off the comment with a meaningful look.

Jess welcomed that news for reasons she didn't dare disclose to her friend. "I'm glad he's going to be okay."

"You are?"

"Of course I am. No matter what's happened between us, I would never wish any harm on Dalton. You have to believe that."

"I do."

The lack of conviction in Rachel's tone drove Jess to further explain the situation, or as much as she could offer without providing all the gory details. "Look, Rachel, I swear to you that Dalton's injuries resulted from an accident. He'd been drinking and he stumbled." With a little help, a fact she opted to leave out of the mix.

Rachel's gaze drifted away. "According to my father, Dalton's tox screen was negative."

A surge of panic swelled in Jess's chest, making it difficult to draw a breath. She could see a criminal case against her building with every disclosure. "There has to be some mistake. I've been with Dalton a long time and I know when he's had too much to drink."

Rachel sent her a weak smile. "Well, I didn't hear the doctor say it, and it wouldn't be the first time my father made an effort to save Dalton's reputation, usually to no avail."

How well she knew that about her former father-in-law. He'd lie to a clergyman if it meant saving face.

Needing a diversion, Jess began rearranging the canned goods according to contents. "It really doesn't matter as long as Dalton recovers. Danny's completely torn up over this, so much so he hasn't spoken since it happened."

Rachel reached over and patted her hand. "If you're really concerned about him, I have a friend from college who's a child psychologist. She lives in Vicksburg and I'm sure she'd be more than willing to see Danny."

"I've thought about counseling," Jess admitted. "But I'd like to wait a few days until he's had more time to recover. I'm not sure turning him loose on a stranger would help matters right now."

Rachel hopped down from the counter. "Just let me know when and I'll give her a call. And one more thing."

She wasn't sure she could handle one more thing. "What?"

Her friend's expression went somber. "If something happened last night that caused you to lose your temper, I would never blame you for lashing out at my brother. I know how he operates. He spent our childhood deriding me for being Daddy's little girl because he's always been Daddy's tow-the-line target. He's never understood that after my mother died giving birth to me, our father was bound to coddle me a little more. To hear Dalton tell it, I got away with murder."

When mortification passed over Rachel's face, Jess was determined to reassure her. "I'm sure he'd say the same thing about me, but he would be wrong on both counts."

The sound of a blaring horn caused Jess to physically jump while Rachel muttered, "My husband has no manners. The last time he honked to summon me, we were dating and he did it just to spite my father."

Jess tried hard to smile but it didn't quite take. "Men. Can't live with them, can't find anyone else to take them."

Rachel braced her hands on her hips. "Well he can just wait while I help you get the house in order."

"You've already done enough, Rachel. And there's not much else to do. I've spent most of the day clearing the cobwebs and dust and disinfecting the bathrooms with some cleaning products I found here and there. Of course, I still have to tackle the oven."

Rachel put a hand to her ear and pretended to listen. "I do believe I hear my husband calling my name."

Jess laughed. "I knew I couldn't count on you to clean the oven."

"You know me so well." Rachel leaned over and gave her a hug. "Hang in there, Jess. Dalton's going to be fine and then you'll be able to get on with your life."

If only she could share her friend's optimism. "Thanks for everything. And in the meantime…" She patted Rachel's belly. "Take care of junior and I'll see you soon."

"You better believe it," Rachel said. "We still have to go baby shopping before this little one makes an appearance in about eleven weeks."

Jess had no idea where she would be in eleven weeks. Preferably not in jail. "It's a deal."

After Jess saw Rachel off and waved to Matt, who

obviously didn't feel comfortable enough to come in for a visit, she went back inside the house to check on her child and resume her cleaning.

Yet an all-consuming guilt plagued her when she considered the details she'd intentionally withheld from the people who cared about her the most. She'd begun to dig a hole so deep she might never find her way out of the abyss. If Dalton never regained his memory of the events that led to this mess, she might be able to keep that secret. What she did with the other secret still remained to be seen.

Chase had a right to know he could be Danny's biological father, but she worried her failure to acknowledge that possibility a long time ago could send him packing for good. He happened to be the only grounding force in her life at the moment, and she couldn't bear the thought of losing his support. Even now the temptation to see him was so great, she considered calling.

But he had a job to do and she had no right to prevent him from doing it because of her insecurities. At least she'd see him tomorrow.

HE HAD NO INTENTION of paying Jess a visit until tomorrow.

But before he finished his shift, Chase decided to drive by the house to make sure it was secure. And when he noticed all the lights filtering through the windows, he signed off for the night and returned to his cabin to retrieve a spare TV to give Jess. If she was going to be stuck at home alone with a bad case of insomnia, he might as well provide her with some entertainment.

Who the hell was he kidding? He wanted to be with

her, if only for an hour or so. He had to let her know he had no intention of deserting her, even if good sense said he should keep his distance.

As he pulled into the drive twenty minutes later, Chase was satisfied he'd done the right thing when he discovered the place was still lit up like a billboard. Of course, she could be sleeping, but he had his doubts about that. Enough doubts that he got out of the truck, hauled the thirty-six-inch console from the bed, and carried it to the front porch.

After he elbowed the bell, Chance glanced to his right to see Jess pulling the curtain back and peering outside. She opened the door in a matter of moments, sporting a look of surprise. "Is it tomorrow already?" she asked.

Chase didn't know if she was teasing or unhappy to see him. "Thought you could use this for a late-night diversion," he said as he raised the TV for her inspection.

"You could have waited until tomorrow," she said. "Danny's already asleep and I've been reading a book I found in a closet. Not to mention I imagine a satellite dish wouldn't work out here in the boondocks with all the trees. No service, no channels, no reason to have a TV."

He considered himself a fairly strong guy, but the outdated television had to weigh well over a hundred pounds and was top-heavy to boot. At this rate he was going to strain something before she made up her mind. "This set has a built-in DVD player and it's got a converter so you might be able to pick up a couple of channels out of Jackson."

"I guess that's worth something."

It wouldn't be worth a plug nickel if he dropped the

damn thing on the porch. "Look, holding this thing is like bench-pressing your car, so I'd appreciate it if you'd decide if you want it before I get a hernia."

She tipped her temple against the partially-open screen. "Sure. I'd hate to think I gave you a hernia and also made you squander your own sleep to help me out with mine."

Like he didn't have his own problems sleeping. "Now that we have that settled, can I come in or do you want me to toss this to you and leave?"

"Sorry," she muttered as she held open the door, finally allowing him inside.

He avoided looking at her attire—a short flannel nightshirt—and kept his focus on the few available surfaces to support an oversized TV. But the images of her bare legs stayed imprinted in his brain. "Where do you want it?"

"Where do you want to put it?"

That was a loaded question. He nodded toward the low wooden table in the corner near an electrical outlet. "Move that stuff and I'll set it up there."

Jess padded across the room in her sock-covered feet and bent over to clear the table of a candy dish and some cheap figurines. When the blasted shirt rode up her thighs, Chase was forced to lower the TV to preserve his dignity.

He didn't know what the hell was wrong with him. In all the time he'd known Jess, he'd never been turned on by her legs. Well, almost never. He could think of a few times he'd had some fairly male reactions during a swim at the pond together, but he'd always maintained control. And he couldn't forget that one night...

He damn sure didn't need to go there, otherwise he'd be forced to hang onto the television until the pain over-rode his libido.

Jess fortunately straightened to give him some relief, her arms full of knick-knacks. "There you go. I'll just put these in the spare room and be back in a sec. In the meantime, make yourself comfortable."

Even if she returned wearing a black garbage sack, he wouldn't be comfortable. "I've got to get the remote out of the truck."

"Okeydoke," she tossed over one shoulder as she headed away.

Chase put down the TV and stepped outside, hoping the frigid night air would help cool his overheated body. He braced both arms above the passenger door and drew in a few deep breaths while uttering a few choice oaths that would cause his mother to send him into the corner as punishment for his many sins.

Finally feeling more composed, he opened the door and took out the remote along with some DVDs he'd brought with him. He then walked back to the house, slowly, and opened the door to Jess seated on the sofa, her heels propped on the coffee table.

"It's pretty cold in here." Not that he didn't welcome the chill.

She pointed at the black iron stove in the corner. "I wasn't sure how to work that thing, but I did find a space heater in a closet. I put it in Danny's room."

"Do you want me to light your fire?" Damn.

She grinned. "How do you propose to do that?"

"In the stove. With wood and matches."

"I'm fine."

Yeah, she was. Real fine. "I brought a few action movies for Danny but this one's for you." Chase tossed her a DVD featuring a couple in the throes of passion splashed across the label.

After she made a two-handed catch, she surveyed the case for a few moments. "I've been dying to see this."

"I figured it was your kind of movie."

She turned over the unopened package before looking up at him. "I appreciate the gesture, but you shouldn't have gone to the trouble of buying it just for me."

He didn't particularly like having to shatter her assumption for the sake of honesty but he saw no good reason to lie. "I bought it a while ago for someone else."

She frowned. "One of your Friday-night girls?"

No surprise she'd think that. "My mom, for her birthday. I noticed the R rating and gave her something a little less risqué."

Jess laughed. "It's a romantic comedy, not porn. I'm sure it just features some racy language."

"And nudity," he added. "Missy doesn't like naked people in her movies."

Her amber eyes went wide. "You've already seen it?"

"No. It says so on the label."

She tore open the package and her face lit up with excitement. "Let's watch it now."

No way would he watch a bunch of sex scenes with her, especially when he considered the way he'd reacted to her night clothes that most would deem more than modest, even his mother. "I probably should get going."

She patted the space beside her. "It's not even midnight yet, and you said yourself you have a hard time falling asleep."

He'd been having a hard time ever since he walked into the house. "I don't like chick flicks, Jess."

She looked thoroughly frustrated. "And I don't like violent, shoot-'em-up films, but I've watched more than my share with you in the past."

She obviously craved his company but she sure as hell wouldn't if she could read his mind. If he had any decency at all, he'd suck it up, stick around and watch the freaking movie. Decency was a huge problem at the moment. "Maybe later."

She pretended to pout. "Come on, Chase. If you stay, I'll make you some popcorn. Besides, you'll probably be asleep after the first fifteen minutes."

Maybe so, if the first fifteen minutes didn't involve any sex, and that was a big if. "Fine, I'll give you fifteen minutes, but if I'm not asleep or I hate it, I'm out of here."

"It's a deal." She hopped up from the sofa and went into the kitchen while Chase paced around the room with enough nervous energy to power Placid.

After a few minutes, Jess returned with a bag of potato chips and napkins tucked under one arm, a soft drink clutched in each hand. "I just realized I only have the microwave kind of popcorn and there's no microwave," she said as she gave him a can of cola.

He opened the tab and took a drink, wishing he had something a little stronger. "We can pick one up at the hardware store tomorrow when we stop by your house."

She sat back down on the sofa and tore open the bag. "I can live without a microwave. And Rachel brought everything I need so we can forget the house. By the way, thank you for sending her over."

He could only imagine how that visit went. "She wanted to do it."

"I'm glad she did. Anyway, I'll pick up what's left at the house, as soon as I decide where I'm going to permanently reside."

Chase figured she just wanted to avoid the bad memories. "Suit yourself." He set the drink down on the napkin she'd placed on the table and held out his hand. "Give me the movie and I'll start it, unless you want me to show you how it works."

That earned him a sour look. "I'm not a complete moron, Chase. I know how it works. Beside, you're already up so you can stick it in."

Everything she said sounded downright dirty, but then his mind—not her mouth—had taken a freefall into the gutter. "That coming from someone who called me to program her VCR back in high school."

"Shut up and play the movie."

She nailed him with a grin and those crystal-clear amber eyes that sometimes looked green, sometimes gold, like now. Cat eyes, he used to call them. She also had a mouth that the stuff male fantasies were made of. Put the package all together and you had temptation personified. A deadly combination, especially to a guy who didn't need a whole lot of encouragement to throw logic to the wind and climb all over her.

Forcing himself back into cautious mode, Chase plugged in the TV, inserted the DVD and started it rolling with the remote. He thought about claiming the straight-back chair, but it looked about as comfortable as cactus. He opted to join Jess on the sofa and slid as far to the left as he could until he butted up against the arm. Better a furniture arm than her arm.

He pointed the remote and turned up the volume while they watched the opening credits, complete with sappy music that made him want to cover his ears. "Too bad we don't have surround sound," he said with a whole lot of sarcasm.

Jess rolled her eyes. "Boys and their toys. Dalton was always about high-dollar sound systems and woofers and tweeters. The man loves big tweeters. Guess that's part of the reason why the marriage didn't work."

Chase tried to center his attention on the TV but his evil eyes betrayed him, landing his gaze right on Jess's chest. "Your tweeters are fine."

She let go a sarcastic laugh. "Ha! That coming from the guy who told me in the seventh grade that he was sorry my training bra needed to be trained for better results."

Man, he thought she'd forgotten that. "Just a stupid remark from a stupid kid."

She popped a chip into her mouth. "If you think I'm going to buy into that excuse, think again."

"You could be pretty caustic with the remarks, too. I recall you throwing around dumb jock more than once."

"Don't forget tail chaser."

"Shrimp."

She hurled a potato chip at his head. "Dimples."

He'd hated that one the most and that called for bringing out the big guns. "Stop throwing food, Gertrude."

She narrowed her eyes and glared at him. "You know how much I despise my middle name. Now apologize."

When she poked him hard in the ribs, he grabbed her

leg and pressed his fingertips in the sensitive spot above her knee. "Not until you apologize for the dimples remark."

She writhed and laughed until he released the pressure, then straightened and sent him a fierce look. "If you try that again, I swear I'll kick you off the couch."

He leaned closer. "You don't scare me, Gertie."

But with his hand still on her thigh and that lethal mouth only a few inches away from his, she did scare him. Correction. He feared what he might do to her if he didn't get away quick. He hadn't wanted anything or anyone this much since he'd come back to town. But he couldn't compromise their renewed connection all in the name of a quick roll on the couch. Provided she'd even go for that.

She would, he realized when she closed her eyes, drew in a slow breath, and inched her mouth closer to his. If anyone needed to be kissed, she did. If anyone could kiss her the way she should be kissed, he could. If the stakes weren't so high, he'd do it. Now. To hell with the consequences.

Instead, Chase moved back into his original spot and muttered, "We're missing the movie."

Jess adjusted her clothes, pulled the lone throw pillow from behind her back and hugged it. "Like you really care."

No, he didn't care, but at least the video provided a distraction. Too much of a distraction, he decided after the lead guy backed the gullible girl up against a wall and started tearing at her clothes. Pretty soon the clothes were gone and the action was on and that just about sent Chase completely over the edge.

He had two choices—steal the pillow from Jess to put in his lap or make a fast exit. He opted for the exit.

"I've got to go," he said as he pushed off the couch and headed toward the door.

Jess move lightning fast and thwarted his departure before he could even turn the knob. "What's the problem, Chase?"

He didn't dare face her and let her see his problem. "I can't do this."

"Can't do what? Watch a movie with me?"

He tipped his forehead against the door and sucked in a couple of breaths. "I can't pretend everything's the same between us."

"And I can't believe you'd let one night, that by your own admission didn't mean anything, stand in the way of our friendship."

If she only knew how much that night had meant to him. How often he'd thought about it over the years. How much he still wanted her. "I'm not as strong as you think. You deserve better."

"Chase, look at me."

He reluctantly answered her command and realized how damn sexy she looked with her hair a complete mess. "What?"

"We both deserve to be happy, and nothing has ever made me happier than having you as my best friend. Sometimes you have to fight for the things in life you consider worthwhile." Her gaze and confidence wavered. "Unless you don't view our relationship that way."

He sighed. "Yeah, I do."

She took his hands into hers. "Then can we at least try to start over again and regain our trust in each other?"

He'd like nothing better than to start over, but easier said than done. Still, he owed her that much and more. "I'll try, but it's going to take time."

Her smile went straight to his heart. "We've got all the time in the world, at least for now."

Chase worried spending that time with her could lead to betrayal, if he didn't keep a chokehold on his desire. But she was right about one thing—their friendship was worth a second shot. He couldn't think of two people who needed each other more. And he could think of all the reasons why needing each other too much could be way too risky.

CHAPTER FIVE

She needed more sleep.

The sound of the TV prevented Jess from pulling the covers back over her head and hiding away from the world. That would mean hiding away from her son, who'd apparently left his room since the last time she'd checked on him.

She'd gone to bed not long after Chase had made his abrupt exit, yet she'd tossed and turned for what seemed like hours on end. That powerful spark of awareness between them had played over and over in her mind like a favorite poem. She'd come so close to falling into the same trap—wanting more from him than he could give her, other than meaningless sex. Meaningless to him, but not to her.

If they'd lost control, she would have been no better for the experience. After all, he'd said he'd been going through a dry spell, and if that happened to be the case, she'd be nothing more than the means to refill his well. She had too much upheaval in her life as it now stood. Becoming just another one of his emotional casualties would only make matters worse.

Sadly, that reality didn't prevent her from wanting to be with him, whenever or however she could.

She pushed aside the sheets that had wound around her body during the night and grabbed the cell from the nightstand. The clock indicated it was five minutes past eight, much later than she'd assumed, but only four hours since her last look. Regardless, she had to get up and face the day.

Jess left the bed, retrieved her robe and headed down the hall. As predicted, Danny had discovered the latest gift, compliments of the deputy. She hoped her child hadn't discovered the movie she'd left in the player last night.

She strolled into the living room and fortunately found that suspect film lying on the floor next to her son, a nice action-packed superhero movie playing on the screen. He was stretched out on his belly, elbows bent and cheeks supported by his palms. He didn't acknowledge her, but at least he appeared somewhat content. He also looked so innocent, so undeniably sweet, she wanted to sweep him into her arms and hold him as she'd done when he was much younger. He'd hate her if she tried, so she wouldn't. She'd simply have to settle for giving him a good-morning kiss.

Before she reached Danny, the doorbell sounded, echoing through the small space. For someone who lived alone in the middle of nowhere, she'd certainly had a lot of visitors over the past twenty-four hours. She assumed that Freddie the propane man had stopped by to replenish the tank and, in turn, save them from another day of ice cold water and a night with no measurable heat.

She discovered she'd been sorely mistaken in her assumption when she pulled back the curtains and peeked outside. The gorgeous guy standing on the porch had been the one responsible for her lack of sleep and, admittedly, her savior in many ways. He hadn't shaven and that only enhanced his unquestionable sex appeal. So did the unbuttoned, untucked navy flannel shirt covering a white tee, the sleeves drawn tight around the bulk of his biceps. The faded jeans, a small rip at the knee, did incredible things for his long legs and narrow hips. Not that he needed any help in that regard. With an axe gripped in one hand and a tool box at his feet, he could pass as one hunk of a handyman. And she knew how handy Chase Reed could be. So did at least half the women in the county.

Jess opened the door and masked her surprise with a mock smirk. "Well as I live and breathe, it's Daniel Boone on my doorstep."

His smile arrived as slow as the sunrise, traveling all the way to those delicious brown eyes framed with sinfully long lashes a little darker than his sand-colored hair. He had the audacity to hook the thumb on his free hand in his pocket, and she had the nerve to look a little left of that pocket. Obviously she'd been visited by the Hormone Fairy sometime during the night.

"That's Deputy Boone, ma'am," he said, followed by a salute. "At your service."

She wouldn't mind being serviced by him. "What's with the axe?"

"Just thought I'd chop some wood before I give you a makeshift shower."

Right now he was giving her some very heady chills. "I was just about to fix Danny breakfast. Have you eaten?"

"I had some coffee."

"Want some eggs and bacon?"

"I wouldn't turn it down. But first, I have a few things to get out of the truck."

Jess peered behind him and didn't see a vehicle in the driveway. "Where did you park?"

"Around the side. I have a surprise for Danny. It's in the truck bed." He leaned the axe against the column supporting the porch. "Come here and I'll show you."

She tightened the robe's sash around her waist. "In case you haven't noticed, I'm not dressed."

He gave her a long once-over. "I've noticed, but you're not exactly naked. And even if you were, I'm pretty sure there's no one else around to see you."

No use arguing with his logic. "Okay, but this better be good."

"It is," he said as he strode away without her.

Jess stepped down the two stairs leading to the yard and picked her way across the gravel drive in her sock-clad feet. She rounded the corner just in time to see Chase lowering the tailgate, preparing to release what she worried might be the surprise.

She'd imagined a new bike or fishing poles or maybe even a baseball bat. She hadn't imagined the shiny, coal-black monstrosity of a canine bounding from the truck's bed, its tongue hanging out and tail wagging like a wind-shield wiper. But the minute its paws hit the ground, Chase pointed at the gravel drive. "Sit, Bo."

The dog remarkably complied and seemed glad to do it.

Jess cautiously approached the pair, just in case Bo mistook her for an intruder—or a meal. "I didn't know you had a dog. After Rory died, you swore you'd never have another one."

"Bo's not my dog."

Her concerns had all but been confirmed. "Please tell me this isn't Danny's surprise."

"Yeah, he is. Something wrong with that?"

He had to be kidding. "First of all, he weighs at least one hundred pounds."

"I'd say about seventy, maybe seventy-five pounds."

Nothing like splitting dog hairs. "Secondly, I'm renting this place and if he tears anything up, I'll be—"

"He won't," Chase said. "He didn't do all that well as a hunter so Jim Creary's offering him as a pet. He's three years old, so he's out of the puppy stage, and he's housebroken. His shots are updated, he's a registered Lab, he's as smart as a whip and he minds better than most kids."

And he most likely ate like a horse. "I'm just not sure this is a good idea. Danny might be completely overwhelmed by him."

Chase streaked a hand over the back of his neck. "Listen, Jess, that little boy in there needs something to get his mind off his troubles. Pets are used all the time for therapy. Bo could be just the thing to draw him out. Nothing else has worked so far."

That made sense, but his insinuation also stung like a hornet. "You're saying that as his mother, I don't have the skills to do that."

He looked somewhat apologetic. "I didn't mean to insult you. I only meant that Danny could use a distraction."

She realized he could be right, but still… "Any chance Bo might be a watch dog?"

When Bo barked, Chase laughed. "Guess that's your answer."

One bark did not a guard dog make, especially with that tail still wagging. Yet Jess acknowledged Chase had made some valid points. Danny could use some companionship. School wouldn't be back in session for another two-plus weeks. Being so far from civilization, she doubted any other children lived nearby, and she didn't feel comfortable arranging play dates in Placid, particularly if rumors had already begun to abound.

If something as simple as giving Danny a dog could bring him back around, then she was game.

"Okay," she said. "We'll see how Bo does on a trial basis. If it doesn't work out, promise me you'll make sure he has a good home." And that in itself posed a huge problem. Once again Danny would be losing a pet, and this time she'd be responsible for the heartbreak, not Dalton.

Chase raised a hand in oath. "I promise I will take Bo myself if it doesn't work. But I'd bet my badge they'll do fine together. He's a great dog and Danny's going to enjoy having him around. You might even enjoy him, too."

We'll see, Jess almost responded but instead headed back toward the house, Chase and Bo following not too far behind. She entered first, thankful to find Danny still planted in front of the TV. Under normal circumstances, she would have encouraged him to go outside. But now she needed to know where he was every minute of the day for fear he might take off to escape her. Paranoid, yes, but his attitude toward her hadn't been at all encouraging.

"Danny," she said. "Chase has something for you and I think you're really going to like it."

As it had been for the past two days, Danny didn't acknowledge her.

Chase moved forward with the dog close on his heels. "Hey, Danny. You have a visitor."

Only then did Danny glance to his left, looking decidedly disinterested, until his gaze landed on Bo. His brown eyes widened and his smile illuminated the room as if Christmas morning had arrived early.

Danny sat up and stared at the dog with blatant awe. "Is he mine?"

She wanted to do cartwheels over Danny's verbal response, the first one since the accident. She had Chase's wisdom, and a dog named Bo, to thank for the breakthrough. "You have to feed him and make sure he has water. Can you do that?"

"Uh-huh."

"Then I guess he's yours."

Chase crouched down and signaled Bo forward. "Danny, this is Bo. Bo, this is Danny, your new owner."

When her son reached to pet the dog, Bo rewarded him with a sloppy lick in the face. Then suddenly Danny did something so surprising, Jess couldn't contain her own excitement—he laughed. She'd always loved that exuberant laugh and she couldn't remember the last time she'd heard it. She vowed to hear it more.

Her child's joy encouraged the dog to dole out more wet canine kisses. As soon as Bo let up, Danny leaned over and hugged the Lab, the grateful look on his face priceless. Chase came to his feet and sent Jess a satisfied look. "I believe it's going to work out just fine."

So did she, much better than expected. "Yes, I believe it will. Good plan. Thanks."

"Don't thank me," he said. "Thank Bo." He looked around the room for a few minutes. "You know what else this place needs?"

"Hot water would be nice."

Chase frowned. "Have you lit the pilot light? Freddie called and said he filled the propane tank around seven."

She'd barely fallen asleep by that time. "I haven't tried that yet, but I hope it works. I had to heat water on the stove last night so Danny could bathe and I toughed it out."

"You took a cold bath?"

"Yes, I did."

"Join the club. I took a cold shower after I left here last night."

"Something wrong with your water heater?"

"Just the opposite. My heaters were working a little too well."

Jess considered that to be an apology. A strange apology, but an apology none the less. "Are they functioning correctly now?"

"So far, but the day is young." He sent her a wink that made her want to both slug him and kiss that cocky look on his face. The old Chase had clearly returned, quite possibly to her own detriment.

"You never said what you think the house needs," she added to move away from a conversation that could land them both in trouble the next time they were alone— if they were alone. "Maybe a good coat of non-yellow paint?"

"I'm thinking something that's a quick fix."

She shrugged. "I give up."

"A Christmas tree."

Jess had yet to be visited by the holiday spirit. Maybe a tree would help, and so would some presents to put under the tree. Too bad she didn't have either. "Even if I did have a tree, I have no decorations readily available and I'd rather not make a trip to the house to get some. I could string popcorn, but I still don't have that microwave."

"Not a problem," he said. "I'm sure Mom has some extra decorations in the attic. She's out of town right now but I could give her a call."

Jess frowned. "Where is she?"

"In the Smoky Mountains with her sisters for a Christmas craft fair and last minute shopping. They're staying at Rachel and Matt's cabin."

Good for Missy and her girlfriend getaway. Jess wished she'd made more effort to stay connected with her own friends. Only one of the many things Dalton had made difficult. "So Buck's having to manage everything alone, huh?"

"Yeah. That's why he's been in such a foul mood."

That and the fact he'd had to deal with a family friend's daughter whom he viewed as uncooperative— and more important, a criminal.

Chase regarded Danny who'd gone back to watching the TV, Bo lying beside him as if they'd always been fast friends. "Hey, bud, why don't you and me go to the tree farm over at Wilson and pick out a nice one?"

Danny looked back over his shoulder. "Can we take Bo?"

"You bet."

Jess couldn't quite believe that her baby boy had finally reclaimed his voice, all because of a four-legged creature. "You can go right after breakfast."

When Danny wrinkled his nose with disdain, Chase added, "We can pick up something at the diner and take it with us."

She'd been thrown over for a dog and suspect food from a greasy spoon. "Fine. Go get dressed, Danny."

He was off like a racehorse with Bo by his side, leaving Chase and Jess alone.

Feeling generous, she faced Chase with a smile. "I'm amazed and I'm very grateful. I was beginning to think I'd never hear him speak again."

"Not possible since he's your son."

She punched his arm and he let go an exaggerated wince. "That's a weird way to thank me."

Jess could think of a few ways she'd like to thank him, none that were advisable for the situation or appropriate for the setting. "You better be glad I'm out of shape."

"I'd have to disagree." He finished off the comment with a rake of his gaze down her body and back up again, shades of the old Chase, only he'd never been quite so attentive to her in the past.

Jess felt a major blush coming on and she couldn't do a darn thing to stop it. "While the two of you are off tree hunting, I'm going to stay here and make a to-do list."

Chase groaned. "For me?"

She patted his whisker-shaded cheek. "Of course. You have to put those tools to good use."

"Good point. A man's tools are meant to be used on

a regular basis." The wicked sparkle in his dark eyes punctuated his suggestive tone.

"I'm not going to even justify that remark with a response." But, boy, did she want to. "I am going to see if my son is dressed and ready to go. And please make sure you return him to me in one piece."

His suddenly serious expression bordered on angry. "Any reason why you think I wouldn't?"

"You do have a habit of driving fast and—"

"I'm more than capable of being careful with a kid in the passenger seat."

She couldn't quite peg the extreme change in his demeanor. "I'm sure you are but I worry about him. If you had children, you'd understand."

His jaw tightened so much Jess thought it might break. "I may not have a clue about raising a child, but I value life as much as anyone. If you're that worried, maybe we should just forget it."

She didn't have the heart to disappoint her son, not when he'd made such progress today. "I'm sorry, Chase. I trust you."

"Fine. I'll have him back home by noon."

"Good. Now that we've established that, I'll go get him."

As Jess walked away, Chase called her back, forcing her to face him once more.

"I should be apologizing," he said. "It's just that over the past few years..." He drew in a deep breath and let it out slowly. "Never mind."

Jess did mind. She minded that she'd apparently exposed a nerve, and he seemed to be holding something back. Perhaps some bitter experience during the war.

In light of her deception, she couldn't judge him for not coming clean.

Maybe someday in the near future, after they'd finally come full circle in their friendship, they could both confess.

WITH A SEVEN-FOOT FIR tied down in the bed, the boy and his dog in the front seat of the single-cab Ford, Chase set out for home. He checked the dashboard clock and realized they'd spent more time at the tree farm than he'd intended. He figured Jess was fit to be tied about now, but he hadn't been able to reach her on the cell. The small town of Wilson was forty miles away from Placid, which meant they had an hour's drive ahead of them, unless he ignored the speed limit. He'd be damned if he did that after making the promise to Jess to protect her son.

He'd done everything in his power to do that today, including watching Danny like a hawk when they were picking out the tree. He never let him out of his sight and at times that had presented a challenge. But he wanted to prove to Jess that he could be a proper guardian to her son. Maybe even prove it to himself.

As he traveled down the main highway, he glanced at Danny, half expecting him to be asleep. Instead, the boy stared out the windshield, looking like he might be returning to that internal refuge where he'd been for the past two days. Chase knew that sanctuary well. He'd visited often, before and after he'd ended his military service, and he learned it wasn't always a good place to be. Sometimes it was necessary for self-preservation.

But he'd made good progress today with Danny and he didn't want to ruin him by letting him withdraw again. "What kind of sports do you like?" he asked, although he knew the answer from the memorabilia in Danny's former bedroom.

"Baseball," he answered without taking his eyes off the scenery.

"What position do you play?"

"Second base. My mom says I'm good at it, but she's wrong."

Chase immediately picked up on the animosity in his voice. "I imagine you're good at it, otherwise you wouldn't play the infield. Besides, Mom's are usually right about those things."

"She's wrong," he said adamantly. "She's wrong about a lot of things."

He wasn't sure whether to move forward, or halt the conversation right there. If he did continue, he could be heading down a treacherous path leading right into what happened the night Dalton was injured. But if the kid wanted to vent, he shouldn't stop him. Any information passed between the two of them would have to remain private, the best thing for all concerned, especially Jess. Even if it meant he'd have to lie to her, and for her.

"Are you mad at your mom for some reason, Danny?" He took another quick look to gauge the boy's reaction.

Danny only responded with a nod.

"That's okay," Chase said. "Moms aren't perfect. Sometimes they make mistakes, but that doesn't mean they don't love us. If she did something you didn't like, maybe you should talk to her about it."

After a short span of silence, Danny declared, "I'm mad because she married my dad."

Chase shouldn't be all that surprised by his response. "Why's that?"

"Because my dad hates me," he said quietly.

If the bastard made his own kid feel unloved, that was sinking to an all-time low, even for Dalton Wainwright. For a brief moment, he regretted he wasn't Danny's father, until he remembered why that wouldn't be a good thing. At one time he'd questioned if that might be a possibility due to the timing. After his mother had told him Jess was pregnant, he'd almost went straight to the source and asked. Almost. But he'd believed that Jess would never withhold that kind of information from him, in spite of what he'd said to her the one and only night they were together.

Jess could be too spontaneous for her own good, and sometimes forgetful, but she leaned toward being brutally honest. Exactly why he had a hard time buying she had anything to do with Dalton's injuries. And as far as he could tell, her son couldn't implicate her, either.

Returning to the problem at hand, he grappled with finding some consolation to offer Danny. "My dad's always been pretty hard on me," he began. "At times we haven't liked each other very much." He could think of one instance in recent history—when Buck had questioned Jess's innocence. "But I'm still his son, and I know he loves me. He just doesn't know how to show it."

"My dad doesn't love me at all."

The boy sounded so certain, he was inclined to believe him. "Are you sure about that?"

He kept his eyes lowered, like he was ashamed. "He told me so."

Chase gripped the steering wheel tighter with the

force of his fury. He didn't know how to respond, so he chose to say nothing.

They rode the rest of the way in silence, and when they pulled into the drive, Jess came out the front door. She didn't exactly looked pleased over their tardiness, but as soon as Danny slid out of the truck, that all changed. Her face instantly lit up over the sight of her son. Unfortunately, she didn't afford Chase the same enthusiasm.

She folded her arms over her chest, looking every bit the school teacher, except for the tight, long-sleeve, stretchy top and dark form-fitting jeans. "Did you forget how to tell time?" she asked.

He pretended to be the contrite student while trying to keep his eyes off her cleavage. "It took longer than we planned, but feel free to stick me in the corner and make me write 'I will not be tardy' a hundred times." Or she could send him to bed early, which would be okay if she joined him.

And there he went again, acting like a man who'd been stranded on a desert island for months, lonely and lusting for his former best friend. A friend who had more problems than she could count.

Jess ignored him and peered into the back of the truck. "It's a gorgeous tree. You're forgiven."

"You can thank your son for the tree. He picked it out."

She turned to Danny, who stood beside the truck, kicking gravel while Bo sniffed around the yard, anointing every bush in sight. "You did good, sweetie."

Danny sent her a "whatever'" look before calling the dog and bounding back into the house.

Pure frustration showed in Jess's eyes. "Did he say anything to you during the trip?"

He'd have to play it by ear when it came to how much he disclosed of the disturbing conversation. "Yeah. He talked quite a bit on the way back."

"About?" she asked.

"Your sorry ex-husband. He told me Dalton said he didn't love him."

Jess's gaze slid away. "Not in so many words, but the insinuation was there. At first, I was the target for his verbal attacks. But when Danny got older, he ended up in Dalton's line of fire."

"Son of a bitch," he muttered. "There's not one damn excuse for that."

"I see it as the 'kick the cat' syndrome," Jess added. "His father bashed him on a daily basis, and then he came home and bashed us."

Chase began to seethe inside over the thought of Wainwright belittling his wife and child—and wondered if there might be more to the story. "Did he ever hit you, Jess?"

She shook her head. "Not physically, but words can wound all the same. There were a few times I thought he might punch me, but fortunately he refrained."

Chase wanted to punch something, namely Dalton Wainwright. "I'm just glad you finally came to your senses and left him. But I can't understand why it took you so damn long."

"I tried to leave after Danny started school," she said. "I'd finished my degree and student teaching. I felt like I could finally make it financially. When I told him I wanted a divorce, he threatened to ruin my parents' business if I didn't do his bidding. I couldn't risk them losing everything they'd worked so hard for all their lives. Eventually Edwin bought them out and they had more than enough money to retire in style."

Chase knew her folks well and he had a hard time with their apparent abandonment. "They left you here to fend for yourself?"

She twisted the ruby ring around her finger. "I gave them my blessing when they decided to join Gary and his family in the Carolinas. They deserved a change of pace."

"And you deserved to have their support while Dalton was doling out all his crap."

She leaned back against the truck. "They didn't know how bad it was, Chase. No one really knew, except for Danny. Not a day goes by that I don't hate myself for subjecting him to a cold, uncaring father."

And not a minute had gone by when he hadn't shouldered some of the blame for her decision, too. "At least now he's out of your life for good."

She sighed. "Sometimes I think he'll never be out of my life."

He draped an arm around her shoulder. "Let's forget about the demon today and concentrate on decorating a tree."

Finally, she smiled. "You're on. And I'm going to make you fried chicken for dinner."

"No mac and cheese?"

Her smile faded into a frown. "If you're worried I can't fry chicken, don't. I learned a lot in your absence."

Yeah, she had. A lot about her ex's faults the hard way. "I'm impressed."

"Don't be until you eat it."

"That doesn't give me a whole lot of confidence in your culinary abilities." When she dropped his arm from her shoulder and started to walk away, he added, "I've got another idea, Jess."

She turned and continued to step backward. "Fast food?"

"No. Why don't we take Danny into town tonight for the Christmas tree lighting ceremony?"

She stopped cold. "I've already thawed out the chicken."

"We can pick up something to eat there, and you can save the chicken for tomorrow night. I'm working the seven-to-seven shift and I can fix your shower after I'm off."

He was walking a tightrope by inviting himself back over for dinner. In fact, she'd be better off if he stayed away from her. But he didn't see that happening any time soon. At least not until she was cleared of all wrong doing.

"I'm not sure walking around town is a good idea," she said after a few moments. "Word about Dalton has bound to have gotten around and who knows what people are saying about me."

She had a valid concern, but Chase had never known her to back down from a challenge before. He wanted to see a glimpse of the old Jess, the one who could tell everyone to go to hell so sweetly that they thanked her for it later. "Look, you and Danny need to get out of the house. We don't have to stay long and if anyone harasses you, I'll arrest them."

"Now that would make for a really fun night, especially if we run into my father-in-law."

"Edwin's probably at the hospital with Dalton."

Her face fell. "You're right."

Damn, he'd spun her mind back onto her troubles. "I hear the furniture store's going to have a train display this year and Mayor Crenshaw's going to be Santa."

"With that beer belly of his, he won't need a suit."

"And we can't miss cow-patty bingo."

She wrinkled her nose. "Speak for yourself."

"The volunteer fire department's auxiliary ladies will be serving pies."

"I can make a pretty good pie from the comfort of my own kitchen."

He saved the best for last. "They're going to have a silent auction and I believe I saw a microwave on the list of donated items."

She raised her hand. "I'm sold."

"Good." He pulled the work gloves from his back pocket. "I'll get this tree set up in the house, go home and clean up and I'll be back in a couple of hours with some decorations."

"Chase Reed, you should've been a used car salesman."

He shot a look over his shoulder. "I'll keep that in mind in case Buck decides to fire me." And he very well could if he showed up tonight and got into a fight to defend Jess's honor.

Not likely that would happen. People respected Jess and they hated the Wainwrights. He couldn't imagine anyone faulting her for Dalton's current predicament. Hell, they might even applaud her.

CHAPTER SIX

SHE FELT LIKE A PARIAH.

From the moment Jess stepped onto the downtown street with Danny and Chase, she'd noticed people talking behind their hands. Some of her students' parents only murmured polite greetings and kept right on walking. Some of the older folks were blatant in their disapproval, doling out looks that made her want to climb beneath the nearest craft booth. Some simply ignored her. On the other hand, they treated Chase with admiration, offering up handshakes and general hero-worship.

Luckily, Danny seemed completely unaware of the snubs. He was too busy playing in the fake snow surrounding the giant, elaborately lit Christmas tree positioned in the center of the parklike town square.

As she and Chase stood on the sidewalk, Jess pulled her denim jacket closer to her body in response to the gust of winter wind. "I'm freezing to death," she said. "I think we should go."

Chase took a drink of coffee, wadded the paper cup and tossed it into a nearby bin. "It's not that cold."

"Easy for you to say since you've always been hot-blooded."

His responding smile was clearly cocky. "That's the rumor."

Once a bad boy, always a bad boy. He wore his baseball cap turned backward and a high school football letter jacket in keeping with the nineteen-fifties-themed Christmas festival. That attire clearly revealed he had the "boy" part down pat tonight. A very mature boy with a physique that warranted a second look, or ten, as evidenced by a nearby group of young women who couldn't seem to take their eyes off of him. They giggled and he smiled, displaying those darn dimples that made many a female want to be bad right with him. Jess included.

She tapped him on the shoulder in an effort to tear his attention away from the admiration society. "Do I have a third-eye growing in the middle of my forehead?" Her tone held enough sarcasm to offend the most practiced cynic.

He narrowed his eyes and surveyed her face. "Not that I've noticed. Why?"

"Because I could swear everyone's talking about me."

He leaned a shoulder against a tree and brought his attention to Danny. "Just ignore them."

If only she could. "Kind of hard to do when the whispering's so loud it makes my ears hurt."

"If you'd worn a poodle skirt, you would've blended in better."

If she saw another poodle skirt tonight, she'd hurl. "Sorry. I don't happen to have one lying around."

"What about your cheerleader uniform?"

Like she could actually get the thing over her expanded butt. "I have no idea where it is. Even if I did, and it still fit, I'd worry someone might ask me to do a back flip. I haven't been that limber in years."

He sent her a sideways glance. "You could try it when we get back to the house."

"And you can kiss my megaphone."

He cracked a killer grin. "Just stick with me, babe, and I'll do wonders for your reputation."

That deserved a serious sneer, which she gave him. "It appears you picked up an extra case of ego while you were out buying the tree."

"I'm just saying that if I have no problem walking around with you, then I obviously don't think you're guilty of anything other than poor taste in men."

She imagined people assumed he'd been assigned to guard her, in case she decided to run. "Present company excluded, of course."

"Damn straight."

She prepared to pose a question she'd been withholding all day for fear of the answer. "Have you heard anything more on Dalton's condition?"

He shifted his weight slightly, a sign of his uneasiness. "I talked to Buck earlier. He says Dalton's alert and they've upgraded his status to stable. He also said he plans to interview him tomorrow morning."

Jess shuddered and it had nothing to do with the weather. "Does he still not remember what happened?"

"Guess we'll find out tomorrow."

She dreaded tomorrow. "Guess we will."

"Look at it this way," he said. "Now that Dalton's out of the woods, and after he clears everything up, the rumors will die down, and so will all the speculation. Everyone will move on to the next gossip target."

Or those rumors could heat up, depending on Dalton's account of the night in question. "I hope Buck realizes that my ex-husband can be fairly vindictive. There's no telling what he's going to say about me."

"You've got enough to worry about without borrowing trouble."

Lately trouble just seemed to follow her around, like a recurring case of the flu. Yet obsessing over the impending interview tonight would only serve to ruin everyone's mood, including her son's if he picked up on her distress.

Jess checked her watch, amazed to find two hours had already passed since they'd arrived. "We really have to go. We still need to decorate the tree and Bo needs to be fed."

"Unless he's already raided the fridge."

Jess couldn't imagine the dog being that smart. "Or eaten half the contents of the house."

"I still have to show Danny the train," Chase said.

She wouldn't feel right denying her son that opportunity. "Fine, but let's make it quick."

Chase stuck both pinkies in his mouth and let go an ear-splitting whistle, then called Danny's name to gain his attention.

In a matter of moments, Danny raced across the park and joined them, cheeks rosy from the cold and eyes alight with excitement. Jess loved that he seemed so carefree, and prayed nothing would happen to crush his enthusiasm tonight.

Chase laid a large hand on his shoulder. "Let's go see the train, bud."

Danny sent the deputy a grin and like everyone else in town, disregarded his mother.

Jess kept a few steps behind Chase and Danny as they traveled the block to the furniture store, amazed at the similarities between boy and man. Both walked with hands in pockets in a slow, leisurely gait, their gazes focused straight ahead. To any casual observer, they'd definitely pass as a father and son spending quality time together. That could very well be an accurate assumption.

Once they reached brightly lit glass windows, Danny took on look of awe as the elaborate train traveled around the track through a storybook town decked out in holiday regalia. He turned that look of wonder on Chase. "Cool."

"Real cool," Chase added with a satisfied smile.

Jess almost laughed when she noticed the brass plate propped up in the corner of the display.

Made possible through the generosity of Edwin Wainwright.

Not a shocker that her erstwhile father-in-law would require his *generosity* be acknowledged. She was surprised he hadn't demanded a life-size portrait be included with the exhibit.

She started to comment on the miniature village, yet words escaped her as she glanced to see Chase crouched down on Danny's level, one hand resting on her son's shoulder. Her heart took a little tumble over the memorable scene—the tall, strong deputy and the soft-spoken, self-doubting little boy, connecting on a level she'd only dreamed about. The more she viewed the two together, the more she became certain that Chase, not Dalton, had fathered Danny. And she desperately wanted to tell them both. Right here, right now.

This wasn't the time or the place to make that revelation. Besides, she had no real proof aside from identical dimples, a mother's instincts and a good deal of wishful thinking. Maybe she wanted it to be true so badly, she'd let her imagination play tricks on her mind.

"I want another corndog, Mom."

He'd addressed her for the first time in two days. She recovered quickly from the shock and went into mother mode, even though she wanted to throw her arms around him and praise his effort. "You've already had two, Daniel. Don't you think that's enough?"

He actually smiled at her. "I'm a growing boy."

"Yes, you are." And a beautiful, precious boy.

Chase straightened, fished through his pocket, and withdrew a dollar bill. "I used to eat four or five when I was his age. Besides, they only cost a buck. That's a bargain these days."

Normally she might resent Chase usurping her parental power, but she was too thrilled over Danny's breakthrough to argue. "Fine. If he has a stomachache, I'll be calling you in the middle of the night."

He placed the money in Danny's open palm. "Knock yourself out, kid."

"Thanks, Chase!"

After her son hurried away, Jess's euphoria dissolved as several horrible scenarios began to bombard her brain. "Go with him, Chase, and make sure he's okay."

He countered her request with a frown. "The booth's just across the street, and the street's blocked off to traffic. He'll be fine."

She noticed the crowd gathered around the concession stand and her panic began to escalate. "People don't always think before they speak, especially kids. I'd hate for someone to say something that might upset him after he's made so much progress today."

Comprehension finally dawned in his expression. "I'll make sure that doesn't happen."

"Thanks. I'll wait right here." Perhaps she was taking the coward's way out, but she also didn't want to subject Danny to anyone who might harangue her about Dalton.

After Chase left the sidewalk, Jess returned to train-watching for lack of anything better to do. For the first time in a very long time, she felt as if the tide might be turning in her favor. That maybe everything would work out after all.

"Hey, pretty lady."

She didn't have to turn around to know who owned that voice—Buster Eustace, the creep who'd made walking into the girls' locker room during high school a daily sport. He'd also spent a lot of time making verbal passes at her, and she'd spent a lot of time telling him where to shove his suggestions. Seeing no way out, she faced Buster with a smirk. "Fancy meeting you here, Buster." And most unfortunate. "I'm surprised Sally May let you roam the streets alone. Are you lost?"

His seedy smile revealed several missing teeth. "It's real good to see you too, Jessa Belle."

That insulting endearment had almost cost him a few teeth back in the day. "Now you've seen me, and now I have to go." She'd rather face a group of gossip mongers than to spend another second with Buster.

When she took a step forward, he caught her arm, preventing her departure. "Not so fast," he slurred. "I gotta ask you a question."

The smell of smoke and booze on his breath caused Jess's stomach to roil. "I'm in no mood for questions, so please unhand me."

"I hear tell you hit old Dalton in the head with a baseball bat," he said, ignoring her command. "Is it true?"

She yanked out of his hold. "Don't believe everything you hear, Buster boy."

He inched closer, practically trapping her between his bone-skinny body and the display window. "Did Dalton finally grow a pair and try to put you in your place?"

Her last thread of composure snapped. If he didn't back off, he'd find himself in need of a new pair.

Jess put on a syrupy sweet smile and spoke through it. "Let me ask you something, Buster. Do you and Sally May want to have more children?"

That seemed to momentarily sober him up. "We already got three girls, but I'm aimin' to try for a boy."

Lovely. Like the world could use another little Buster. "Then I suggest you head back to your wife before my knee becomes personally acquainted with your crotch."

When he still refused to move, she tried to push him away, but he wouldn't budge. He might be only a few inches taller than her, and maybe twenty pounds heavier at best, but he was a lot stronger than he looked.

Buster swayed slightly before he invaded her personal space even more. He continued to stare at her like she was a glass of whiskey, and he was about to go through withdrawal. "I have a good mind to bring you down a notch. Show you what it's like to be with a real man. You were always too high and mighty for your own good."

The minute he grabbed her butt, Jess thrust her mighty knee high, jabbing it squarely in the intended target.

She tried to wrest away but Buster took an unexpected swing, landing the back of his hand directly below her left eye. The force of the blow threw her off balance and she blindly grabbed for the brick ledge below the window. The pain shooting from the point of impact made her feel as if her head might explode.

After her vision came back into focus, she straightened and caught sight of Chase shoving Buster against the glass, a murderous look on his face. "You're under arrest, you son of a bitch."

To her mortification, a group of onlookers had gathered in response to the commotion. And to her horror, she looked to her left to see her son seated on the sidewalk, arms wrapped around his legs as he rocked back and forth, staring off into space.

After all the progress Danny had begun to make, Jess felt as if she'd lost him again. Maybe this time for good.

"IS HE OKAY, CHASE?"

After closing the door to the hallway, Chase crossed the room to where Jess had stretched out on the couch, a bag of ice pressed against her cheek. "Hard to tell," he said as she bent her knees, allowing him enough space to sit on the sofa. "He looked like he could use some company, so I let Bo stay in the bed with him. He was drifting off when I left."

"But he didn't say anything?"

"Not a word." And that worried Chase as much as it worried Danny's mom.

Jess raised the bag and touched the red welt below her eye. "I can't believe this happened."

Chase bore most of the responsibility for the disaster. If he hadn't pressured her to go to the festival, then she wouldn't be lying here, nursing a wound inflicted by a worthless jackass. And since he'd turned the official arrest over to another deputy, he didn't have all the details. He didn't like asking her to recount the events, but he needed to fill in the blanks. If she faced criminal charges, Buster could be called to testify, and he'd probably twist the story to make Jess appear to be the perpetrator. "Tell me what happened with Buster, beginning to end."

She blew out a slow breath. "He made a few snide remarks, I issued a few warnings. Then he grabbed my butt and I kneed him. That's when he slapped me senseless."

The thought of Eustace putting his hands on Jess made his blood boil. The image of the bastard slugging her was still fresh in his brain, refueling his anger. If he hadn't remembered where he was, or who he was—a deputy who'd sworn to uphold the law—he might've wrapped his hands around the guy's throat and applied enough pressure to make his eyes bulge.

"It's my fault," he said. "I should've known some of Placid's sleaziest would show up and give you grief."

Jess held the bag to her cheek and grimaced. "Buster's genetically predisposed for sleaziness. Buster Sr. is still serving a ten-year sentence for two home invasions and forgery."

And everyone thought Placid had a low crime rate. "Now they can have a family reunion when Junior joins him."

Jess shook her head. "That's not going to happen. Maybe if he'd backhanded his boss, dear Edwin, he'd find himself incarcerated. But because it was me, the ex-daughter-in-law who gravely wounded his son, Edwin will make sure he walks away. He might even give him a bonus."

Boss? "What does a scumbag like Buster do for the old man?"

"He does Edwin's dirty work." Jess lowered the bag and returned it to the table. "For instance, Edwin hired him to take pictures of Horace Breedlove walking into the motel with Janie Adams. The scuttlebutt has it he used those photos to blackmail Horace into selling him a prime piece of real estate adjoining Potter's Pond. As it turned out, Horace's wife found out and divorced him anyway."

Placid had become a regular hotbed for scandal, thanks in part to the wealthiest family in town. And the fact that Eustace worked for Wainwright could make matters even worse for Jess.

He retrieved the bag and pressed it against her face, causing Jess to wince. "You need to use the ice so it doesn't swell."

"You're going to freeze my mouth shut."

"That would take a glacier."

When she tried to smile, she flinched again. "Please don't make me laugh. It hurts."

It hurt him to see her in any kind of pain. "At least one good thing came out of the chaos."

"I caught you up on all the small-town drama?"

"You have a new microwave." After lowering the bag to give her a reprieve, he tipped her chin up to get a better look at her injury. "You also have a black eye."

She dropped her head back against the sofa's arm. "Great. I'd gladly give back the microwave if it meant not having the black eye. Better still, I'd give anything if Danny hadn't witnessed that horrific scene. I feel like he's take ten steps forward, only to be pushed back a mile."

Chase straightened her legs and draped them over his lap. "I think it's time to consider calling that counselor, before he withdraws even more."

After she lifted her head, he witnessed a flicker of alarm in her eyes. "You're right. I wanted to give him a few more days, but after what happened tonight, I realize I can't wait. I'll call Rachel tomorrow and get the number. By then we should know how your dad's interview went with Dalton."

If Dalton didn't support Jess's story, or if he still maintained he had no recollection of the events leading up to his injury, then Buck would go after Danny for answers. All the more reason for Jess to find her son a good counselor.

After Jess yawned and stretched her arms above her head, Chase considered that his cue to leave, even if he didn't particularly want to. "You look like you could use some sleep."

"Not really." She sat up and shifted to face him, her arm resting on the back of the sofa. "I need a new life."

He brushed a lock of hair from her cheek and tucked it behind her ear. "You'll have that as soon as this garbage with Dalton goes away."

The first sign of tears welled in her eyes. "What if it doesn't, Chase? What if he makes allegations that aren't true?"

He had the same concerns. Dalton didn't possess one ounce of integrity, especially when he had an agenda.

The Wainwright men always had an agenda. "Then it's going to be up to Danny to tell Buck what he saw."

"I can't put him through that," she said. "I'd rather go to jail than have him suffer more than he already has."

"You might not have a choice, Jess."

She tipped her forehead against his shoulder. "Maybe it's time I accept the inevitable. If Dalton has his way, he's going to gain full custody of Danny."

Chase framed her face in his palms. "Don't you dare give up, Jess."

She looked as if she already had. "What's the point, Chase? I don't have the means or the clout to take on both Dalton and his dad, if it comes to that. You can bet Edwin's going to be right in the middle of it before this is all over."

He recognized how easy it would be to kiss away her concerns. To provide the means to make her forget, at least tonight. But that would only complicate matters more.

He dropped his hands from her face to maintain some distance. "The point is, when you see an injustice done, you just have to fight through it, no matter what the outcome might be."

"It's the possible outcome that worries me," she said.

She had the right to be worried. "Believe me, I know what you're going through. You wait for the other shoe to drop until you think you might go crazy. You know it's going to be bad, but not knowing is worse." And the reality was always much worse than anyone could ever predict.

The images came back to him, sharp as a switchblade, and that was all he could see. Unknown enemies. Children playing amid the violence. One minute, a normal day. The next, sheer chaos. Flashes of gunfire, civilians taking cover, weapons drawn. The bloodcurdling screams…

"Chase?"

Jess's voice thrust him back into the present. "What?"

She studied him with concern. "Are you okay?"

Not in the least. "Yeah. Why?"

"You looked as if you went somewhere else."

He should've known she'd see through him. Then again, he'd been fairly transparent, at least for a moment. "I was just remembering something."

"About the war?"

He could attempt to lie, but he probably couldn't fool her. "Yeah."

"Did something happen over there?"

"It was war. What didn't happen?"

She released a frustrated sigh. "It's more than that. I saw the same thing the other day. At times there's a part of you that's completely unreachable."

"I'm still the same old me." What a load of bull. Truth was, war claimed numerous victims, and not just fallen soldiers.

"No, you're not the same," she said. "No one expects you to be. But when you're with Danny, it's as if you understand what he's going through. I sincerely believe it's because you've been through something similar."

In some ways he had, but he couldn't provide any details. Disclosing the fatal mistake might be his undoing. So might the random flashbacks, if his father ever found out. "I watched a lot of people die, Jess. Men and women who had families waiting back home. Sometimes

I wonder how soldiers ship out knowing they could be seeing their spouses and children for the last time. It's a good thing I wasn't cut out to be a husband and father. It made it a helluva lot easier to do what I had to do."

She touched his face. "You'd make a good father, Chase. Just look at the way you've handled Danny. I can tell he worships you."

The boy would do well to focus his misplaced admiration on someone who deserved it. "I'm just being a friend to him, Jess. That's not nearly as tough as being a father."

"I agree. Raising a child is a tough job. But the rewards are worth all the trouble."

"Again, I'm not equipped for fatherhood. I never have been."

"It breaks my heart that you really believe that," she said. "And I personally believe you're wrong."

He needed to turn the topic back to her issues. "The point is, you're a good mother. Don't let this mess with Dalton make you doubt that."

"I do doubt it, Chase, thanks to the ongoing war I've been having with Dalton for years. And now I'm facing one more battle that's chipped away at my confidence. A battle that I might not win."

Her dejection was killing him. "If you promise to stay optimistic, I promise to help you get through this." A penance he needed to fulfill. A promise he hoped he could keep.

"How can I stay optimistic if I might lose my son? He's all I have."

As he watched a lone tear slide down her face, he wanted to say, *You'll always have me.* But that commitment wouldn't benefit her in the long run. He'd returned home a broken man who'd erected walls for self-protection. Unfortunately, Jess had begun to see through his guise, and that could be dangerous. If she only knew what he was capable of, what he had done, she'd never view him in the same light again.

Chase tugged a tissue from the cardboard box on the side table and handed it to her. "You're a lot stronger than you realize, Jess." Stronger than him, at least on an emotional level. "You have to hang in there and fight."

She dabbed at the tears with the tissue. "How do you propose I do that?"

"I'm pretty sure that cheerleader's still in there somewhere."

She tucked the tissue in her pocket and raised her fisted hand. "Rah. Rah."

Her attempt at humor through her tears was classic Jess. "That was sorely lacking in school spirit. Maybe you ought to try that back flip."

She sent him a shaky smile. "I'd probably hit the floor facedown and give myself another black eye."

He glanced over his shoulder at the bare tree centered in the front window. "Want to put that microwave to good use? We could make some popcorn decorations to go with the ones I found in my parents' attic."

He turned to see her shaking her head. "I can't decorate a tree without Danny."

He should've known she'd say that. "Then that leaves you going to bed, and me going home. I'll come by tomorrow night for that chicken dinner and we can all decorate the tree together."

"I just hope I'm here and not in jail."

Just when he'd thought she'd made some decent strides. "Don't go there, Jess."

"All right," she said. "I promise I will think nothing but positive thoughts."

"Good."

After Chase rose from the sofa, Jess stood and followed him to the door. "Thank you for saving me from Buster, Deputy."

He barked out a laugh. "Best I recall, you saved yourself. You might want to register that knee as a lethal weapon."

She slid her arms around his waist and laid her head against his heart. "I don't know what I'd do without you, Chase."

There could come a time in the very near future when she'd be forced to find out, maybe sooner than he'd planned. But if her fears about Dalton came to pass, they'd wind up on opposite sides of the law.

Last night, he'd promised her a fresh start, but he realized that wouldn't last past the short term. He could continue to offer her support until she no longer needed it. Beyond that, he couldn't offer her anything but a lifetime of grief.

He pressed a kiss against her forehead and let her go before he lost his will and asked her if he could stay. "Try to get some sleep."

JESS TIP-TOED DOWN THE HALL, muttering a silent oath every time the wood floor creaked beneath her feet. She didn't dare wake Danny, but she couldn't go to bed until she made sure he was okay.

When she opened the door, ribbons of light streamed across the bed, revealing the sweetest scene. Danny slept on his belly, his face turned toward the wall, one arm draped over the dog. Bo opened his eyes but didn't stir, aside from a slight wag of his tail.

Maybe Bo lacked in the watchdog department, but he obviously gave Danny the comfort she couldn't give him. And after the downtown debacle, she doubted her son would ever trust her again. Yet he did trust Chase.

After taking a seat in the chair at the foot of the bed, she recalled Danny's and Chase's interaction, and how many times tonight she'd almost told Chase the truth. But that truth had died on her lips when he'd insisted he wasn't father material. She wondered if his attitude would change if he did know Danny might be his son. Or would he simply walk away?

She couldn't afford to risk that now. She would need Chase's support in the coming days. Especially tomorrow.

CHAPTER SEVEN

"HE WANTS TO SEE YOU ASAP, Deputy Reed."

Chase didn't have to ask the dispatcher who "he" was. Nor did he have to ask why he'd been summoned. "How long as he been back?"

"About ten minutes."

So far the morning had been uneventful—a couple of traffic tickets, chasing two heifers out of the road. He figured that was all about to change. "Did he say anything about how it went?"

"You'll have to ask him."

He shouldn't have expected Sue to offer any information, even if she did know what had transpired between Buck and Dalton. "I take it he's in his office."

"Yeah, and a word of warning. Be prepared."

He would if he knew what the hell to prepare for.

As he strode down the corridor, a million possibilities tore through his brain, not a one of them favorable. Either Danny, or his mother, would soon be on the hot seat.

When he reached the closed door, he didn't bother to knock. Instead, he pushed his way in and found his father seated behind the desk, wearing his usual poker face. "Tell me what you know," Chase said, not bothering with formality.

Buck gestured toward the opposing chair. "Sit."

"I'll stand."

"Suit yourself."

Buck snatched a pen and began tapping it on the wood surface, a sure sign of trouble. "You know, for a guy who suffered a head injury a few days ago, Dalton Wainwright's doing pretty good."

He didn't give a horse's behind about Dalton's condition. "Just tell me what he said."

"The good news is, I won't be bothering Jess's boy. Not in the near future, anyway. Dalton tells me he's not going to be any help."

Chase braced himself for the bad news, because as sure as grass was green, bad news was coming. "Then he remembers what happened."

"Yeah, he remembers. Right down to the last detail. Pretty interesting details at that."

His dad seemed determined to try his patience. "Stop beating around the bush and get on with it."

Buck again pointed to the chair. "I still think you should sit."

He'd stand on his head if that would speed up the process. After yanking back the chair, he dropped into it and glared at Buck. "Okay, I'm sitting. Now get to the point."

Buck sat back in the chair and sighed. "Dalton says Jess said she was going to kill him, then she attacked him, plain and simple."

There wasn't anything simple about it. "And you believe him?"

"No reason not to believe him."

Chase could think of at least a hundred. "You're saying that a woman who's a few inches above five feet could take down a man well over six feet? Not to mention he's got to outweigh her by at least eighty pounds. If you're buying that, then you're probably padding your retirement fund with swampland."

Buck's ears began to turn red. "You are about this far—" he held up his pointer finger and thumb an inch apart "—from finding yourself suspended."

Any other time, he might've told him where to stick the job. But he couldn't. Not if he wanted to protect Jess. "I'm only saying that I don't believe Jess is physically capable of inflicting that kind of injury."

"She could if she had a weapon."

A weapon? "I was the first on scene and I didn't see a weapon."

"I checked the log," Buck said. "You didn't get there until five minutes after Jess placed the 9-1-1 call. That gave her plenty of time to get rid of it."

Even if he didn't believe Buck's theory, he couldn't argue the possibility. "What was the object supposed to be?"

"Dalton's not sure. He just remembers her hitting him in the head with something."

He thought back to that night and Dalton's position. "That doesn't make any sense. I found him on his back."

"He could've rolled over. I'll have to ask Barkley if that fits with the crime scene."

Like that sack of manure had enough sense to analyze evidence. "Maybe you should run it past the county D.A. before you jump to conclusions."

Buck scowled. "I've been doing this job since you were a tadpole, son, so give me some credit. I stopped by the courthouse on the way back and reviewed the case with Millsap."

"And?"

For the first time during the meeting, Buck refused to look at him straight on. "A warrant's been issued for Jess's arrest."

Chase took a moment to absorb that information before coming to terms with the inevitable. He couldn't stop the system, but he sure as hell wasn't going to let Jess go through this alone. "I'll bring her in."

Buck tossed the pen aside. "It's too late for that. I sent Barkley to pick her up five minutes before you walked in here."

Chase sprung into action and headed out the door, slamming it shut behind him. He ignored the sound of Buck's warning to stay out of it. Ignored Sue, who also tried to stop him by claiming he had a message. He only knew he had to get to Jess.

He opted to take the cruiser instead of the SUV to save time. With lights flashing and siren blaring, he raced down a back street through town and increased his speed when he hit the winding country road. The ten minutes it took to reach the house seemed like thirty. Once he arrived, he discovered another cruiser parked in the drive, next to a plain navy sedan that he didn't recognize.

As he slammed the car into park and exited the cruiser, a strong sense of dread hit him with the impact of a gut punch. The same dread he'd experienced when this nightmare had begun to unfold. Only this time, he knew what to expect.

But nothing could ready him for the scene that played out before him. A scene that stopped his blood cold.

Jess came out the door in handcuffs, flanked by Barkley and a young deputy named Mike. A gray-haired woman followed, leading Danny away as he reached for his mother, calling her name over and over. Barkley recited her rights as Jess begged for a moment with her son, the pleas falling on deaf ears.

But Chase heard everything, from Jess's gut-wrenching attempt to reassure Danny, to the dog barking furiously behind the screen door.

He remained frozen for a moment, until he caught sight of her struggling against the restraints. "Don't fight the cuffs, Jess. And don't say anything."

The minute her gaze connected with his, and he saw the abject terror in her eyes, adrenaline kicked back in, sending him straight toward the trio. But he didn't get far before Barkley handed her over to Mike, and then headed Chase off at the pass.

Barkley raised his hand, palm forward. "Hold it right there, Deputy. I'm in charge of this arrest."

He wanted to knock the cocky look off the jerk's face. "Uncuff her, Barkley."

Barkley stroked his mustache like a pet. "Well, now, Chase, you know I can't do that, even if she is your girlfriend."

He saw no sense in correcting him about their relationship. His main concern was Jess's well-being. "She's not going anywhere, so take the damn cuffs off her."

Ignoring the demand, Barkley turned and headed toward the cruiser, while Mike pushed Jess's head down as she slid into the backseat.

Chase automatically followed him to the car. If Barkley wanted to stop him, then he'd have to do it with force.

When he tapped on the window to garner Jess's attention, she looked at him with tear-filled eyes and mouthed one word. "Danny."

"I'll take care of him," he said as the car began to back down the drive. "I'll take care of everything."

Chase glanced to his right and realized the sedan had yet to move. That meant he still had the opportunity to speak with Danny. His words might not offer the boy much consolation, but he had to try.

He walked to the driver's side to find the window halfway open. "Excuse me, ma'am."

At first the social worker seemed startled, until she noticed his badge. "May I help you, Deputy?"

He peered into the car and spotted Danny in the front seat, his head lowered and his shoulders shaking. Every broken sob shot straight to Chase's soul. "I'm a family friend. I'm just wondering what the next step will be."

She pushed her glasses up on the bridge of her nose. "Since Danny's father is currently hospitalized, I've contacted the child's aunt, a Mrs. Rachel Boyd. She's agreed to assume emergency custody until the time Mr. Wainwright is able to care for Danny. I'll be taking him to her home immediately."

He hoped Dalton's recovery took a long time. Living with a father who didn't give a damn about him was the last thing the kid needed. A lying, worthless father. "Mind if I have a word with Danny before you go?"

She looked almost relieved by the suggestion. "That might make the transition a little easier for him. Normally we ask a relative to be here, but there wasn't enough time."

Thanks to Buck, who couldn't wait to toss Jess in a cell. "I'll do what I can to calm him down."

"Wonderful. And if you can convince him to wear his seat belt, I'd truly appreciate it."

As soon as Chase heard the lock trip, he rounded the hood and opened the passenger door. Danny immediately flew out of the car and wrapped his arms around his waist. He stayed that way for a few moments, letting the boy cry and cling to him as long as he needed to.

Chase loosened Danny's grasp before lowering to his level. He rested his hands on his thin shoulders and waited for the boy to make eye contact. "I know this is bad, kiddo, but you're going to be okay. Your Aunt Rachel's going to take good care of you until your mother comes home."

Danny swiped at his nose and sniffed. "When is she coming home?"

He wished he had a more positive answer to hand him. "I'm not sure, but hopefully soon. I'm going to do my best to fix this." His best might not be good enough.

"Will you come see me?"

The boy looked and sounded so hopeful, no way could he refuse. "You bet. And as soon as you're settled in, I'll see if your aunt's okay with me bringing Bo over. In the meantime, I'll take him home with me."

Danny lowered his gaze to the ground. "It's all my fault."

He hated seeing a nine-year-old kid taking the blame for something completely out of his control. "No, bud, this isn't your fault. It's no one's fault."

"But—"

"Try not to worry too much, Danny. It's all going to be over soon." What *over* entailed was anyone's guess.

Danny didn't look like he believed him, but who could blame the boy? His life had been a series of disappointments. And lately, one trauma after the other.

Chase needed to give him something to look forward to. Something to get his mind off his troubles. "Tell you what. I'll come over in the next couple of days and play some catch with you. And if Aunt Rachel says it's okay, you can come to my place and I'll show you how to drive a few nails into wood. I could use some help building the new room on my house."

"Really?" Both his smile and voice reflected his gratitude.

He smiled back. "Really."

Danny's expression suddenly turned sour. "My dad never did that for me. He never did anything for me."

One day in the near future, Chase planned to confront the rat bastard over all the misery he'd caused Jess and Danny. If Dalton wanted to pick on someone, he'd give him a target his own size. Then Wainwright could see exactly how it felt to be on the losing end.

"You're going to be okay," he assured Danny again. "You'll be with your aunt and uncle real soon. Last I heard, they have a new foal in the barn."

The social worker emerged from the car. "We need to go, Deputy."

Chase gave Danny another solid hug and a pat on the back. "Hang in there, bud," he said as he straightened. "And buckle your seat belt."

Danny nodded, climbed back in the car and secured the belt without any argument.

Chase waved at Danny as he watched the sedan drive away, and then started to turn to retrieve Bo. But another car caught his attention, stopping him dead in his tracks. A black luxury car parallel-parked near the end of the drive. He'd seen that vehicle around town, front and center at the bank. He recognized the silver-haired driver immediately. Arrogance in an expensive suit. He despised the millionaire almost as much as he despised the millionaire's son.

Chase wondered how long Edwin Wainwright had been there, and how much he'd seen. He also questioned how he'd found out about Jess's arrest. Then again, Wainwright made it a point to know everyone's business. He wouldn't be surprised if he had a mole in the sheriff's department. Enough money earned unlimited access to information.

Whatever the man's motives might be, he had no reason to be there, and Chase had no problem informing him of that fact. As soon as he strode down the drive, Wainwright pulled away, but not before displaying a sickening, satisfied smile.

Chase recognized Jess was about to undertake the fight of her life. A fight with the devil himself.

SHE NOW KNEW THE MEANING of true humiliation.

Dressed in county-jail orange and her hands bound by cuffs, Jess left the cracker-box hell with an armed guard at her side—a mountain of a guard named Bill, whom she'd known most of her life. Although respectful, he'd still treated her as if she were any other common criminal. In his eyes, she probably was.

She traveled down the cell-lined corridor to the sound of cat-calls and comments so crude, she wanted to cry. But she refused to cower. Instead, she walked with her head held high, keeping her gaze focused forward. They might have taken her dignity, but she wasn't going to let them take what was left of her pride.

Bill opened a steel door and escorted her into a small room containing a table and two chairs—as well as one of her very best friends. Savannah Greer looked every bit the successful attorney, from the sleek blond hair pulled back in a low ponytail, to the tailored, brown wool suit and diamond stud earrings.

Jess couldn't remember when she'd been so glad to see anyone. Had she not been shackled, she would have launched herself into her friend's arms.

Savannah came to her feet, gave Jess a smile and favored Bill with a frown. "Please uncuff my client."

Bill pulled out a chair for Jess and guided her into it. "Now, Miss Savannah, you know that's against the rules."

"Now, Mr. Bill," Savannah countered, "in case you don't remember, this is the former Jessica Keller. You know her folks well. I believe Ronnie Keller helped you dig a new well a few years back. And Cathy used to play bridge with your wife."

Jess was floored that Savannah remembered all those details, not that any of it mattered to Bill. He had yet to make a move to remove the silver bracelets that made her wrists ache beyond belief.

He rubbed the top of his bald head and sighed. "That's

true. But I also recall that you and Jess and that group...
What did you call yourselves?"

"The six-pack," Jess and Savannah said simultaneously.

"That's right," he said. "You two and Miss Rachel and the three boys, Chase, Matt and Sam. You were all responsible for me having to clean toilet paper out of my trees, and eggs off my front porch, after that Halloween a few years back."

Savannah tapped her chin. "Ah, yes. I also recall your son accompanying us that night, and the eggs were his idea. I still have the photos of Willy hurling those things."

Muttering under his breath, Bill fished the keys from his pocket, unlocked the cuffs and slid them from Jess's wrists.

She worked her wrists in circles, grateful for the temporary relief. "Thank you, Bill. I promise I'm not going anywhere." If only she could.

Savannah reclaimed her seat and folded her hands before her. "Now if you don't mind, I'd like a few minutes with my client."

Bill pointed a beefy finger at her. "My job's on the line, so don't you two do anything stupid."

She raised her hand as if swearing in. "I promise I don't have a file hidden in my shoes. I assure you Ms. Wainwright will be right here when you get back."

The guard muttered again and finally left them alone, closing the heavy door behind him.

Savannah leaned forward and studied her a long moment. "How are you holding up? Aside from the whole booking process, which I imagine is pretty dreadful."

Dreadful was a colossal understatement. Being poked and prodded, stripped of all personal effects and then finger-printed, ranked right up there with a root canal. "I'll be better when I know where they took my son."

"He's with Rachel," Savannah said. "She wanted me to send you her love and tell you that you have hers and Matt's full support."

"I appreciate that so much." She also appreciated her pregnant sister-in-law taking care of her baby boy. "At least I know he's in good hands."

"Chase stopped me before I came back here," Savannah said. "Basically he told me the same thing, that he'll help in any way he can. He also said don't try any back flips because the cell is too small."

Jess stopped short of laughing. "He's been a godsend. I couldn't have survived these past few days without him." And she longed to see him again. "Is he still here?"

"No. Buck told him to go home and not to come back until the day after Christmas. Something about his lack of objectivity."

Her guilt increased. "I should have never dragged him into this mess."

"He's one of your closest friends, Jess. He'd never abandon you when you needed him."

"I understand that, but I still hate that he's going to take the heat for supporting me."

"Chase is tough. He can handle it." Savannah lifted a briefcase from the floor and pulled out a pen and yellow legal pad. "Time to get to the business at hand. I have a few questions I need to ask."

Exactly what she'd been dreading. "Ask away."

"First of all, I want you to know that I'll only be handling the arraignment since corporate law is normally my thing. But since I'm the only game in town, you're stuck with me for the time being."

"I couldn't imagine having anyone else represent me, Savannah."

"Again, I'm only going to take you through the initial proceedings. However, I've spoken with a defense attorney from Jackson, and he's agreed to take your case. Unfortunately, he'll be out of town until the latter part of next week."

Her stomach clutched from anxiety. "I'll have to stay here until next week?"

"No, but you will be here overnight. The county judge only hears pleas twice a week, Tuesdays and Thursdays. I have you on the docket for first thing tomorrow morning. Depending on the bail, you should be out after lunch." Her gaze momentarily drifted away. "If all goes as planned."

She swallowed hard. "Are you saying something could happen to change those plans?"

"The judge could decide to remand you into custody until your trial, especially if he feels you're a flight risk."

Not only would she have to spend the night in a virtual cave, she might be incarcerated for months. "That's ridiculous. I have nowhere to go. My parents are on vacation and I don't even know where I put my passport. I would never leave my son and—"

Savannah laid a palm on Jess's hand, halting the tirade. "It's only a remote possibility. I just want you to be prepared if the D.A. argues that you're a threat to society, and your son, due to the attempted-murder charge."

Attempted murder? "I didn't attempt to murder Dalton. In fact, I didn't do anything to him."

Savannah clicked the pen and rested her hand on the pad. "That brings me to the night of the alleged attack. Tell me everything that happened to the best of your ability."

Though she trusted Savannah, she couldn't reveal everything. Not yet. "Dalton has Danny every other weekend, so he stopped by last Friday night. He was two hours late and he'd been drinking."

Savannah looked up from the notes she'd been taking. "Not according to Edwin Wainwright."

"Rachel told me Edwin claims that Dalton's tests were negative for alcohol. But I swear to you, Savannah, either he replaced his aftershave with bourbon, or he'd tied one on after work."

"We'll subpoena the medical records."

That might suffice under normal circumstances. Unfortunately, she hadn't married into a normal family. "What if Edwin paid someone off to alter the results?"

"That's highly unlikely," Savannah said. "Regardless, we'll worry about that later. Go on."

She'd had nothing to do but worry. "Anyway, I had no intention of letting my son get into a car with him. That's when he threatened me."

Savannah continued to jot down the facts without missing a beat. "What kind of threats?"

"He said that if I didn't agree to go back to him, he'd take me back to court to gain full custody of Danny."

"What did you tell him?"

"I told him no, and then he claimed that since Danny

didn't look a thing like him, I must have cheated on him before we married."

Savannah stopped writing and released a caustic laugh. "That's so rich. Of course, it's been my experience that men who cheat usually believe everyone does, including their spouses. It's nothing more than a skewed justification of their own infidelity. Dalton knows you'd never cheat on him."

She could gloss over her friend's assumption, or she could tell her the truth. She desperately wanted to tell her the truth. For ten years, she'd never confided in one soul, and she was tired of carrying around the secret.

She drew in a deep breath and exhaled slowly. "He's right."

The shock took a while to subside from Savannah's face. "You cheated on him?"

"Not exactly, although he wouldn't see it that way. We broke up for a month. It happened then."

"When was this?"

"Ten years ago. Two weeks before we married."

She hadn't been struck by lightning, and the roof hadn't caved in. Yet she'd run the risk that by confessing, she could have lost her friend's respect.

Savannah put down the pen and laced her hands together atop the paper. "I realize it's none of my business, but do you mind telling me the identity of this mystery man?"

"As long as you promise not to tell anyone. Not even Sam."

"Anything you say to me in this room is protected by attorney-client privilege." She traded her serious demeanor for a smile. "Besides, you know how my future husband feels about gossip. The less he knows, the better."

The less anyone knew what she was about to reveal, the better for all concerned. "We were friends. The night before he left for Afghanistan, he came to see me at my dorm. We were both scared and sad, and we turned to each other for comfort. Neither of us intended for it to happen. It just did."

Savannah's mouth dropped open before she snapped it shut. "Are you telling me you slept with Chase?"

Jess could only nod.

She could see the calculations turning in Savannah's mind. "If this happened ten years ago, then there is a possibility that Danny—"

"Could be Chase's son. But I'm not sure since the timing was so close. I haven't let myself believe anything other than Dalton was Danny's father."

"You didn't think Chase had a right to know the possibility existed?" Savannah's tone held no judgment, only sincere interest.

"I only knew he was away fighting a war," Jess said. "And I knew he might never come home. In the meantime, I'd already married a man I thought I loved. A man who was going to be around to provide for my son, while Chase kept volunteering for more tours of duty."

"And you thought that was best for Danny."

She paused and sighed. "Even after the marriage began to deteriorate, and it became apparent Dalton didn't care one whit for Danny, I was still stupid enough to believe any father was better than no father at all. Guess I was wrong about that."

Savannah remained silent for a few moments, as if

weighing her words. "As your friend, I'd encourage you to tell Chase as soon as possible. As your attorney, I'd advise you to wait until after your legal issues are resolved. Otherwise, it could compromise your case. The D.A. could claim the paternity question served as your motive for attacking Dalton."

"I didn't attack Dalton. And how could he use that against me when I divorced Dalton months ago?"

"Easy. Dalton could claim he voiced his suspicions about Danny's paternity, and you decided to do away with him to retain any alimony or child support that would be challenged in court, if it's determined Chase is Danny's father."

All the more reason to keep her second secret. "I can't win for losing, can I?"

Savannah picked up the pen again. "Let's return to what transpired after the threats."

Now came the part where Jess could only tell a partial truth. "I ordered him out and he grabbed my arm. It's like I told Chase and Buck, after that, it's all a blur. I think he stumbled and fell backward and hit his head on the raised hearth."

"You didn't see it happen?"

She had. The images still haunted her. "I was distracted. I thought I heard Danny calling me."

"Dalton stated that Danny wasn't around. But if what you say is true, then Danny may have witnessed the fall."

She suddenly realized she'd said too much. She also realized that either Dalton didn't remember any details at all, or he was bent on ruining her. "I don't want Danny involved in this."

"In light of what you just told me, he could be called as a witness."

"And I hope you'll make sure that doesn't happen. He's so traumatized now, I'm not convinced he'll ever be the same again."

"I'll do what I can."

That was all Jess had to rely on. "Is that it?"

"I have one more question before we wrap this up. A very important question."

Nothing would surprise her at this point in time. "Go ahead."

Savannah retrieved a document from the briefcase and turned to the second page. "According to Dalton's most recent revelation, you hit him in the head with a fireplace iron."

Of all the ridiculous accusations. "He's lying. In fact, he's making this up as he goes."

"That could be, but that iron is missing."

Jess racked her brain to recall the last time she'd seen that tool, and then recalled she'd used it the night before Dalton's fall. "It had to be there when I left the house with Chase that night."

"Well it's not there now, and that's a problem. If it turns up, we can prove through forensics that it wasn't used to injure Dalton. But if it's going to show traces of his blood, then we don't want it to surface."

Her own friend sounded as if she doubted her. "I promise I did not whack Dalton in the head with anything." Not that the thought hadn't crossed her mind before. "But I can think of a number of ways that the iron could have gone missing. With enough money on hand, anything could disappear."

"I suppose that's true. Does anyone else have the key to the house?"

"Only Rachel and my parents. But that doesn't mean Dalton didn't have copies made without my knowledge."

When the sharp rap came at the door, Jess jumped like a jackrabbit.

"That means my time's almost up," Savannah said as she slid the notebook back into her briefcase. "But I need to ask you to do something, and you might not like it."

Right now she was so appreciative, she'd do anything for her friend, short of murder. "What?"

"Stop seeing Chase. I don't care how innocent your relationship might be, a rumored affair is the last thing you need."

Jess fought the urge to burst into tears. Chase had been her touchstone, the one person she could rely on to make her feel better. The only person her son seemed to trust. "If that's what we have to do, we'll do it."

"I'll let Chase know." Savannah took her hands and gave them a gentle squeeze. "I'll do whatever I can to help your new attorney win this case. Then you can get on with your life."

If only she could count on that promise, yet the future seemed ominous. She would probably lose her job. She would most likely go to trial. She could end up in prison—unless she revealed the piece of the puzzle that could free her, and possibly imprison her son.

When she thought back to that awful Friday night, Dalton's words echoed in her head.

The kid's a wimp. A whiny mama's boy. He's worthless. I'd wager my last dollar that he's not even my son....

No weapon had been involved, only an angry little boy who'd suffered enough verbal abuse to last a lifetime. A sweet, insecure little boy who, with all the strength he could muster, shoved the only father he'd ever known, sending him backward to suffer a blow to the head. A precious little boy who'd been born into a family that embraced lies and deceit. And revenge.

The world might forgive Danny for his actions, but Edwin Wainwright surely wouldn't—especially if he learned that his presumed grandson could be another man's child.

CHAPTER EIGHT

HE'D BE DAMNED if he let him get away with this.

Chase stormed into the department and went straight to Buck's office. When he didn't find him there, he retraced his steps and located him in the break room. As usual, he was seated at a round table, drinking his morning coffee and reading the Placid newspaper.

"We need to talk, Sheriff."

Buck continued to scan the page without bothering to look up. "I thought I told you yesterday to go home and not come back until Monday."

He still didn't care for that directive, then or now. "And I thought I told you Buster Eustace belonged in jail."

"Yep, that's what you said."

Buck's lack of concern only fed Chase's anger. "So why is it that he's still roaming the streets?"

He flipped to another page. "We only arrest 'em. We don't decide how long they stay. "

He thought about Jess spending last night in a hell-hole, while Eustace was free as a bird, having breakfast in the local diner. "How long did he stay, Buck?"

Buck folded the paper in precise creases and put it aside. "Not too long after you turned him over to Jones and he hauled him in. I was in bed when I got a phone call from the D.A.'s office. They said a couple of witnesses came forward, claimed it was a misunderstanding, and I was then instructed to let him go."

In all probability, bought-and-paid-for witnesses. "A misunderstanding? He slapped the hell out of Jess right there on the street."

"You probably should count your lucky stars that Buster didn't file charges against her. From what I hear, she started it. She's already in enough trouble already. You don't need to borrow more for her, so leave it alone."

He planted his palms on the table and leaned forward. "You can bet Wainwright had something to do with Buster's exoneration."

"Maybe so, but I learned over the years not to ask too many questions."

That had to be the sorriest excuse he'd ever heard coming from a peace officer's mouth. "And during all those years, you just bent over and took it."

Buck gave him a look as hard as steel. "I did what I had to do to put food on the table and keep a roof over your head. Some battles aren't worth fighting if you stand to lose more than it's worth. You'll learn that when you take over this job after I retire next year."

His own father had pretty much looked the other way to save his own ass. Disgusted, he straightened and backed away from the table. "I don't want this damn job. Not if it means turning my back on the law."

"Where are you going now?" Buck asked as Chase headed toward the door.

"To Jess's arraignment."

"You're already in too deep."

Chase turned, slowly. "I'm not going to desert her, so just lay off."

Buck inclined his head and narrowed his eyes. "Are you in love with her?"

The hesitation in his response was pretty damn telling. "I care about her." And he couldn't imagine not having her in his life, something best left unsaid.

Buck looked like he'd just caught a ten-pound bass. "It's more than caring about her. I can see it in your eyes. But you need to remember one important thing. She's been a Wainwright for a decade. She's bound to have learned something about lying."

"I don't have time for this," he said as he strode out the door.

He didn't have time for Buck's unwelcome advice, or to ponder his father's questions about his feelings for Jess. He'd have to take those out and examine them later.

Chase left the department the same way he entered, in a hurry. The hearing was scheduled to being in less than five minutes. Fortunately, the county courthouse was right next door.

Wearing civilian clothes and a baseball cap, Chase kept a low profile as he stood at the rear of the packed courtroom. The only courtroom. One-stop shopping for all things legal. He suspected a lot of bartering between the Wainwrights and the powers that be went on behind closed chamber doors.

Word of Jess's arrest had traveled like a wildfire through town, drawing every Tom, Dick and Bubba to the proceedings. Including Edwin Wainwright, who was seated two rows back, studying his nails like he was contemplating his next manicure.

Chase had half a mind to plop down right next to the

rich bastard just to see him squirm. Maybe get in a few digs while waiting for Jess's case to be called. Instead, he stayed rooted in the same spot in order to prevent a scene. He'd already landed on Buck's bad side as it was. Any job was better than no job at all.

The drunk driver he'd arrested two nights ago stepped forward, announced his innocence, followed by a very loud and drawn out explanation. Considering the jerk was slapped with the maximum bail allowed, the outburst apparently didn't set well with the circuit judge. Or maybe the judge was in a foul mood. The honorable R. J. Perkins wasn't always known for his good humor, or impartiality. He was known for his ties to Edwin Wainwright. And that might not bode well at all for Jess's release.

The bridge officer rattled off a docket number, followed by, "The People versus Jessica Keller Wainwright. Attempted murder in the second degree."

When the side door creaked open, all heads turned toward that direction, the crowd falling suddenly silent.

Savannah entered the courtroom first, with her cuffed client and the rail-thin bailiff trailing a short distance behind. Chase expected Jess to look battered and broken. Instead, she kept her chin raised and her eyes focused forward. "That's my girl," he muttered, thankful she hadn't lost her pride.

Savannah and Jess moved behind a table while the D.A., Jed Millsap, stood on the opposite side. After the judge flipped through the file, he glanced up over his glasses and looked squarely at Jess. "How does the defendant plead?"

"Not guilty, Your Honor," Jess stated, her voice clear and concise and confident.

She's been a Wainwright for a decade. She's bound to have learned something about lying....

Chase forced away the thoughts and concentrated on the proceedings.

"Your Honor, the defense requests that the accused be released on her own recognizance," Savannah said. "She has no prior record, she's a valued second-grade teacher, and she's well-known for her volunteer work with—"

"Might I remind the defense this is an attempted-murder charge, not a botched bake sale," Millsap chimed in. He waited for the chuckles to die down before he added, "Mrs. Wainwright's reputation doesn't take precedence over the fact that she tried to kill her husband. The People request remand."

"Ex-husband," Savannah corrected. "And might I remind the district attorney that the defendant *allegedly* tried to kill her *former* husband. Not to mention, your case has more holes in it than a ten-year-old pair of underwear."

Perkins rapped his gavel in sharp succession. "Might I remind you both, counselors, to save it for the official trial. Bail is set for four-hundred thousand dollars. Next case."

A collective intake of breath echoed in the courtroom and for the first time, Chase witnessed Jess's armor begin to melt. She walked out with her shoulders slumped and her head lowered, like she was just about ready to deflate.

Before the crowd moved toward the exit, he pushed through the double doors and strode down the corridor toward the holding cell. He arrived just in time to meet Savannah head-on in the hall.

"Four-hundred grand?" he said before she even came to a stop. "What in the hell is that all about?"

Savannah gestured Chase over into a small alcove and set her briefcase at her feet. "It's higher than usual, but it could have been worse if she'd been charged with first-degree attempted murder, not second."

"And it might have been more reasonable if Wainwright wasn't a major contributor to Perkins's campaign."

Savannah took a quick visual survey of the area. "Be careful what you say, Chase. Accusing an officer of the court of misconduct is serious business."

He didn't give a damn who he offended. The truth was the truth. "Is Perkins going to preside over the trial?"

"No, he won't. That will be handled by a superior court judge."

Chase couldn't think of one judge in the county who'd qualify as superior. "Guess it doesn't matter who it is. Edwin prides himself on filling his pockets with local officials."

"That's why I intend to encourage Jess's new attorney to file a change of venue."

New attorney? "I thought you were going to handle the case."

She shook her head. "As I told Jess, I'm not experienced enough in criminal law to defend her beyond the preliminary phase."

He understood what she was saying, even if he didn't like it. "Who is this new attorney?"

"A hotshot named McDonough out of Jackson. I'm hoping we can move the trial there."

"She'd be better off staying in Placid." Closer to her friends. Closer to him. "If you throw her at the mercy of strangers, then she's as good as convicted."

She looked like she didn't appreciate him telling her how to run the show. "Sure, Chase. Let's put her fate in the hands of her peers who rely on Edwin Wainwright's bank to keep their businesses and farms afloat. A jury filled with folks who are terrified of him will not encourage a just verdict."

He wanted to debate that point but couldn't come up with a single argument. "Fine. Back to the bail. I have some cash in savings and I can put up my land. I can also draw on a line of credit through—"

"It's taken care of, Chase."

Unless Jess had a secret stash or a serious benefactor, he couldn't imagine anyone coming up with that amount on a moment's notice. "It's a hell of a lot of money, Savannah."

"Yes, and Rachel has it all, in cash. She received the balance of her trust fund when she turned thirty. She volunteered to use those funds and claims there's plenty more where that came from."

Chase rubbed his chin. "I'll be damned. That means—"

"Edwin Wainwright is indirectly paying for Jess's defense. Isn't that ironic and highly amusing?"

They exchanged a smile before Chase asked the most important question. "When will Jess be ready to go?"

Savannah checked her watch. "Probably in less than an hour."

"Good. I'll drive her home."

Savannah looked as stern as a spinster schoolmarm. "No, you won't. I'll drive her home."

"Dammit, Savannah, I need to do something for her."

"The best thing you can do for Jess is stay away from her."

Not acceptable. "No way am I going to abandon her when she needs all the support she can get."

"She has support from her friends, myself and Sam included. Your presence in her life might cause more harm that good."

"How do you figure that?"

"I don't have to tell you that this town thrives on gossip. If anyone misunderstands yours and Jess's relationship, that could open a huge can of worms. Besides, you're the law, and right now, she's on the wrong side of it."

Everything she'd said made sense, but Chase couldn't stomach the thought of leaving Jess high and dry. "We're just friends, Savannah. Everyone knows that."

Something about his words made Savannah frown. "Jess is vulnerable, and you're still too charming for your own good. Under the current circumstance, that could be a lethal combination."

She was basically accusing him of being a womanizer who couldn't control himself. "I'm not that same guy, Savannah. People change."

"Yes, people change. And so do relationships between people. That's what worries me."

Chase wondered if she knew about that night he spent with Jess. Nah. As far as he could tell, Jess had never mentioned that to anyone. If she had, the guys would've ribbed him about it a long time ago. "I'm not going to do anything to hurt her, if that's your concern. She's already been hurt enough."

"I don't believe you'd hurt her, at least not intentionally." Savannah picked up the briefcase and gave him a quick hug. "Unfortunately, the hurt might not end today. I just heard that Wainwright's called an emergency school board meeting to determine what they're going to do about Jess's teaching position."

Hell, that's all she needed. "I have a good mind to barge in and try to convince them why they should hold off on doing anything."

Savannah wagged her finger at him. "Now, now. Let's control our temper and not make matters worse. I assume the most they could do right now is temporarily suspend her. If she's officially indicted, the contract could allow the board to terminate her position immediately."

Only another phase Jess would have to endure. "Do you think they'll have enough to return an indictment?"

"We won't know until the grand jury convenes after the first of the year. Right now, it's not looking good for her."

"Even if the case is built on the word of an expert liar?"

"A wealthy liar with a father who basically owns the town."

So much for an impartial justice system. "Maybe he'll grow a conscience between now and then and clear Jess."

Savannah looked as skeptical as Chase felt. "And maybe I'll strike oil in my front yard. In the meantime, we'll just have to keep Jess as upbeat as possible."

"Kind of hard to do when I'm not allowed to see her."
When he was feeling anything but upbeat himself.

"I don't see any reason why you can't pick up the
phone and call her now and then." She pointed at him.
"But only phone calls."

Chase would agree to that, but only because he had
no choice.

History definitely had a way of repeating itself.
Once again, he was forced to leave her alone. Only this
time, he'd be damned if he turned her away if she really
needed him.

"YOU'RE NOT SUPPOSED to be here."

Not exactly the greeting Jess had hoped for when
she appeared at his front door. Yet she shouldn't be all
that surprised. In less than twenty-four hours, she had
already broken the cardinal rule set out by Savannah—
stay away from Chase.

"I know I'm not supposed to see you, but the house
was so quiet, I just couldn't take it. I thought about
watching a movie. I even considered going to bed, but
it's not even nine o'clock. Besides, I'm too keyed up to
sleep."

He remained as immovable as a boulder. A gorgeous
rock of a man dressed in a navy T-shirt and a pair of
camouflage pants, reminiscent of the time he'd made
that surprise visit to her dorm. "I don't have to tell you
what Buck's reaction will be if he sees your car."

She slipped her hands into her jacket pockets, feeling
as contrite as a teenager who'd just blown curfew. But
not so contrite she would turn around and leave before

she had the opportunity to spend some time with him. "I didn't drive. I walked."

He looked completely incredulous. "That's got to be five miles."

"Probably only three, if you take a short cut through the Allworth's land, which I did."

"Not smart, Jess. That's rugged terrain. You could've fallen and broken your pretty neck. Or found yourself on the wrong end of Frank Allworth's shotgun."

At least he thought her neck was pretty. "As you can see, I made it just fine, all in one piece. Don't forget I ran cross-country my sophomore year in high school. And I was one heck of a tumbler in my day."

"How many years ago was that?"

She shrugged. "Okay, it's been a while. I'm only saying my ability to walk several miles proves that I'm in better shape than I thought."

"And that you've lost your mind."

Close, but not quite. "Look, if you'll let me in, I won't stay long." Did it count that she had her fingers crossed behind her back?

"This is still a bad idea, Jess."

Time to play the guilt card. "After the day I've had, I just need to talk to someone. They won't even let me call my own child. And when you didn't call, I felt so isolated. I had to get out of that place."

The guilt card worked. He hesitated only a moment before stepping aside. "You've got an hour, and then I'm driving you home."

She didn't come here for an hour of his time. She wanted all night, right or wrong. But if his cranky attitude didn't improve, she might not last five minutes.

Jess brushed past him and walked into the den, where a floor lamp and a roaring fire provided the only light in the room. Only then did she notice how cold she really was. Slogging through ankle-deep water through part of her journey, in thirty-five degree weather, certainly hadn't helped. Her cross-trainers had dried. Her socks, however, had not.

She shrugged out of her coat and hung it on a spare hook near the door, right next to Chase's jacket. "I would've been here sooner if Frank hadn't dug a trench right in the middle of his pasture." She turned and came face-to-face with his frown. "Wading through the slush slowed me down."

He glanced at the bottom of her frayed jeans now caked with mud. "Do you want to borrow a pair of my pants?"

She'd have to pin up the hem to keep from tripping. "If they fit, I'd be even more depressed than I already am."

His stoic expression softened somewhat. "That bad, huh?"

"I'm okay." And she was, now that she was with him.

"Are you sure?"

"I'm sure." She decided to share her latest accomplishment to prove she hadn't completely collapsed into a worthless puddle of gloom and doom. "I actually lit a fire all by myself in that old stove. I even chopped some wood with your ax. It's not as nice as your fire, but it warmed up the house fairly well." Yet it hadn't done a thing to rid her of the ongoing chills that had accompanied thoughts of her tenuous future.

"I knew you could do it," he said. "You can do anything if you set your mind to it."

Except keep myself out of prison. She halted the comment before it left her foolish mouth. She didn't want to spend these moments with Chase, drowning in self-pity. "Sam and Savannah stayed most of the afternoon after they brought me home. We had a nice visit."

"That's good. You probably needed the company."

She needed his company.

He gestured toward the sofa facing the fire. "Have a seat."

Using the back of the couch for support, she toed out of her shoes, stripped off her soggy socks, and set them near the door. She returned to claim a spot at the end of the sofa, discarding all decorum when she rested her heels on the edge of the coffee table to thaw her frozen feet.

Chase joined her, keeping a fairly wide berth between them. "What's going on with Sam and Savannah these days?"

She appreciated his attempt to avoid talk of literal trials and tribulations. "They're completely enamored of each other. In fact, they couldn't seem to keep their hands off each other." And she'd been stung by the jealousy bug just watching them. "I did appreciate having them around. But, honestly, I was glad when they finally left. I felt like an intruder in my own home."

He smiled, but only halfway. And it didn't last long. "You should've told them to get a room."

"I almost did. But I was afraid they'd end up in mine and I'd have to endure the sounds of heavy breathing."

Finally, he grinned, showing his dimples to supreme advantage. "I guess they're making up for lost time."

Jess truly couldn't fault the couple for that. Not after what they'd gone through to find each other again. But she couldn't deny she was jealous of the way Sam looked at Savannah, as if she were the most special woman on the planet. Dalton had never looked at her like that. No one had.

"Savannah did say they're moving forward with the wedding plans," she added. "They're going to wait until the spring so they can marry on that rickety bridge that joins their farms."

"I was beginning to wonder if they were actually going to do it."

She pushed up her sleeve and checked her watch. "They left my place several hours ago, so I imagine they've already done it. Probably more than once."

"I meant get married."

She faked confusion. "Oh, that. I certainly hope so. Then they can officially move in together and make-out in the privacy of their own home." She sounded like an envious harpy. "Don't get me wrong. I have nothing against public displays of affection. I'm just not used to it."

Chase rested his arm on the back of the sofa and shifted to face her. "Old Dalton wasn't into that, was he?"

She barked out a sarcastic laugh. "Dalton's idea of affection involved slapping me on the butt, right before he told me he needed his shirts ironed."

Chase's loathing for her ex-husband was palpable. "He's a real romantic guy."

"He can be, when he wants something."

"Like sex?"

The word went straight to her head like a shot of tequila. "What's that?"

His dark eyes looked even darker in the flickering firelight. "Do you want a summary, or the dirty details?"

Before she did something totally insane, like tell him she preferred a hands-on demonstration, she switched the subject. "By the way, do you have Bo?"

He shifted his weight, as if the query made him uncomfortable. "I took him to Matt and Rachel's this afternoon. They both agreed it might help Danny if I left Bo there for the time being."

She was starved for news of her son, and not altogether happy he'd withheld that information. "Why didn't you tell me you'd seen him before now?"

"Because I wasn't sure how you'd feel about it when you're not allowed."

She laid a hand on his arm. "I'm glad you checked on him. He thinks you hung the moon."

He pulled his arm back and faced forward, as if he couldn't stand her touching him. "I didn't have the chance to speak to him. He was taking a nap and I didn't want to bother him."

Her heart broke all over again when she thought about Danny weathering the storm without her. "He's probably exhausted. Did Rachel say how he was doing? Is he eating?" Had he asked about her, or had he'd written his mother off entirely?

"She told me he hasn't spoken much at all," he said. "She also said she's going to call that counselor she told you about. She'll try to set up an appointment, but it might be after the holidays. I need to let her know by Monday if you're okay with it."

She could barely think beyond the next few days. "Anything to help him through this." And she prayed her son didn't make any disclosures. That could present too many complications to count.

"Speaking of eating," he said. "Are you?"

She hadn't had much of an appetite, but she didn't dare mention that to him. She didn't want to encourage a lecture. "They fed me watered-down eggs and stale toast at the jail this morning. I can't remember when I've had such an interesting gastronomic experience."

"That doesn't account for the rest of the day."

"Savannah and Sam brought burgers from Stan's." And she'd thrown out over half the sandwich, another fact she would keep to herself.

"Just make sure you take care of yourself," he said. "You can't afford to get sick."

So much for avoiding a lecture. "True. I wouldn't want to miss work." She snapped her fingers. "Oh, wait. I no longer have a job."

Chase scowled. "Savannah told me about the board meeting, but she said they couldn't fire you unless you've been officially indicted."

Just more bad news to add to the rest. "They suspended me. Without pay. The principal called and apologized. It took her two whole minutes. But it's only a matter of time before they dismiss me for good, if Edwin has any say-so in the matter, which he does."

"Guess we're in the same boat. I'm on leave until Monday. Buck's orders. If I keep pissing him off, I might find myself without a job, too."

And she carried most of the responsibility for that. "Savannah mentioned that to me, right before she told me we couldn't be around each other."

"And that's why you shouldn't be here."

She wasn't so needy that she couldn't take a hint. Clearly he didn't want her, not in the way she wanted him. "If my presence is bothering you that much, I'll be glad to leave right now." She pushed off the sofa and stood. "And don't worry about driving me home. I prefer to get there the same way I got here, on foot."

He clasped her hand and pulled her down next to him. "You're already here, so you might as well stay for another hour. And I am going to drive you home, whether you like it or not. You don't need to be traipsing around all alone in the dark."

"I had enough light to see." She could also see she'd begun to wear him down. With a little luck—and a lot of convincing—her plan might work after all.

"A word of advice," he said. "The next time you decide to go for a late-night walk, and you don't want to risk falling over a log, do what I do."

"Pack night-vision goggles?"

"I have a flashlight in my pocket."

She should keep her mouth shut, but she couldn't seem to contain the questionable thought. "I bet you say that to all the girls."

When he patted her thigh, she felt it all the way to her tingling toes, and all points in between. "Glad to see your smart-ass switch still works."

He'd turned on her libido switch with only an innocent touch and devilish smile. "Do you take a lot of walks at night?"

"Not since my Army days."

She decided to pose a question she'd wanted to ask for ages. "Exactly what did you do over there?"

His gaze drifted to some unknown focal point across the way. "I trekked through mountains and deserts, looking for bad guys."

"Did you find them?"

"Yeah, and they found us. Unfortunately, sometimes it's hard to identify the enemy. Mistakes are made when that happens."

Jess watched as Chase went to that place again. A place in his head that she couldn't go, unless he agreed to take her there. "If you ever want to talk about it, I'm here."

After a brief bout of silence, he came out of his momentary mental fog. "I'll make a deal with you. I'll talk about it, as long as you tell me everything that happened that night with Dalton. All the details."

A deal she couldn't—wouldn't—make. "I thought you said you didn't want to know details that you might be forced to reveal in court."

"If I do have to take the stand, I'll claim I don't know anything."

She couldn't believe he'd break his code of honor for her. "You'd lie under oath?"

"If that's what it took to save you."

She could be beyond saving. "Don't worry. You don't have to lie. I've already told you everything." Everything she was willing to tell him.

"Are you sure about that, Jess? Because I'm sensing you're withholding something."

For once in her life, she wished he didn't know her

so well. "I didn't attack Dalton. I didn't touch a hair on his perfectly-styled head. And I have no problem saying *that* under oath."

He kept his gaze centered on hers for a few moments, as if searching for hidden truths. "I believe you." His lack of conviction said otherwise.

"Thank you," she told him anyway. "And now it's your turn to talk about what happened to you over there."

The sound of breaking glass brought the conversation to a standstill and sent Chase off the sofa to investigate. Jess stayed close behind him as he flipped on the light and opened the front door. Since his broad shoulders blocked her view, she leaned to her right to see a large, ornamental black vase in pieces on the porch.

"I told Savannah not to put the damn thing there," he muttered. "But she thought it gave the entry character."

"Not anymore," Jess said. "There's barely a breeze blowing. I can't imagine how something so heavy would just fall over."

"Probably a raccoon or a possum looking for food knocked it over."

That sounded plausible, but it didn't completely alleviate her fear that a human might be lurking in the shadows. "It had to be that. I highly doubt someone would try to break into a deputy's house. Unless they were incredibly stupid."

He faced her again, putting them in very close proximity since she'd failed to move. "I'll grab a flashlight and take a look around, just to be sure."

"Okay. But be careful. I'd hate for you to get ambushed."

"Yeah. Gotta watch those killer possums."

She would rather watch his killer smile. All night.

They returned inside where Chase retrieved a flashlight and put on his jacket. After he left out the front door again, Jess dropped into a nearby chair and contemplated her next move. She'd always believed in the "there are worse things than being alone" adage, but she'd never been in this situation before—without her son, and facing possible prosecution for a crime she didn't commit. She wanted the opportunity to escape her troubles, forget the tenuous future. To ignore the world in the arms of a man who could easily erase all her worries. Problem was, he could very well reject her request. She wouldn't know unless she tried.

"All clear," he said after he came back in the house. "Whatever knocked over the pot is probably long gone."

Jess came to her feet and walked to the window. She pulled back the heavy brown curtain and peered into the night, needing some time to gather her courage, to implement her plan. "If you say so."

"Don't you trust me?"

She did. Otherwise, she wouldn't be here, planning to invite herself into his bed.

After she turned to find Chase hadn't removed his coat, she suspected he was ready to boot her out. "I trust you. I'm just a little jumpy tonight." For obvious—and not so obvious—reasons.

"Do you need anything before I take you home?" he asked, confirming her suspicions. "I have some extra cash."

She needed something all right, but strictly from a non-monetary standpoint. "I'm fine on that front. I used to sock away money when Dalton and I were still married. A rainy day fund." She hadn't realized she'd be swept up in a hurricane at the time, otherwise she would have saved more.

"Just let me know if you run short." He glanced at the clock hung over the bookshelves flanking the fireplace. "It's getting late. I better get you home."

Now or never had arrived. She opted for now. "I don't want to go home. Not now. Not tonight."

She'd expected a resounding refusal, yet he seemed to be mulling it over. "If you're that worried about being alone," he said, "I guess I can lend you my couch. But you'll have to be out of here before dawn."

"I'd rather be in your bed."

"Then I'll take the couch and you take the bed."

If he insisted on being obtuse, she'd simply have to be straightforward. "I don't want you to sleep on the sofa. And I don't want you to sleep in your bed, either."

"You're not making any sense, Jess."

She wasn't making any progress, either. "You're really out of the loop if you don't recognize a proposition when you hear one."

He started to pace around the room, his hands laced behind his neck. "We can't do that, Jess."

"Yes, we can. If you recall, we already have. But then, you did tell me that night we should forget it ever happened. But here's a flash, Chase. I didn't forget, even if you did."

He spun around, frustration etched in his face. "You really believe I've forgotten?"

She leaned back against the door to block the exit, in case he decided to leave when she refused to go. "It wouldn't surprise me in the least if it never crossed your mind. After all, I was just one of your many conquests. A mistake you made along the way."

He stood right in front of her before she realized he'd moved. Bracing both hands above her head, he trapped her between solid wood and his equally solid body. "First of all, there haven't been as many women as you think. Secondly, not a day's gone by when I haven't thought about that night."

Years of pent-up emotional pain, prompted by his careless disregard, drove her to bait him. "Funny, you never mentioned it again. Not one time in all the letters we exchanged." Then again, neither had she.

"What did you expect me to do after you ran off and married Dalton? You're right. I've made mistakes in my life, but staking a claim on another man's wife isn't one of them."

She might not have been another man's wife if she'd meant more to him than a quick round of send-off sex. "I still have a difficult time believing you."

He pressed his body flush against hers. "Here's a flash, Jessica," he began, throwing her words back at her. "At night in the barracks, when there wasn't a woman in sight and I had to take matters into my own hands, do you know what I fantasized about?"

"Supermodels?"

He leaned closer, his warm breath a whisper on her ear. "You."

Jess had a difficult time composing herself enough to catch a breath. "Then you don't regret being with me?"

"I regret that I didn't take my time with you."

She felt remarkably empowered. Bold and brash. And

sexy, for the first time in years. "You can make up for it now. I'm not asking for forever, just one night."

"I don't want to hurt you, Jess."

"You won't unless you tell me no. I assure you, I'm going into this with eyes wide open. You don't even have to pretend you care about me more than you do."

"If I didn't give a damn about you, I would've had you naked and flat on your back long before now."

His intense expression, the rapid rise and fall of his chest, told Jess she was about to taste triumph. "Let me stay, Chase. I'll make it worth your while."

"You're making it real hard to say no."

All a part of the master plan. She traced the indentation in his cheeks, then feathered a fingertip across his lips. "I gave you comfort that night before you left. This time, I need some comfort, too. I need you."

A storm of indecision reflected in his eyes, and she knew the very moment he conceded defeat. When kissed her.

After ten long years, she would finally get what she thought she would never have again. Another night with Chase Reed.

CHAPTER NINE

HE HAD JESS DOWN for the count on the couch in a matter of minutes, one hand up her shirt and the other poised on his fly. And then he had a moment of clarity. A big one.

He raised his head and locked into her gaze. "Are you on the Pill?"

"No."

The next question was a long-shot at best. "You didn't happen to bring any condoms with you, did you?"

"No. They're at home in the cookie jar."

"I'm serious, Jess."

She looked seriously ticked off. "No, I don't randomly keep condoms in my pocket."

"Then we can't do this," he said as he climbed off her, leaving Jess looking as perturbed as he felt. But he wasn't mad at her. He was mad at himself.

She sat up and glared at him. "You mean you're just going to kiss me like that and then not follow through?"

He'd had every intention of following through, until he remembered something too important to neglect. "We don't have a choice. The last thing we need is for me to get you pregnant."

A strange, unreadable look passed over her expression. "Yes, that would definitely be inadvisable. But my question to you is this. Why in the heck don't you have a condom cache? You're the confirmed bachelor, not me."

Because he hadn't been with a woman in well over six months. "Like I told you before, I've been in a—"

"Dry spell. I know." She grabbed her hair with both hands, like she wanted to pull it out by the roots. "This is a fine time for you to ignore your Boy Scout motto."

How could he have prepared for her blatant seduction? Not that he wasn't willing to scratch her itch. But the cost was way too high to throw their clothes, and caution, to the wind. "Maybe this is a sign we shouldn't be doing this."

She came to her feet, looking as determined as ever. "It's not a sign. It's a minor inconvenience that can easily be remedied. That's why they invented convenience stores, hence the convenience part. There happens to be one this side of the county line, and it's open until midnight. I'd go, but by the time I walk there and back, I could be too tired to tango. And that, Deputy, just won't do."

She was definitely serious about seeing this through. No one ever accused him of not giving a lady what she wanted, even if this could be a catastrophe in the making. If anyone found out what they were doing—what they were going to do—they'd be instant grist for the rumor mill. Just like Savannah had predicted.

What the hell. No one would find out. The closest neighbor lived over a mile down the road, and he doubted anyone was out driving around. Besides, if he backed out now, he'd have to live with disappointing Jess. Again. She needed him, and he needed her, and that was a good enough reason to go for it. Then he'd have to find a way to break all ties in order to protect her.

He put on his jacket, fished the keys from his pocket and faced her again. "I'll go. You stay here."

She sent him smile that was so damn sexy, he almost said goodbye to the store and hello to poor judgment. "Marvelous idea," she said. "My socks are still wet, and I don't do wet socks."

Old habits came home to roost. "Sweetheart, sometimes wet isn't a bad thing. I'll show you what I mean when I get back."

That seemed to shut her up, but it didn't stop her from tagging along behind him as he walked out the door. Before he reached the first step, she tapped him on the shoulder, drawing him back around to receive an all-out assault on his mouth. If she didn't let up soon, he'd never be able to walk into the store with his dignity intact.

"What was that for?" he asked when she finally broke the kiss.

"I just wanted to remind you what you'll be missing, in case you decide to keep going and not come back."

"I'll be back." She'd pretty much cemented that with her wicked mouth. "In the meantime, get naked and get in bed."

She saluted him like a drill sergeant. "Do you want any shirts ironed before I do that?"

Damn. She'd just pointed out he wasn't any better in the romance department than her sorry ex-husband. "Come to think of it, I'm going to take off your clothes, real slow, and then I'll carry you to bed. If we make it that far."

Without waiting for a response, Chase strode to the truck, unlocked it with the remote and slid inside the cab. For once he wished he had the cruiser at his disposal, but he'd been forced to leave that at the department after his temporary dismissal. Permanent dismissal, if Buck got wind of this little rendezvous.

He waited a few minutes to start the ignition, closing his eyes to reclaim some calm. When he opened them, he saw Jess standing on the porch, tapping her foot. Patience had never been one of her stronger virtues. Evidently the same held true for her modesty, he realized, when she shimmied out of her jeans. The oversize, long-sleeve T-shirt she still wore covered her enough, but also revealed a lot of bare leg. That sight was enough to ignite a fire that shot straight to his groin. So much for cooling his jets.

He backed out of the driveway in a rush, spewing gravel and dust as he hit the main road. As bad luck would have it, he'd only traveled a few yards when a beat-up, aged, tank of a sedan pulled out in front him. The driver had to be going a good ten miles under the speed limit, which made Chase wonder if the person behind the wheel had been drinking. But the car held steady to the curve of the road, which thankfully shot holes in that concern. Probably just some geezer with bad eyesight going out for milk at his wife's request.

The car finally pulled over to the shoulder, allowing Chase to pass him. He punched the accelerator and made it to the store in record time, fortunately finding the parking lot deserted. He sure as hell didn't want an audience when he made the purchase. Unfortunately, he recognized the clerk behind the counter. A tall, lanky seventeen-year-old who played guard for the high school basketball team.

Chase grabbed a cup of black coffee from the pot near

the soda dispenser before heading down the candy aisle. After picking up a box of chocolate-covered mints—Jess's favorite—he made his way to the display near the front of the store. Might be nice if they put the damn condoms in a less obvious place, but he figured they had a lot of teenagers trying to steal the things. Right now he felt like a sneaky teenager. But he wasn't. Not even close. Maybe guilt had something to do with the return to his youth.

After snatching a couple of packets from the long metal hooks, he set them on the counter, along with the candy and coffee.

"Evening, Deputy Reed."

Chase looked up to meet the clerk's obnoxious grin. "Evening."

"It's party time, huh?"

He withdrew his wallet from his back pocket, pulled out a twenty and offered it to the kid. He also offered him a mind-your-own-business glare. "Why are you working this late on a school night?"

The kid looked like he could crawl under the counter. "It's the holidays, sir. Do you need a sack?"

He needed to stop being such a hard-ass, otherwise he'd end up just like Buck. "No thanks, and keep the change."

Chase pocketed the items, grabbed the coffee and then pushed through the double glass doors and walked into the frigid night. Before he stepped off the curb, he noticed a car sitting near a flickering guard light in the corner of the lot. A car that looked a lot like the one he'd passed on the road. He couldn't make out the driver's features that were set in shadow, but he did recognize his gender from the hairy hand holding a lit cigarette out the open window.

He could be lost, which would explain why he'd been driving slowly. Or he could be up to no good.

Chase thought about the boy in the store, alone and probably unarmed. Some mother's son who needed someone to look out for him. With that in mind, he opened the door, and leaned into the cab to retrieve his gun from the locked glove box. After he put the coffee cup in the holder and stuck the weapon in his back waistband, he straightened to see the car pull away. He didn't make another move until he watched the taillights fade out of sight.

Satisfied the clerk was safe, he climbed back in the truck, put away the gun and sped back to the house without encountering anyone on the road. He cut off the ignition and paused to down the last of the coffee. By the time he reached the front door, he was high on caffeine, adrenaline and a whole lot of anticipation.

The sound of crackling wood filled the otherwise silent den, the dying fire providing the only real light. Chase assumed Jess had decided to wait for him in bed, but that assumption was splintered when he caught sight of a lock of auburn hair draped over the arm of the sofa. He almost called her name, but decided to wait until he assessed the situation. As expected, she was stretched out on her side, eyes closed, a throw pillow supporting her head, and both hands curled beneath her cheek. The T-shirt had ridden up high on her thighs, exposing a lot of bare leg and the lace edge of a pair of jet-black panties. The ache way down south returned. An ache that only she could alleviate.

As badly as he wanted to wake her—as badly as he wanted her—he decided to let her sleep. Aside from making the three-mile walk to get to him, she'd been put through the emotional wringer over the past five days. She needed her rest, regardless of how bad he needed her.

He retrieved a white wool blanket from the bedroom closet, and after making sure she was sufficiently covered, he claimed the club chair adjacent to the couch.

She reminded him of the girl he once knew. The girl who'd played angel to his devil. When he'd defended her honor on the playground, she'd kicked him in the shin for disrupting her flirtation. After she'd suffered a number of break-ups with childhood boyfriends, he'd been in charge of bandaging her broken heart. And she'd been the one to scold him when he'd broken someone's heart. They'd been thick as thieves, and the best of friends— until Dalton Wainwright rode into her life in his shiny red sports car, sweeping her away with priceless gifts and promises the bastard had never intended to keep. To Dalton, she'd been nothing more than a pretty possession. The girl many a boy wanted, but could never have. Including Chase.

He knew the exact moment he'd begun to see her as more than a friend, and it had happened long before the eve of his first deployment to the Middle East. She'd come to the party his parents had thrown the day before he'd left for basic training. He remembered what she'd been wearing—a white sleeveless dress with black polka dots. He remembered the last thing she said to him, too.

If you ever get lonely, just think of me thinking of you and wishing you were back home with me.

In that moment, he'd viewed her as a woman worth waiting for. As someone he loved, and not only as a friend. He hadn't admitted it then, not even to himself, but he realized it now. And that scared the hell out of him.

When she stirred, he thought she might wake up and expect him to finish what they'd started. Instead, she rolled onto her belly and sighed in her sleep. He couldn't deny his disappointment, but he also couldn't deny that maybe this wasn't meant to be.

He pushed out of the chair, kissed her cheek, and set off to bed alone. But not completely alone. As sure as the dawn would come, he'd be visited by the horrors of war that often infiltrated his dreams—and the face of the little girl who had died in his arms.

The little girl who had died by his own hand.

JESS CAME AWAKE WITH A START, jolted from sleep by a tortured voice filtering into the room from down the hall. After she got her bearings, she moved toward the sound. Toward Chase.

She felt blindly along the wall until she found the switch and flipped it on. The light allowed her to see the partially-opened door, and the bed where he thrashed about. She perched on the edge of the mattress and watched the anguish form on his face as he muttered unintelligible words. But a few were crystal clear—"save her" and "too late."

The dog tags resting on his bare chest glinted in the limited light, a symbol of what he stood for. A reminder of a war he clearly still fought in his dreams. She wasn't sure how to wake him. She wasn't sure she should. Yet she couldn't bear his torment any longer. But as she smoothed her hand over his damp forehead, he grabbed her wrist and bolted upright, almost scaring her out of her skin.

"It's Jess, Chase," she whispered softly. "It's okay."

He loosened his grip as his dark eyes finally focused on her, and awareness dawned in his expression. "Did I hurt you?" he asked, his voice grainy from troubled sleep.

"No, you didn't hurt me."

He collapsed back onto the pillow and stared at the ceiling. "I'm sorry."

"You don't have to apologize. I'm just worried about you."

He shifted toward the middle of the bed and opened his arms. "Come here."

He didn't have to ask her twice. She curled up close to his side on top of the covers, and rested her arm across his belly where the sheet barely covered his hips. She was content to just hold him. To be held.

But as he stroked her arm, back and forth in a steady rhythm, she was no longer satisfied with the limited contacted. She wanted more. She wanted everything he could give her. What he would have given her if she hadn't foolishly fallen asleep. The question was—would he still be willing?

She shifted restlessly against his side and an odd sound slipped out of her parted lips before she could stop it. He showed her that he understood her need when he framed her face in one palm and kissed her. Gently at first, before it deepened to the kind of kiss that told her he wanted more, too. He wanted her.

Without saying a word, she rose up and tugged her shirt over her head, then removed her bra, all under his watchful eye. Having a baby, and age, had softened her in places, widened her in others. She definitely wasn't as thin as she had been when he'd made love to her the first time. But amazingly, she didn't feel at all self-conscious or shy. She just felt…hot. Really hot after he tossed the sheet away, revealing that he was several steps ahead, as far the undressing went. He was also very aroused, but then so was she. And she became even more aroused when she returned to his side and he slid her panties away.

As they faced each other, he teased her with a kiss, then another, before he skimmed his palms down her body. He caressed the curve of her hip with a feather-soft touch, never taking his gaze from hers.

"You're beautiful," he whispered. "Did you know that?"

Not until now. But she actually did feel beautiful, and desired. All because of him.

She wanted so badly to touch him, too. She was dying to touch him. But when she reached for him, he caught her wrist again, more gently this time. "If you put your hands on me right now, it won't last long enough." He nudged her onto her back and rose above her. "And I want this to last a long, long time. Unlike the last time."

The reference to that long-ago night wasn't completely lost on Jess. Everything had happened so fast back then, she hadn't had time to really enjoy the experience. She'd also been racked with sadness and fear for his safety. Later, with more than a little remorse.

Right now, she couldn't consider anything beyond the

downward path he was traveling with his lips. He paused to linger at her breasts before he moved to her belly, but he didn't stop there. As he approached his final destination, Jess knew exactly what he was about to do. She was powerless to stop him, even if she wanted to. She didn't want to.

This ultimate act of intimacy required a good deal of trust, and the willingness to let go, to follow wherever he cared to lead her. She did trust him, and she did let go as he brought her to the brink with his incredibly talented mouth.

As the climax began to build, a thousand heady feelings rushed through her. Her heart beat at a rapid pace. Every breath became an effort. She wanted to savor each sensation, wanted it to go on forever, but the release was so powerful, so quick, she could only surrender to it.

So lost in the afterglow that had eluded her for a long, long time, she hadn't realized Chase had moved, until she heard the sound of tearing paper. She looked to her left to see him seated on the edge of the bed, keeping his beautifully sculpted back to her. She waited eagerly for the all-important pay-off, although she'd already been paid in full. Now it was his turn to reap the rewards.

Yet instead of doing what she'd expected, he moved over her and braced on bent arms, leaving too much space between their bodies. "Tell me your fantasies," he said in a low, sensuous whisper.

She wasn't accustomed to talk during sex. Dalton had never made a sound, except to snore after the fact. She banished her insignificant ex-husband from her brain, and tried to come up with an answer to Chase's question that didn't sound totally off the wall. "I really don't have any fantasies."

"Sure you do," he said. "Everyone does. Maybe a place where you'd like to make love, but never have. A way you'd like to make love, but you've never been brave enough to do it."

One thing did come to mind. She should be embarrassed to share, but she wasn't. Okay, maybe a little. "Do you promise not to laugh?"

He kissed her forehead. "Babe, right now, laughing is the last thing I want to do." He rubbed his lower body against hers, sending a strong message, loud and clear.

"I've imagined having sex on top of Dalton's desk down at the bank," she rattled off. "But not with Dalton."

"Then with who?"

Oops. "With you."

He looked rather pleased by her answer. "Babe, I can't physically take you there right now, but imagine we're on that desk while I take you to a place you've never been before."

She managed a weak smile. "A little cocky, are we?"

"Just confident."

Chase had the skill to back up that confidence, she soon realized, as he finally slid inside her with an easy glide and built steady momentum with his powerful body. He practically blew her mind with very descriptive words that were somewhat crude but oh-so-sexy. As promised, he did take her to a place she'd never been before, right into the throes of another climax, the second equally as strong as the first. And he wasn't far behind her, she realized, during her slow journey to recovery. With one last thrust, every muscle in his body tensed, and a low groan escaped from somewhere deep in his throat. And then he collapsed, giving Jess all his weight after giving her the experience of a lifetime.

They stayed that way for a while, as closely joined as two people could be, until he moved away and took her back into his arms. She couldn't imagine anywhere else she wanted to be in those quiet moments. She couldn't imagine any man ever measuring up to him.

"Are you okay?" he asked, finally breaking the silence.

"I am, but are you?"

"Couldn't be better."

Oh, but he could. And as much as she wanted to stay steeped in bliss, she needed him to open up, now more than ever. After what they'd just been through together, maybe he would.

Covering herself with the tangled sheet, Jess leaned over and turned on the bedside lamp, then scooted up against the headboard. "I have something I need to ask you."

He honored her with his trademark dimpled grin. "Yeah, I bought another condom. Just give me fifteen minutes and we'll put it to good use."

As tempted as Jess was by that suggestion, she had a more pressing issue on the table. And as badly as she hated to ruin the mood, she had an urgent need to know the story behind his night terrors.

She drew in a deep breath, let it out slowly, and started down the path possibly leading to the truth.

"Who was the woman you couldn't save?"

CHAPTER TEN

Right when he'd finally had a few minutes of peace, she'd forced him to remember.

Chase instinctively wanted to shut down. Shut her out. The need to guard his emotions overrode his need for absolution.

He draped one arm over his eyes to avoid her scrutiny, only to see the never-ending horrors. "Let it go, Jess."

"I can't, Chase. You need to talk to someone about this. Why not me?"

"I've already talked about it." But not all of it. Never all of it. "I've talked to doctors and counselors. I even took the pills they offered for a while, but I didn't like the way they made me feel. Or I should say, the way they kept me from feeling."

"I see. You want to relive it, whatever it is, because you have some absurd need to punish yourself."

She had that one nailed. "Just forget what you saw, and what you heard, and let me deal with it."

"How can I forget it when you obviously can't? And it's more than apparent you're not dealing with it."

Fine. If she wanted the gritty details, he'd give them to her. He'd been looking for a way to cut her off, to discourage this situation from happening again. Once he divulged the facts, and his downfall, she wouldn't hold him in such high esteem. An easy out. Not an easy story

to tell. But one that had to be told so she would understand.

He climbed out of the bed, grabbed some clothes from
the bureau, and went into the bathroom to clean up. He
ran the risk she might take off before he was finished,
but that wasn't likely. She was prone to digging her heels
in when she wanted something. She'd proved that tonight
with her proposition. And he'd given in to her wishes
without that much thought. Sad thing was, if she hadn't
witnessed his nightmares, or at least overlooked them,
they might still be in bed, making some more real, sweet
love. He needed that a whole lot more than a sorry trip
back into the past.

When Chase returned to the bedroom, she was still
in the same spot, looking as mad as a soaked hen. And
sexy as hell. Her hair was a mess and her cheeks were
flushed. She looked like she needed to be kissed again.
Everywhere.

"Going somewhere?" she asked when he failed to
move.

Yeah. He was about to board the insanity train.

He gathered her clothes from the floor and tossed
them on the bed in front of her. "Get dressed."

Anger as turbulent as a tornado flashed in her eyes.
"Oh, so that's it. Now that you've had your wicked way
with me, you just pat me on the butt and take me home.
Heaven forbid I want to be your friend, not just your
one-night lover."

He sensed a tirade coming on. "Put your clothes on,
Jess."

She didn't disappoint. "Perhaps, Deputy Reed, you
believe keeping your emotions locked tight is the manly

thing to do. That needing someone is a sign of weakness. In my book, that's darned arrogant. And dangerous. One day you might crawl so far inside yourself, you won't be able to feel anything. But I guess that suits you just fine, doesn't it? All a part of your skewed macho persona."

She didn't know the half of it, but she would. Provided she kept quiet long enough for him to have his say. "If you want to know the truth, you've got it. But if I'm going to tell you what happened, we're going to do it somewhere other than in a bed."

Otherwise he'd be too distracted. To tempted to persuade her to drop the whole admission thing. He had the means and the know-how to do it. But that would only be a temporary diversion. She'd eventually hound him about it again.

"Meet me in the den when you have your clothes on," he said.

Then without another word, he walked into the kitchen and went straight for the bottle of tequila someone had left during a card game back in the summer. He wasn't one to drink hard liquor. He'd seen the effects of too much booze on fellow soldiers and friends and even enemies, namely Dalton Wainwright. And he sure couldn't forget Matt Boyd's dad. But in this case, desperate disclosures called for desperate measures.

He poured a shot, drank it fast and then had one more. The tequila burned his throat and left a foul taste in his mouth. As much as wanted to be numb, he didn't want to be drunk when he tore open old wounds, and that could be the case if he downed another shot.

After he dumped the rest of the tequila into the sink, he set the glass aside and returned to the den. The fire had gone out completely, but he didn't have the will to start another. The pile of ashes scattered in the hearth seemed like a proper backdrop for the confession.

He sat on the sofa and waited for Jess. Waited to drop the information bomb that could blow her opinion of him right out of the water. She came into the room a few minutes later, bypassing the space next to him, choosing the chair instead.

She sat straight as a stick, hands gripping the chair's arms. "I'm here, and I'm ready to listen. Feel free to begin when you're ready." The speech was so dry, no one would believe they'd been about as close as two people could be only a short time ago.

Chase had a hard time believing it himself. He also had a hard time believing he was about to let her in on his secrets. Let her in, period. But he'd come this far, he wasn't going to turn back now.

Leaning forward, he draped his arms on his knees and focused on the beige area rug beneath his bare feet. "It was near the end of my second tour of duty. It happened on a day like any other day." The air had been thick with dust and the usual tension. Weapons loaded and readily on hand. Everyone prepared to spring into action on a moment's notice. Everyone but him.

"We were patrolling the streets that afternoon, keeping the peace," he continued. "The open-air market was crowded with civilians. That's the first time I remember seeing her, at least on that day. She'd been around before."

"The woman?"

He looked up to discover Jess had scooted to the edge

of her seat. "Not a woman. A girl. She was maybe a year younger than Danny."

He could tell that struck a chord with her, but she still remained calm and attentive. "Go on."

Consciously living those moments, step-by-step, was akin to walking across burning sand without shoes. He wanted to rush through the events to avoid the pain, but the terrain was too vast. "Anyway, she was a little thing with big brown eyes and a huge smile. She used to come around when we'd hand out treats to the local kids. As far as I could tell, she only knew one English word. *Candy.*"

He allowed a smile over the few good memories, and that didn't escape Jess's notice. "I guess the love of candy is universal," she said. "She must have been a special little girl if she stood out from the crowd."

"She was special. They all were in their own right. Survivors of a living hell. But they could still get excited over a gumball."

"Maybe we could both take a lesson from that."

He was too jaded to believe he could be that resilient. He'd proven it every night. "A lot of the kids were orphans. But that little girl always had her mother nearby. That day was no exception."

As the events unfolded in his mind, the visions were razor sharp, as if they'd happened only hours, not years, before. The fortress he'd built for self-protection began to crumble, one memory at a time. Ironic that for years, he couldn't talk at length about it. Now he couldn't seem to stop.

"She handed me a piece of paper," he said. "A drawing she'd done. I knelt down to take it from her."

Thank you, sweetheart. That's really pretty.

"She was smiling when the shooting started."

Mass chaos. Bullets ricocheting all around him. Sheer terror.

When Chase leaned his head back against the sofa, Jess came over and sat beside him. "Do you want to take a break?"

"No. I want to get this over with."

He waited just long enough to collect his composure before he began again. "People starting scattering when the gunfire erupted. I grabbed her hand, pulled her behind me. I could hear her mother screaming *Safa* over and over again. Funny, I didn't even know her name until that moment."

He paused to draw a breath, then let it out slowly. "I saw one of the insurgents shoot one of my men, then he tried to escape when he saw me. I don't know for sure, but I believe he was out of ammo."

His mind momentarily froze when the next images began flashing in his brain, like some freak slideshow.

"Go on, Chase."

Jess's voice thrust him out of his stupor. "I was so damn determined to stop him, I let go of Safa's hand. She ran into the street, trying to get to her mother. I discharged a round, and she took a bullet. Right in the heart."

Jess gasped and covered her mouth with her palm. "Oh, Chase."

The words kept flowing like water from a busted dam. "I dropped to the ground and crawled over to her. I picked her up and held my hand on the wound, but I couldn't stop the bleeding. She was still alive at the time, and I watched the life drain out of her eyes. And, God, her mother…"

He streaked both hands over his face. "Her mother kept screaming. I've seen a lot in my time, but I've never heard that much agony coming from another human being."

When he glanced at Jess and saw her tears, he thought for a moment he might just join her. But he didn't dare cry. If he did, he might never stop.

"And you know what's so damn unfair?" he said after a time. "The gunman I shot survived, while an innocent little girl died. Helluva world we live in, huh?"

She took his hand into hers and held it against her damp cheek. "This wasn't your fault, Chase. You couldn't have known what would happen."

He'd tried to convince himself of that for years, but so far it hadn't worked. "I could've held on to her hand. I could have let the bastard go. Then she'd still be alive."

She tipped her head against his shoulder. "I understand why you feel the way you do, but I don't understand why you won't give yourself a break."

"Because I can't. I took that child away from her mother, the same as if I'd intentionally turned the gun on her. And that's what I see at night, that moment I let go of her. The fear in her eyes a split second before she left this world. I hear her mother's screams." Sights and sounds that would never go away.

No longer able to sit still, he stood and walked to the fireplace where he gripped the edge of the mantle. On one hand, he felt drained of energy. On the other, he could punch the wall with the force of his despair.

"Why on earth did you go back again?" Jess asked.

That could be answered with one word. "Absolution."

"But you didn't find it, did you?"

He'd stopped searching when he recognized he didn't warrant it. "No."

"And why would you take a job in law enforcement? That has to make matters worse."

"Because I promised Buck I'd do it. Because it's always been expected of me." Being the best soldier. Being the best deputy. Eventually being the best father. He'd failed at two, he wasn't going to set himself up to fail at the other.

"Then Buck doesn't know about what happened."

He shot a quick look at her over his shoulder. "Hell, no. I couldn't tell him that his hero son isn't a hero after all."

When he felt the light touch on his shoulder, he tensed from the contact. "You are a hero, Chase. Just think of all the other lives you've saved. You're certainly Danny's hero."

He dropped his arms and faced her. "Danny needs to find someone else to admire. I'm only a man who made an unforgivable mistake."

"I forgive you."

He'd underestimated her compassion. Looking back, he wasn't sure why he had. "I don't deserve your forgiveness, Jess. I don't want it."

She tipped her chin up and glared at him. "Well you've got it, whether you want it or not. And you can either beat yourself up, or you can finally accept the fact that you're mortal. You never meant to hurt that little girl, and the fact that you're still mourning the loss only demonstrates you're a good man."

That brought him to a question he needed to ask her. "What about you, Jess? Have you ever done something you regret? Something that keeps you awake at night?"

She instantly looked away. "If you're talking about what happened with Dalton, I've already said all that I want to say about that."

He didn't know where the anger had come from. He only knew it hit him like a left hook. "Great. You force me to expose my soul, and you're not willing to do the same. That's kind of unfair, don't you think?"

That earned him her attention. "Everything I've done in my adult life, good, bad or indifferent, I did to protect a child. Maybe it hasn't turned out the way it should, but my intentions were good, and so were yours. I have to keep telling myself that to keep going."

That wasn't exactly a confession, but in Chase's opinion, it was darn close. "You know what they say about the road to hell and good intentions."

"They can shove it. I believe if your heart is in the right place, anything can be forgiven."

He wanted to adopt her optimistic attitude. He wanted to go to bed at night knowing he hadn't completely botched his honor. Right then, he wanted to sweep her back into his arms, carry her back to bed and forget everything aside from making love to her. But he had to stay away from Jess or risk failing her, too.

"I need to take you home," he said. "I'll go warm up the truck while you put on your shoes."

When she moved closer and cupped his jaw in her palm, he saw the sympathy in her eyes. "I can stay a little longer. It's still dark outside."

Now came the hard part. He clasped her wrist and

took her hand away. "This is the last time we're going to do this, Jess. I don't want to be responsible for ruining your life, too."

She crossed her arms over her middle and sighed. "Okay. We can't take the risk again. But I'm not worried about you ruining my life, because you can't. You don't have that much power over the cosmos, or me. I'll go home now, but as soon as this thing with Dalton is settled, I'm going to help you through this guilt. The same way you've helped me in the last few days. Even if I have to do it from jail."

The thought of her being thrown into a cell made him sick. "Most of the time, I'm not fit to be around."

She smiled. "Only when you haven't had your coffee, or you can't watch a playoff game. But in my eyes, you're still about the best thing going when it comes to being a friend."

He wanted to fight her on the issue, but he was too damn exhausted. In spite of what she'd said, he vowed to keep his distance, at least for the time being. If he had any sense whatsoever, he'd take a permanent hiatus from her life. But the fact that she knew his well-kept secret and still didn't think any less of him, made leaving her alone all the more difficult. And so did the feelings that had begun to surface. Feelings as hard to ignore as the night terrors.

Buck had been right—he was in love with her. He just didn't have a clue what to do about it.

HE WAS CLEARLY DONE with her.

Jess had come to accept that over the past three days. Chase hadn't bothered to call. Hadn't bothered to answer her calls, until a half hour ago. And he certainly hadn't paid her any surprise visits. Pride had prevented her from visiting him. That and the fear that, this time, he would turn her away. For good.

Yet the rain that had steadily fallen for a good part of the previous night, and most of the day, had presented her with an opportunity to see him again. Thank heavens for backed-up plumbing, a leaky roof and a landlord who refused to pay a repairman's double rate during a holiday.

She stood at the window and waited for Chase, the overcast skies contributing to her melancholy mood. But her spirits lifted when she spotted the truck coming up the drive. They went into a free-fall when she became aware that it wasn't Chase's truck after all. His was silver with a single-cab, while this one had an extended cab. And as the mystery vehicle drew closer, she recognized the truck by the magnetic sign adhered to the door that read, Matthew J. Boyd, DVM. Rachel's veterinarian husband. Jess's former brother-in-law and recent surrogate father to her son.

At first she experienced a twinge of panic when she considered something might have happened to Danny. Then blessed relief arrived as Chase emerged from the passenger side. So did the heightened awareness that had become all too familiar. He looked so good, she had to wrangle the urge to run to him. Yes, he needed a shave. And yes, he wore a plain chambray shirt over his white T-shirt, along with his usual dark wash jeans. But since she'd recently seen, up close and extremely personal, what lurked beneath that non-descript clothing, she viewed him in a whole new light. Lately, she'd been seeing him unabashedly naked in her very vivid imagination.

Shaking off those thoughts, Jess walked outside and waited for the pair on the porch. Matt arrived first, tool box in hand, and gave her a quick peck on the cheek. "How are you holding up, Jess?"

"With both of my legs, Matt." Though her legs could give out on her at any moment, thanks to the deputy's appearance.

When Chase didn't even bother to say hello, she turned back to Matt. "How is my son?"

"I'm pretty sure Danny misses you," Matt said. "But Chase has been coming over to play some catch with him. He took him over to his place yesterday, right, Chase?"

To that point, Chase acted as if he'd lost his voice. "I gave him a hammer and showed him how to pound some nails into a two-by-four. Didn't take him long to get the hang of it. He's got good hand-eye coordination."

She could use a couple of two-by-fours and a hammer to vent her irritation. She was grateful Chase had paid special attention to Danny. She wasn't so thrilled by his inability to look at her. "That's great," she said. "Thanks."

Still no eye contact, but he did say, "You're welcome."

Matt pulled at the collar of his shirt, as if he were a bit uncomfortable over the obvious tension. "Chase says you have a roof leak."

"Yes, I do. Water's dripping from the ceiling in the middle bedroom. I called Gabe and he basically said to put a bucket under it until Monday." And she'd wanted to tell him where to shove the bucket. Sideways. "To top it off, now the sink in the kitchen is overflowing, and after I bathed this morning, the tub wouldn't drain."

Chase looked directly at Matt. "You check out the roof, and I'll see about the plumbing."

"Good idea, Reed," Matt replied. "I don't like to deal with plumbing, and you're damn good at it."

Finally, a way to force Chase to engage with her. "You never told me you had plumbing skills."

When he answered with a noncommittal lift of his shoulders, Matt jumped back into the conversation. "Yeah, he's real good at it. He knows his way around plumbing about as well as he knows his way around a woman." He gave her a wink. "But I'm not telling you anything you don't already know."

Jess's mouth dropped open and Chase practically sneered. "The roof is calling you, Boyd."

Matt hooked a thumb over his shoulder. "I'll be gettin' the ladder out of the truck now."

Jess planned to get Chase alone to play a game of twenty questions. And if she found out that he'd been playing kiss and tell, she'd give him a piece of what was left of her mind.

Without further acknowledgment, Chase picked up the tool box and walked into the house, practically slamming the screen door in Jess's face. She tried to catch up to him, but his legs were too long and his determination to flee her, too great. Well, too bad. She'd corner him eventually.

And she did, in the kitchen. He'd stopped to investigate the sink although he didn't appear to be doing anything, other than staring at the faucet.

Jess leaned a hip against the counter and let the frustration flow like a fountain. "Did you tell Matt about the other night?"

"Didn't say a word. He was just making a dig at my reputation."

His well-deserved reputation. She'd gained literal first-hand knowledge of that.

But that still didn't explain why he hadn't afforded her even a passing glance. "Then why won't you look at me?"

"Because if I did, then he'd know."

A ridiculous assumption. "Yeah, right. He's going to know you got me naked and made a woman out of me, all because of a look."

"We can sense that kind of thing. We have a built-in radar when it comes to sex."

Men. "Look, I know this thing between us is a mess, but we're going to have to be adult about it. There's no need to stress over it."

He planted his palms on the edge of the sink and shifted his weight from one leg to the other. "About the only stress I'm having right now is the stress going on behind my fly. When I saw you standing on the porch, wearing those holey jeans, it took every ounce of strength not to tell Matt to get lost. I was ready to take you down right there on the front porch."

She shivered in some places, heated up in others. She hadn't given a thought to putting on her favorite rainy-day jeans. The ones with the rip across the upper right thigh, and another just below the back left pocket. How could she have known that a few tears would turn him on?

She should have known. The produce department

at the grocery store could turn a man on. "Since having wild sex out in the open isn't wise, albeit tempting, you're going to have to man up."

He groaned and finally met her gaze. "Poor choice of words, Jess."

It took a minute for her to catch on to his comment. "Maybe I should have said down boy."

He went back to the sink-studying. "It's killing me not to be able to touch you."

He could join her celibacy club. "I'd hate to think I'd be the cause of your premature death, so I'm going to go now."

Before she could take one step, he had her in a body vise against the counter. He had his hands on her butt and his mouth locked tightly with hers. The things the man could do with his tongue. The things he could do to her with just a slight tilt of his hips. Yes, he had definitely manned up, and she needed to stand down, before they took it way too far.

The sound of the slamming screen door effectively sent them to opposite ends of the kitchen. And Chase conveniently walked right out the back door, leaving Jess to face their friend.

She pulled a cloth band from her pocket and twisted her hair into a knot at her neck, hoping to appear a little more put together. Regrettably, she couldn't do a thing about the whisker-burn.

"Where's Chase?" Matt asked as he entered the kitchen.

Hiding out. "He went in the yard to check something."

"I found the missing shingle where the water's coming through," he said. "But he's going to have to help me fix it."

"Good." When she noticed Matt staring at her mouth, she had to come up with something to distract him. "Where's Rachel?"

"She took Danny downtown for the afternoon. Edwin's got her helping out with a blood drive."

"On Christmas Eve?"

"Yeah. They figured they could catch the last-minute shoppers and solicit donations. Edwin claims this is the family's efforts to replenish the blood they gave Dalton while he was in the hospital."

She just couldn't resist. "Dalton's always been somewhat of a bloodsucker."

Matt grinned, his teeth flashing white against his perpetually tanned face. "I agree, but I wouldn't have chosen the word *blood*."

Something occurred to Jess. An important question that could potentially be a paternity clue. "You know, after all the years we were married, I never knew Dalton's blood type."

"It's type O," Matt said, unknowingly taking the bait. "Same as Rachel's."

More important, the same as Jess. If her hunches were correct, the possibility that Dalton had fathered Danny was growing dimmer and dimmer.

Chase finally reappeared, looking quite a bit calmer than he had when he'd abandoned her. "The plumbing's going to require a backhoe," he said. "Looks like there's a big-time drainage problem."

"Sounds like a job for a professional," Matt replied. "Now you can climb on the roof and help me patch it."

"Not a problem."

Jess saw a huge problem. If the plumbing couldn't be repaired, she couldn't bathe. That was the least of her concerns. She had some sleuthing to do. First, she had to search for what could prove to be a pivotal piece of the puzzle.

Before the pair could leave, Jess addressed Chase. "Matt tells me Rachel's overseeing a blood drive for Dalton. I thought you might like to help. They specifically need type O. That's Dalton's type."

His expression turned lemon-sour. "I'm A. And even if I had the same type, I wouldn't give him a drop, unless I thought it would kill him."

Type A. *Danny's blood type.*

"Too bad you didn't know that before they gave Dalton the transfusion," Matt added. "I can start an IV. I would've hooked you right up."

"Actually, they're not looking for direct donations," Jess said, after she recovered from the stunning revelation. "They need to replace the blood bank's supply."

"By the time we get through here, it's going to be too late," Matt said. "We plan to have a nice dinner with Danny tonight and open a few presents."

"That reminds me." Reminded her that she wouldn't be spending Christmas with her son. "I went to the outlet mall yesterday and bought Danny a few gifts. Could you take them to him?"

Matt shook his head. "This isn't right."

She'd never known her former brother-in-law to be unreasonable. Just the opposite. "I can't see where it would hurt if I give him Christmas gifts."

"That's not what I meant," Matt said. "You should be

with Danny during the holidays. And I far as I see it, you can deliver the presents in person tonight."

"That's risky, Matt," Chase interjected. "She's not supposed to contact him. I'll take them by."

Matt frowned. "The CPS workers have more to do than police our house. You can bring Jess over in your truck. You've already been there several times this week, so it wouldn't look out of the ordinary."

Chase turned his gaze on Jess. "If you're okay with the plan, I'll drive you over."

She was more than okay with it. She was thrilled over the prospect of seeing her baby boy. "It's worth the risk of getting caught."

She couldn't help but notice the meaningful look Chase gave her. He was mostly likely reflecting on the risks they took last night.

Matt cleared his throat. "We better get started on that roof. If I'm late getting home, Rachel's going to cook my goose instead of the one she bought for dinner."

After Chase and Matt walked away, Jess waited a few minutes before she seized her cell phone from the counter and sneaked into the bedroom. Since she had no Internet access, or a computer on hand for that matter, she'd go straight to the source.

She plopped down on the mattress and punched in a college friend's number. A nurse who happened to live in Alabama, so she shouldn't be privy to the recent legal issues.

The minute the woman answered, Jess launched into her query. "Libby, I'm sorry to bother you on a holiday, but I need to ask you something."

"Jess? How in the heck are you doing? It's been six months since we've talked."

She had no time for pleasantries. "I know, and I'm sorry. I've been very busy since the divorce. But I'm great. Danny's great. Merry Christmas. Now can you help me with a medical question?"

"Sure. I was just about to head to the in-laws, but believe me, I'd welcome the delay."

"This won't take long. I just need to know that if two parents have the same blood type, say O positive, could their offspring have A-type blood?"

"Have you been watching soap operas?"

Her life had certainly been one during the past few years. "Actually, I'm asking for someone else." Not a lie at all. This was for her son's sake. "It's a paternity issue."

"No, it's not possible for two parents with type O blood to produce a child with type A. I could go into the hows and whys, but I'd put you to sleep."

After hearing this particular verdict, she didn't expect to get much sleep in the immediate future. "You're absolutely sure?"

"Totally. My parents didn't pay for my education for nothing."

"You've been a great help, Libby. Give Johnny and the kids my love."

After Jess ended the call, she couldn't move. She just sat in the middle of the bed, steeped in shock.

Chase was Danny's father.

Short of an official DNA test, there was no doubt about it. And tonight, when she finally had the chance to see her son, she would do so knowing that today, he'd received the best gift he could possibly get—the opportunity to sever all ties, biological and otherwise, from a man who wasn't fit to be a father.

Problem was, she couldn't give her son that gift. She would have to indefinitely keep the news to herself until the time was right. She also couldn't tell Danny's real father. Just one more secret among many. And she feared that someday soon, at least one was bound to come back to bite her.

CHAPTER ELEVEN

THE RAIN HAD STOPPED and the skies had cleared, revealing a sliver of moon and a host of stars. Jess appreciated the beautiful night in ways she never had before. And for the first time in ages, she felt almost giddy. In less than a minute, she would finally be reunited with her son.

Chase steered the truck up the drive leading to Rachel and Matt's place, an expansive stone ranch house with more Western flair than Southern charm. Jess had always thought it looked as though it should be in Texas, not the Mississippi Delta. Rachel had outdone herself this year with the Christmas decorations, from the team of horses and wagon composed of tiny white lights, to the life-size Santa, sporting a cowboy hat, set in the middle of the yard.

She could imagine Danny's delight over spending the holidays in such a beautiful home. He'd probably hung out in the barn with his Uncle Matt, and helped his Aunt Rachel make gingerbread men. If he couldn't be with her, at least he'd been in the presence of people who genuinely cared about him.

As soon as Chase stopped the truck, Jess reached into the backseat for the bag filled with gifts. Most were for Danny, but she'd managed to find a couple of items for her hosts. She'd also made a few impulse purchases, including the little black dress she wore with the red stiletto heels that Rachel had brought to her a week ago. In fact, she'd acquired several new outfits to replace those that still hung in the closet of her former residence. She was ready for a new beginning, and new clothes seemed to be a good step toward that goal. With any luck, she wouldn't have to wear those new clothes in court.

Determined not to spoil her rare good mood, Jess banished all negative thoughts as she walked with Chase to the front entry. Rachel opened the door wearing a free-flowing red silk blouse that complimented her long, dark hair. She possessed that proverbial pregnancy glow that reached all the way to her brown eyes.

After they stepped inside, Rachel gave out hugs to Jess, then Chase. "Merry Christmas, you two," she said. "I'm so glad you're both here."

Jess couldn't express how glad she was to be there. "Thank you so much for letting me come tonight. I know you're breaking the rules."

"Stupid rules," Matt said as he entered the room. He kissed his wife on the neck, and handed Chase a beer. "I thought you'd want this instead of eggnog."

"You thought right," Chase said, his first words since they'd arrived.

He'd been unusually somber when he'd picked her up, and extremely quiet on the drive. She had no reason to believe she'd done anything earlier today to make him particularly angry. But she wouldn't even try to second-guess a man who still had many demons to conquer.

"What can I get for you, Jess?" Matt asked.

"I'm fine right now." Or she would be. She searched the great room for signs of her son. All she saw was tasteful décor and a towering tree with myriad gifts surrounding the base. "Where's Danny?"

After a grim look passed between Rachel and Matt, Jess sensed something was terribly wrong. "What is it?"

"Maybe you should have a drink first," Matt said.

"I don't want a drink." She hated that she'd sounded so snippy, and made an effort to temper her tone. "I'd just like to see him as soon as possible. We can't stay that long, and this may be the last opportunity I have for a while." Maybe even months, if the court decided she wasn't fit to raise her child. Longer if she was imprisoned.

Rachel put an arm around Jess's shoulder. "He had a bad day. When we were downtown, one of the boys said something to him. He was very upset."

If only she could have been there to console him. She would have to settle for comforting him now. "What did they say?"

Rachel shrugged. "He wouldn't tell me. I wouldn't have even known if someone hadn't told me about the fight."

Fight? "Was he hurt?"

"It was only a scuffle," Matt said. "He doesn't have a scratch on him."

She could count her blessings for that. "Did anyone talk to this boy's parents? He shouldn't be able to walk away without suffering the consequences."

"Danny started it, Jess," Chase said.

Her son had never been prone to violence. But he'd probably been beaten down so far, he'd decided to battle back. "I'll talk to him about it."

"He doesn't want to see anyone," Matt added. "After

we told him you were stopping by, he went into his room with Bo, and he hasn't come out since, even for dinner."

Jess had never felt so helpless in her life. But when it came to her child, she refused to throw in the towel. She handed Chase the presents, took off her coat and gave it to Matt, then pushed up her sleeves as if preparing for her own fight. "I can't leave here until I speak with him."

Chase handed the beer back to Matt and set the bag on a marble end table. "I'll talk to him."

She'd rather handle it herself. Or at least try. "If he doesn't respond well to me, then you'll have my blessing."

"He's in the room across from the nursery," Rachel said. "You know the way."

She did. She'd helped stencil the wild horses along one wall of that nursery not more than a month ago. It seemed like a century ago. "Thanks. Just put his gifts under the tree, and I'll be back soon." Perhaps sooner than she planned.

After Jess reached the room, she paused with her hand on the knob. She didn't know if she should knock, or just make an entry without identifying herself. Knocking seemed the better part of valor, but he might not let her in. She compromised by rapping lightly on the door before opening it a few inches to peek inside. "Danny? It's Mom."

"Go away."

She might be deterred if she hadn't heard that before. "I'm not going away, Daniel. In fact, I'm coming in now."

She entered the room to find him sitting on the floor, legs crossed in front of him and an open book in his lap. At least the dog looked happy to see her. He was stretched out at Danny's side, his wagging tail beating a steady rhythm on the carpet. Her son, on the other hand, didn't bother to acknowledge her.

Oh, how she wanted to hug him. To kiss his sweet face and tell him how much she'd missed him. How very much she loved him. But since he still hadn't bothered to look up from the book, she would talk now and save the affection for later.

If she hadn't been wearing a dress, she'd join him on the floor. Instead, she perched on the edge of the queen-size bed. "What are you reading, sweetie?"

He stared up at her with soulful brown eyes. "Are you going to jail?"

If she answered no, she could be giving him false hope. If she said possibly, she'd completely shatter his security. She'd have to meet in the middle. "I don't know what's going to happen, Danny. I do know that I have a team of people working for me. They're going to do everything they can to keep that from happening."

He closed the book and tossed it aside. "I should be going to jail. I'm the one who pushed my dad."

How easy it would be to tell Danny that Dalton wasn't really his dad. Yet she couldn't lay that on him now. "Oh, sweetie, don't say that. You were just upset with him, and you had every right to be. You didn't mean to cause him any harm."

Pure defiance showed in his expression. "I did mean to hurt him. He hates me and I hate him."

Regret and fear pelted her like a hailstorm. If he ever admitted to anyone that he'd pushed Dalton with malice, he could face a term in a juvenile facility. And she could lose her custody rights.

Disregarding the dress, she pushed off the bed and lowered herself to her knees. But when she reached for him, he leaned back to avoid the contact. He might as well have slapped her. "Danny, I know you're really mad right now. And I also know a boy said something to you today that made it worse. Do you want to tell me about it?"

He lowered his eyes. "He said we were trash. He said you're a husband-killer and then he called you a bad word."

She could only imagine what that word might be. "Who was it?"

"Austin Prather."

The son of Edwin's second-in-command at the bank. "He doesn't know what he's talking about."

"He should've called me a criminal. You didn't do anything."

That brought about another major concern. "Did you tell him that?"

Thankfully, he shook his head no.

"Good."

He gave her a look so desperate, it stole her breath. "But I want to tell Chase. He'll make sure I don't go to jail."

She was mortified to think that he might follow through. "You can't tell him, sweetie. He doesn't need to be involved." Not any more than he already was.

Jess was torn over what to do. Had she given Danny too big a burden to bear in order to protect him? Should she finally let someone know the details, and hope that her son didn't suffer for his actions? She simply didn't know which road to take.

"You're going to have to trust me, Danny," she said. "Just give me a few days to sort this out. Besides, I understand your dad is doing okay, so that's a good thing. Right?"

His desperation turned to anger. "I have to see him tomorrow at Grandpa Edwin's house, and I don't want to."

The second shock of the day. "He's home from the hospital?"

He nodded again.

Jess accepted that Rachel would want to be with her father on Christmas, and that she would take Danny with her. But she hadn't dreamed that Dalton would be there. If only she could find some way to prevent it, but she had no control over the situation.

She gently tipped Danny's chin up, forcing him to look at her. "You don't have to be alone with your dad. You don't even have to talk to him if you don't want to. He's not going to say anything about what happened to him." And she could be giving Dalton too much credit.

But she still truly believed that Dalton didn't remember anything about that night. Otherwise, he would have implicated Danny. Or perhaps he did remember, and he was bent on punishing her, knowing she would never accuse her own son. It would be so like him to use the child to get to the mother.

She couldn't leave until she made one more attempt to make her baby boy feel better. "I have to go now, but I left you a few presents under the tree. It's not a lot, but I'm sure your grandfather will have some very special things for you." Edwin had never shown Danny much affection, but he'd always been generous when it came to gifts.

Tears began to form in his eyes, breaking Jess's heart. "When are you coming back?"

"I don't know, sweetie. It might be a while."

"Am I going to have to live with Dad?"

A very real possibility. One that made Jess ache with regret. "Let's just take it one day at a time."

She leaned over to hug him, and this time he didn't pull away. "I love you, honey. Never forget that."

"HE HATES ME, and I don't blame him."

Chase took his eyes from the road to see that Jess was trying hard not to cry. "He doesn't hate you. He's a scared kid whose life has been turned upside down. He wants to blame someone, and you're a safe target. But if anyone's to blame here, it's that prick, Dalton."

"He's been released from the hospital," Jess said. "He'll be with the family tomorrow, and that means Danny's going to be forced to see him."

He tightened his grip on the steering wheel. The world was sorely lacking in justice when a jerk like Dalton Wainwright could spend the holiday with a son he didn't want, and Jess couldn't. "Maybe I should show up and invite myself in for Christmas dinner."

"I'd buy tickets to that."

He heard a hint of a smile in her voice, but he suspected she was only trying to cover her distress. By all rights, he should drop her off at the house and then go home. But he'd determined that morning she shouldn't be alone tonight. He'd also made plans to make the evening as special as possible.

After he pulled up the drive and turned off the ignition, he reached over the console and took her hand. "You know what you need?"

She pulled a tissue out of her coat pocket and dabbed at her eyes. "Right now, I need makeup remover. And two tickets to Bolivia."

If he thought he could get away with helping her escape with her son, he'd damn sure do it. "I was thinking more along the lines of a party. Just me and you in attendance."

The smile she sent him was soft and sexy. Maybe even a little suggestive. Or maybe he wanted her so badly, he was jumping to conclusions. "That sounds interesting. Are clothes optional?"

Okay, he wasn't imagining it. "That's entirely up to you, babe."

"Did you bring champagne?"

And he just thought he'd remembered everything. "That totally slipped my mind."

"That's okay," she said. "I have some orange juice and ginger ale, so we can fake it. And I could probably scrounge up some cheese and crackers, too."

"Why don't we just skip the refreshments and get right to the celebration?"

She smoothed a hand over her skirt. "You know, for two people who've been warned to keep their distance, we certainly aren't doing very well in that regard."

That had been his original goal, to stay away from her. But he didn't have the will or the want-to. "I just figured we both deserve to have a good time."

"You're not worried we're going to get caught?"

He should be, but he wasn't. "I can park the truck in the shed out back, if it makes you feel better."

"That's probably not necessary. I doubt anyone's going to be snooping around here on Christmas eve, trying to catch me engaged in illicit behavior."

He grinned. "You forgot about Santa."

She returned his smile. "That's all I need, some rotund guy tromping around on the roof that you and Matt just fixed." Her smile suddenly dropped from sight. "I don't know what I'm worried about. Since there aren't any children here, he has no reason to come."

And that only bolstered Chase's reasons to stay. He could attempt to keep her mind off her son's absence, at least for a few hours. Beginning now. "I have a couple of presents for you." He also had a surprise in the house.

Her expression brightened. "I have something for you, too. It's not much, but it's cute."

Cute always meant trouble. "You didn't buy me another pair of reindeer boxers, did you?"

Now she just looked downright mischievous. "You'll have to wait and see."

"Then what are we waiting for?"

No sooner than he'd said it, Jess was out of the truck and onto the porch before he'd even unbuckled his seat belt. He came up behind her as she slid the key into the lock, and turned her around before she opened the door.

He rested one hand on her waist and pointed to the porch's overhang with the other. "You know what that means, don't you?"

She looked up and then her gaze snapped to his. "Where did you get mistletoe and when did you hang it?"

"It's some my mother had lying around the house."

She raised a brow. "She has mistletoe just lying around?"

"Okay, I stole it from the hall. I hung it when you were getting ready tonight."

"Since you went to all that trouble, let's put it to good use."

He slid his arms around her waist, lowered his head and gave her a quick kiss. "How's that?"

Her glare said it all. "That's probably the lamest kiss I've had since I left my ex-husband."

He saw a challenge, and he had no problem rising to it. But before he could prove his worth in the kissing department, the sound of squealing tires drew his attention.

He witnessed panic spreading over Jess's face. "We should have gone in the house."

She was right about that. "It's probably just some kid showing off for his girlfriend. But you're right. We should go inside."

"Good idea."

He reached around her, opened the door, and when he flipped on the light, he was pleased to see his plan had been perfectly implemented. Every inch of the once-bare tree had been covered, from top to trunk.

"When did you do this?" Both her expression and her voice told him she was pleased with the finished product, too.

"I didn't exactly do it," he said. "I hired a couple of

elves to take care of it while we were out. I'm kind of surprised they got it done since they can't seem to keep their hands off each other."

"Sam and Savannah did this? I thought they were spending the holidays with her mother in Knoxville?"

"They are. Their flight doesn't leave until midnight."

She turned her attention back to the tree. "It's absolutely beautiful. I can't believe you pulled this off."

He'd do just about anything for her, and he'd tell her that later. "I know what you said about not wanting to decorate unless Danny was here, but—"

She stopped the commentary when she gave him a soft kiss. "You're here, and that's what matters."

He planned to be here all night. Most of it, anyway. He'd have to be gone before morning came, and that royally sucked.

He moved behind her and wrapped his arms around her waist. "It does look pretty good."

"It's wonderful. Are these Missy's ornaments?"

"Yeah. My mother's taken to decorating in line with the latest trend. She used purple and black this year, with a lot of bows and sparkly crap. I thought my dad was going to stroke when he saw it. Buck doesn't like prissy."

She lifted one ornament from a branch and examined it closely. A homemade ornament made out of a circle of cardboard, trimmed in foil, with a photo stuck right in the middle. His friends could have gone all year without including that one.

"I remember this picture," she said. "You were in the first grade. You wouldn't smile because your front teeth were missing."

"Yeah. My mother was fit to be tied. Serves her right for giving me that chili-bowl haircut."

"It's cute." She looked back at him. "Speaking of cute, I want you to open your present."

"And you can open mine." He released her and knelt to retrieve the two packages underneath the tree. When he straightened, she was nowhere to be found.

"Where you'd go?" he called out.

"I'm getting yours," she called back. "I'll be there in a minute."

He stepped to the side of the tree and looked out the window, still worried someone might be spying on them. With Dalton now on the loose, anything was possible. But he didn't see anyone around. No vehicle parked on the road. No movement aside from the bend of the trees in the wind that had picked up steam earlier in the evening. His gut still told him something wasn't right. Maybe he'd come down with a major case of paranoia.

"I'm ready if you are," Jess said from somewhere behind him.

He turned to discover she'd taken a seat on the sofa, a shiny red gift bag on the coffee table before her. She was still wearing that black, knock-'em-dead dress that fit every one of her curves to perfection. When she crossed her legs, the hem climbed up her thighs, and Chase's temperature climbed right with it. And man, those red high-heels. He could picture taking that dress off her slowly and making love to her while she still wore the shoes. If he didn't kill that fantasy real quick, he'd be ready, all right. Ready to ditch the gift-opening so he could take her straight to bed. That wasn't part of the plan. Not yet.

After setting his presents on the coffee table, he dropped down beside her. "You want to go first?" he asked.

"Of course I do." She sounded as excited as any kid would at Christmas. But she definitely wasn't a kid anymore. She was a woman through and through.

He offered her the larger of the two boxes. "I want you to open this one now, and then the other one after I open mine." Saving the best for last. He just hoped she saw it that way.

Jess tore off the wrapping paper with a vengeance and opened the lid. When she pulled back the white tissue, Chase wished he had a camera to capture the awe in her expression. He didn't realize that something as simple as a picture of him showing Danny how to hold a bat could have such an impact on her.

After she lifted the photo to study it more closely, her eyes begin to mist. "When was this taken?"

"Thursday at Rachel and Matt's. Matt took the picture, and Rachel had it framed. Believe it or not, I wrapped it."

Tears began rolling down her cheeks. "It's the best gift I've ever received, aside from my son."

He put his arm around her and thumbed away a tear. "I'm sorry, Jess. I didn't mean to make you cry."

She swiped at her eyes and sniffed. "These are good tears. I don't remember the last time I've seen him look so happy. And I have you to thank for that."

He should be thanking her for introducing him to Danny. "He's a great kid, Jess. And he's tougher than you think."

She sighed. "He's his father's son."

Dalton didn't deserve any praise for Danny's upbringing, and he was surprised she'd given him any. "He's your son, Jess. He's got that same strong will and determination. He's going to get through this, and so are you. And I'm going to do everything in my power to help." Even if it meant crossing over the legal line to do it. They both meant that much to him.

"I really do appreciate what you've done for Danny. You've paid more attention to him in the past week than Dalton ever did in nine years."

And during time spent with her son, Chase's eyes had been opened to things he'd taken for granted. "Being around Danny brought back a lot of memories of my dad. Maybe Buck was strict and made me tow the line, and sometimes he really pissed me off. He still does now and then. But he never missed one of my games, and he took me camping at least twice a year. We might still butt horns on a regular basis at work, but at the end of the day, I know he has my back."

"That's what good fathers do," she said. "And that's why I know you'd be a wonderful father. You've learned by example."

Yeah, he had. And for the first time in his life, he was starting to think he might be willing to give parenthood a try, somewhere down the road.

He was ready to move away from the heavy stuff, and get back to the party. "Can I open mine now, or are we just going to sit here until it opens itself?"

"I was just about to get to that." Jess propped the photo on the table and then handed him the gift bag. "Don't expect anything quite as good as what you gave me."

She'd given him her time and trust, and the opportunity to get to know her boy. That was enough.

He dug through mounds of paper, and some sort of curly strings, before he finally got to the actual gift—a pair of navy silk boxers, complete with flying, red-nosed reindeer. "You shouldn't have."

She laughed. "I'm sorry. When I saw them in the store, I couldn't resist. And they're much more fancy than the last pair. Besides, I assume that since I gave you those when we were in junior high, you probably outgrew them and tossed them out."

"Yeah, I've outgrown them quite a bit. But since you didn't know me the way you know me now, you'll have to take my word for it."

When he winked, she frowned. "You are so bad, Chase Reed."

She'd know exactly how bad when she opened his next gift. On that thought, he handed her the final box. "Just so you know, this one's as much for me as it is for you."

"Did you buy me a power tool?" she said with fake enthusiasm.

"Not exactly, but it is a powerful tool."

Now she looked stunned. "I know they don't sell those in Placid, so you must have either ordered it online, or bought it in another town."

He was a little slow on the uptake at first, until he finally figured it out. "Sorry, sweetheart. It's not that kind of tool."

"Too bad."

"Just open it already," he grumbled.

She tore the paper away, one strip at a time, apparently just to see him squirm. It worked. By the time she finally opened the box, he was about ready to do it himself.

She held up the silky red, barely-there gown and then turned the empty box over. "Where's the rest of it?"

"That's it, babe. And you better appreciate it. The dress shop was already closed, so I had to sweet talk Polly into letting me have my own private shopping trip."

She dropped the gown into her lap. "Knowing Polly, she would have preferred to give you a private showing of all her wares. She used to service my ex-husband."

With the exception of Jess, Dalton had questionable taste in women. "If you don't like it, I can take it back." And that would be a damn shame. But if that's what she wanted, so be it.

"I love it," she said. "But I can't wear it. I don't have the body to wear it."

He was inclined to disagree. Strongly. "I don't know what Dalton Wainwright said to make you believe that, but he was dead wrong. Just thinking about your body makes me hotter than hell."

A blush started at her neck and spread to her cheeks. "Since you put it that way, I suppose I could try it on. But if it doesn't fit, you'll have to return it."

He had no doubt it would fit. He could judge a woman's size by touch alone, a talent he'd developed over the years. A talent not worth mentioning to her.

"Then go try it on," he said. "I'll be waiting for you."

"In here?"

As badly as he wanted to be waiting in bed, he also didn't want her to think that's all he wanted. "Let's just see what happens when you put it on."

"Okay."

When she left the room, Chase took off his jacket and draped it over the back of the sofa. On afterthought, he yanked off his boots and socks, but he stopped at that. Getting completely naked would send the wrong message.

He collapsed onto the couch, laced his hands together behind his neck, and waited for her return. And waited. And waited.

About the time he thought she'd reconsidered, two feminine hands with red-painted nails slid down his shoulders from behind him. He started to look back, until he heard, "Close your eyes and don't open them until I say so."

That was going to be torture, but he complied. He found himself waiting again, this time for permission to check out the merchandise.

"You can look now."

He opened his eyes to see that she looked exactly as he'd imagined she would wearing that scrap of silk that clung to her like he wanted to. But he didn't care for one thing—she couldn't look him in the eye. "Man, I'm good. And you're damn beautiful."

She afforded him only a fast glance. "Are you sure? Because I think it's a little tight. I'm not convinced it looks good on me at all. Maybe on someone else a little thinner."

Her attitude just wouldn't do. He came to his feet, walked right up to her, and lifted her face with his palms. "In all the time we've known each other, I've never been one to tell you what to think. But that ends now. I never want to hear you say you're not good enough, because you are." Probably too good for him.

She lowered her eyes again, looking shy and self-conscious. "You're just saying that because you tossed the receipt and can't return it."

"I'm dead serious, Jess. And now you have to promise me something else."

Finally, she met his gaze. "What?"

"In a few minutes, we're going to make love. And when we do, don't close your eyes. I want you to see me tonight. I want you to see us, together. We don't need any fantasies because the reality is better. Can you do that?"

"Yes."

He kissed her with more restraint than he thought possible. "Then that's all I need to know."

Taking her by the hand, he led her into the bedroom and set her down on the edge of the mattress. He didn't bother to turn off the light or wait until she climbed under the covers before he undressed. She followed every move he made, watched him release every button on his shirt and then take it off. Her gaze never wavered when he unzipped his fly and stripped out of his jeans. She did smile when he took off his briefs, but she didn't look away for even a second.

"Don't move yet," he told her as he retrieved a condom from his jeans pocket and tossed it on the nightstand. "So we don't have to raid your cookie jar."

She answered him with a shaky smile.

He sat beside her and took her hands into his. "You're in control tonight, babe. I'm leaving everything to you, so do what you will with me."

After he released her, he stretched out on his back and prepared for the best. But when she didn't immediately move, he wondered if maybe he'd gone too far. Maybe she wasn't ready to take command of the situation.

Man, was he wrong. She crawled onto the bed and slowly slid her sweet, silk-covered body up his body, pausing to pay a little special attention to certain parts with a wriggle of her hips. Then she kissed him like there was no tomorrow. By the time she finally took her mouth away, he had no doubt who was in control, and it wasn't him.

She utilized a lot of creativity, with her hands and mouth, while she took care of the condom. Good thing he was still relatively young. Otherwise, his heart could very well give out.

When she knelt beside him on the bed, lowered the gown and shimmied out of it, he automatically went for her breasts. And she clasped his wrists to halt him before he got there. "No touching yet."

Damn. "Are you trying to drive me crazy?"

"As a matter of fact, yes."

She made good on that promise when she straddled his thighs and took the lead. Took him on a wild ride straight into oblivion. She eventually let him touch her, on her terms, and he took full advantage. Not once did she close her eyes. He didn't close his eyes, either, because he wouldn't have missed this for the world, watching as she went from self-doubting to completely confident in her sexuality. He might have let her have all the power, but she had no idea exactly how much power she had over him.

He soon felt the pull of her climax, and saw the absolute pleasure in her face and eyes. That's when he gave up trying to hold back. He could only roll with the tide, and he didn't care if he drowned. He didn't care about anything but Jess.

After they were both spent and winded, she collapsed against him and rested her cheek on his chest, right above his pounding heart. He could think of few instances when the sex was better than he'd expected. He couldn't think of one time when he'd been so blown away that he wasn't sure he could move. So he didn't.

As his body began to calm and his respiration slowed, Chase realized the time had come to kiss Jess goodnight, get dressed and take off. His sex life in a nutshell. Meet a girl, have a good time, say so long and cut out before the dust settled. He'd never had a relationship that lasted more than a couple of months, because he'd never found what he'd been looking for. Until now. Funny thing was, she'd been right under his nose all along. And it was high time he told her.

He couldn't deny that putting his feelings into words scared the hell out of him. Words that he'd never said to another woman. He'd best do it now, before he lost his nerve.

"Jess, I have a few things I need to say."

Nothing but silence. He realized why when he lifted his head. She was out like a light. He reached for the sheet at the foot of the bed, covered them both and dropped his head back on the pillow. Normally he didn't sleep for more than a few hours at a time, so he could afford to stay awhile longer. And that's if he could sleep with her in his arms without wanting to wake her for something other than a conversation.

But his eyes soon grew heavy, and he knew it was only a matter of time before he drifted off.

Just a little while, he told himself. Then he would go.

WHAT WAS HE STILL DOING THERE?

Jess had woken a few minutes ago to find Chase sleeping soundly in her bed, and the morning sun streaming through the window. At some point, he must have turned off the light and turned over onto his belly. And she hadn't turned on the alarm.

When she looked to her left and noted the time, she hopped out of bed, retrieved her robe from the bathroom and slipped it on. She returned to find he hadn't moved an inch.

She leaned over and shook his arm, right above the sexy barbwire tattoo encircling his amazing bicep. That tattoo—and many remarkable details about his incredible body—had captured her fancy when they'd made love with the light on last night. "Chase. Wake up."

"Hmmm."

"It's 7:00 a.m. and it's light outside."

He finally rolled onto his back, but he didn't open his eyes. He did send his palm down his sternum and paused right below his navel. She truly wanted to follow that same path with her own hand, follow that happy little trail and keep going to see what lurked beneath the sheet draped low on his hip. But darn it, she didn't have time for that.

She sat on the edge of the bed, leaned over and kissed him lightly. "Get up, sleepy boy."

His grin slowly arrived and then he opened his eyes. "I already am up. But I guess I should probably get out of bed. Then again, maybe you should get back in the bed."

He caught her by the arm and pulled her down, taking her totally by surprise. When he started showering her neck with kisses, she started laughing. After she finally untangled herself from his hold, she sat up and moved as far from him as she could without falling off the bed. "Stop it. You have to go."

From the sour look on his face, he clearly took exception to her command. "I don't have anything better to do, and neither do you."

"Oh, yes, you do. It's Christmas, and I know Missy and Buck's routine. They'll be expecting you at the house in about an hour to open presents. If you don't show up, they'll come looking for you."

"I'll just tell them I met a she-devil last night and I couldn't tear myself away from her. Buck will understand."

"And your mother will send you to your room for the remainder of the day."

"Wanna come with me?"

He'd clearly lost his mind. "That will go over real well with the folks, me spending the day in your room with you."

He scooted up against the headboard. "I meant come to the house for all the traditional festivities."

At one time, she'd readily accept the invitation. But not now. "You know I can't do that, Chase. Your father will have a total meltdown if I show up unannounced."

He rubbed a palm over his jaw. "You're right. Duty calls, even if I'd rather hang out here."

Without an ounce of shame over his nudity, he left

the bed and gathered his clothes. He did turn his back as he worked his jeans up his long legs. And she had no qualms about admiring his attributes until they disappeared beneath the denim.

Once he was finished dressing, she followed him to the den where he sat on the sofa and put on his boots. After that, she expected him to leave, but he surprised her by saying, "Have a seat. We need to talk before I go."

His serious tone had Jess gearing up for the same old speech about how they couldn't do this again. How he needed to stay away or risk damaging her case. She sat beside him anyway.

He stared at the ceiling for a moment before regarding her again. "After this is over, and we're free to do as we please, I want to continue to see you. And I don't want to sneak around."

Time for the million-dollar question. "What exactly is our relationship?"

"I don't want to be without you, even for a minute."

Jess was totally floored by his assertion. "You want us to be a couple?"

"Yeah. Or a trio. You, me and Danny."

The moment was so surreal, she didn't know what to say. "There's still so much riding on the indictment, I don't think we can plan on anything right now."

He draped his arm around her shoulder. "If you're cleared, and this all goes away, would you be willing to try to make a go of this?"

She didn't have to think twice to come up with that answer. "Yes, but—"

"Then that's all I need to know. Dalton's story isn't

adding up. I plan to dig a little deeper and see if I can punch some holes in it."

The 'digging deeper' part worried her. "I doubt you'll get very far. He's going to stick to it even if it's fabricated." Which it was.

"Just let me worry about that," he said. "In the meantime, if I'm not around, don't believe for a minute it's because I don't want to be here. I can't think of anywhere else I'd rather be than with you."

He deserved a kiss for that, and she gave him a good one. Once they parted, she sensed he wanted to say something else. Instead, he came to his feet. "I'll call you later."

Jess walked Chase to the door, her mind still reeling over the conversation. But before he turned the knob, he faced her again, a solemn look on his face. "I have one more thing to say, and I'll try not to screw it up."

If what he had to say was as wonderful as what he'd already said, she was more than willing to hear it. "Go ahead."

"I might not have known it until recently, but I've been searching a long time for someone I can spend the rest of my life with. That someone is you." He kissed her softly, sincerely. "I love you, Jess."

And then he was out the door before she could even respond. She stood and gaped as he drove away, and continued to stare long after the truck disappeared. After she finally came back around to the real world, she ran through the house like a silly, smitten schoolgirl, considered a cartwheel but settled for a jump instead.

Chase loved her. She couldn't imagine a better Christmas gift.

The thought kept running through her mind during her bath, as she sorted laundry, when she made her breakfast that she didn't even mind eating alone. Everything was looking up, and hope was definitely springing eternal today. All because he loved her.

When the doorbell rang, Jess said a little prayer Chase had come back so she could tell him she loved him, too. Yet when she opened the door, another man stood on her porch. A man with slick black hair and an even slicker smile. His suit was tailor-made, his shoes designer quality, the platinum watch on his arm worth thousands of dollars. His near-black eyes could draw a woman into his web of deceit, before she realized she'd been duped by his charm. He was a chameleon, a charlatan, the consummate devil in disguise.

Her hope no longer sprang eternal, but her hatred did.

"Merry Christmas, darlin'. Did you miss me?"

CHAPTER TWELVE

"What do you want, Dalton?"

His smile was the epitome of condescension. "Is that any way to greet your husband?"

He should feel fortunate she didn't kick him down the porch steps. "Ex-husband. Again, what do you want?"

"I want to have a little chat with you."

Of all the unmitigated gall. "What makes you think I ever want to speak to you again?"

He winked. "Because I have a deal you can't refuse."

He always had a deal, all of them suspect. "Look, you basically had me thrown in jail and now I'm possibly going to prison. I don't have my son and I don't know what the future holds. But I still have enough sense not to let you anywhere near me."

He put on his all-business face. "If you don't hear me out, you'll never have the kid with you again."

He'd found her Achilles' heel, and stomped on it. "Fine. You have five minutes."

She didn't hold the screen door open for him. She just let it slam shut and waited in the middle of the room for him to enter. He strolled inside, hands in pockets, and immediately made himself at home on the couch.

He leaned back, crossed his legs, and looked around with obvious disdain. "I see you've returned to your white-trash roots. How did it feel to go from the top of the mountain right into the sewer in a week?"

How would it feel if I slapped that arrogant look off your face? "You now have four minutes, Dalton. If you don't say what you need to say and get out, I'm calling the sheriff and I'll have you arrested for harassment."

"The sheriff, or his ass of a son?"

Red flags began to wave madly in her mind. "Leave Chase out of this."

"My dear," he said, "I can't do that. Not when he's screwing what's rightfully mine."

Jess thought she might be sick. Her nausea increased when Dalton stood, reached into his jacket's inner pocket, and tossed several photographs onto the table.

"Don't be shy, Jessica," he said. "Take a look at your sex-ploits, captured in living color."

She felt as she were watching some freakish horror film. She wanted to look away for fear of what she might see, but she couldn't.

When she leaned over to get a better look, she experienced blessed relief. She saw nothing but a blurry image of two people in an unknown location. "I don't know, Dalton. These are so out of focus, this could be anyone. Maybe even the mayor colluding with the city secretary, for all I know."

He released a dramatic sigh. "I agree. Buster means well, but his photography skills leave a lot to be desired. That's surprising since he's delivered good product before. Maybe it's that knee-jab to the crotch you gave him that's affected his brain."

Buster's limited brain could probably be found in that immediate vicinity. She suddenly thought back to that night at Chase's house. A possum clearly hadn't been responsible for the broken vase. More like a sleazy snake in the grass.

She folded her arms across her middle and stood her ground. "Again, you can't prove anything with these photos."

"But I can prove something with these." He reached in his side pocket, withdrew more photos, and spread them out like a pornographic deck of cards next to the other pile. "Unlike Buster boy, I have a quality camera with telephoto lens, and a much better knack for capturing the shot at just the right time. One of my many talents. Speaking of that, I didn't know you had so many."

Jess shuddered over the clarity of the pictures. Her and Chase holding each other on the front porch last night. Her modeling the gown Chase had given her. And worst of all, her and Chase making love in various stages, obviously shot through the bedroom window.

"Anyway," he continued, "I went to a lot of trouble to have these made available to you. I had to drive forty miles in the middle of the night to find a twenty-four-hour pharmacy, and I also had to shell out a hundred bucks to get the kid behind the counter to develop them. However, he did have the added bonus of getting off after seeing you in all your glory."

"You're a sick pervert," she hissed around her mortification.

His slimy smirk stopped her blood cold. "I know a few people who'd say the same thing about you if they saw these pictures. They'd make a fine addition to the front page story in the Placid newspaper." He held up his hands as if framing a billboard. "I can see it now.

'Accused School Teacher Takes The Law Into her Own Hands.' Or maybe mouth, depending on which photo they decide to use."

She felt the tears beginning to build, but she'd be damned if she cried in front of him. She wouldn't back down to him, either. "First of all, the Placid Herald isn't a tabloid. Secondly, even if you released these all over the Internet, I'm a divorced, adult woman who's free to do what she pleases, with whomever she pleases."

"Think again, darlin'. If you recall, your boyfriend was the first on scene that night." He tapped his chin with a manicured fingertip and pretended to think. "Wait. I'm having another memory. I'm sure he's the one who hit me over the head with that fireplace iron. Two lovers plotting to kill the ex-husband so she can get her hands on the life insurance he was forced to take out during the freakin' divorce."

He was more twisted than she thought. More ruthless than she ever dreamed he could be. "You and I both know that's not what happened."

He barked out a laugh. "Actually, I have no idea what happened. I was pretty wasted that night."

Exactly as she'd suspected. He'd made the whole story up out of some need for revenge. At least Danny was safe. And she might be, too, since he'd also made a grave error in judgment. "That's interesting, Dalton. I'll be sure to let Buck know about the whole memory thing when he comes to remove you from the premises."

He pinned her in place with a deadly glare. "You really think Buck's going to believe a little whore like you? Even if he did, remember that my father owns most of the judges in the county and he plays golf with the D.A. The truth walks when money talks."

Dalton had always worked tirelessly to be like his father. To earn his father's approval, usually without success. But he'd never stooped this low. She had to wonder what she ever saw in him. Why she had ever married him in the first place. But then, he hadn't been this far gone in the beginning. Or had she been too blinded by what she thought was love to see it?

"I'll take my chances with a jury," she said.

"Are you sure you want to do that when I'm about to offer you a way out?"

She didn't trust his way out any more than she trusted him. "Short of you dropping the charges and handing over my son, I don't want to hear what you have to say."

"That's exactly what I was going to say. I'm willing to drop the charges and reunite you with the brat."

This was way too easy. "What's the catch?"

He slowly sauntered over to her and laid a hand on her hip. "You come back to me, we get remarried and we both move back into our house, just like nothing ever happened."

She yanked his hand away. "Why would you ever think I'd even begin to consider those terms? And why would you even want that after you agreed to the divorce, no questions asked? You just signed the papers and went on your merry way." On to the next merry widow.

"I divorced you just to piss off my father," he said. "For some strange reason, he actually liked having you as a daughter-in-law, even in light of your sad, working-class background."

That certainly made perfect sense, at least the part

about pissing off Edwin. "Oh. I thought maybe your latest girlfriend dumped you after she discovered the rumors of your assets were a complete exaggeration. The manly assets, of course."

He glossed right over the insult. "As far as us remarrying, I missed having you around. You aren't a bad cook and you do a good job ironing my shirts. The sex wasn't great, but I can take care of that outside the comfort of our home."

He always had. "Well, I don't miss having you around. I don't miss being made to feel like I'm worthless. And I certainly don't miss you deriding my son."

"But you do miss him now. And even if you manage an acquittal, which I seriously doubt you will, I'll sue for full custody and I'll get it. Either way, you'll never see him again, unless you agree to my offer."

The thought of never again being with her son was so painful, she almost gave in. Almost. "Why would you even want custody of Danny when you've all but said you can't stand the sight of him?"

"Because I've invested a lot of money and time in him, and I don't like to lose on an investment. I'm also tired of Edwin riding me about being a crappy father, like the bastard has any room to talk. As far as having Danny around, that's why they invented boarding schools. I'm thinking he'd do well in a military academy. He could use a good attitude adjustment."

Don't cry... Don't cry... "I don't know what happened to you, Dalton. I only know that you're not the man I married."

"Maybe that's true, but I am the man who holds your future in his hands. So what's it going to be? A life of luxury and raising the brat? Or a possible life behind bars and never laying eyes on him again?"

If she agreed, she would be trading one prison for another. She would be doomed to a life with a man she couldn't bear to be around. A life without Chase. But she would still have her precious son, and no one would ever have to know the role he'd played in his father's injuries.

Yet she still wasn't completely powerless. She could accept Dalton's terms and send Danny to live with her parents. She could visit him frequently since Dalton wouldn't care, as long as he could continue his exploits. He only cared about finances, and his father's opinion. She would also be taking him away from his biological father. But then, she couldn't reveal that, either. How unfair that Chase would never know he had a son.

She needed time to think, to weigh her options. In the meantime, she would pretend to go along with Dalton's plan, until she could come up with her own.

"All right," she said. "I'll do what you say. But I'll need proof that you're dropping the charges, and I won't make a move until Danny's with me again."

He patted her bottom, gathered the photos and put them back in his pocket. "I knew you'd come around. As far as proof goes, I can't do anything about that until tomorrow when the city offices are open again. But I'll be back around three with the kid. In the meantime, you pack up your things."

She couldn't wait to see Danny, but she dreaded Dalton's return.

He spun around to leave before he suddenly faced her again. "Oh, and when we're back in our own bed tonight, I expect you to give me the same attention you gave your boyfriend."

Over her cold, dead body. "Anything you say, honey pie."

"One more thing. If I ever see that ass-wipe anywhere near you again, the deal's off."

He left her with another seamy smile and an overwhelming sense of anxiety. But what was done, was done. She had one last important thing to do. A heartbreaking task.

Tell Chase it was over, before it had barely begun.

"WHAT DID YOU JUST SAY?"

"I said I'm going back to Dalton."

He'd been shocked as hell to see her standing on his porch in broad daylight. But that didn't compare to the shock of hearing her utter those unbelievable words. "Did the bastard threaten you?"

She dropped her gaze to the ground. "He promised to drop the charges and return Danny to me."

"And you agreed?"

He saw absolute desperation in her eyes. "I don't have a choice, Chase. He has pictures."

"What kind of pictures?"

"Of us, making love. He managed to turn something special into something ugly and sordid. I've never been so humiliated in my life."

And he had never been so ready to kill someone in his life. He should have listened to his gut last night. He should have stayed away from her. "If he even dares to show anyone those pictures, I'll arrest him for trespassing."

"And he'll claim that he hired Buster Eustace to do it, which he did. Only Buster's photos weren't quite as clear. I assume they were taken at your house, but I couldn't really tell."

The broken vase. The squealing tires. It all made sense. Every risk they'd taken to be together had blown up in their faces. "Come inside and let's talk about this."

"I can't come inside," she said. "He'll be at the house with Danny in less than an hour. I need to pack my things and be ready to go when he gets there."

He felt like he'd been dumped in the middle of a living hell. "I'll find another way to get you out of this, Jess. You don't have to give in to blackmail."

"There isn't another way, Chase. He's threatened to claim that you and I conspired to kill him for the life insurance policy he had to purchase in accordance with the divorce terms."

The fact any life insurance policy existed only strengthened the prosecution's case against her. "Don't worry about me. I'll handle him. We know he's lying about the plot, so he has to be lying about you forcefully injuring him. We just need some way to prove it." When she refused to look at him, he grew more concerned. "Dalton is lying, isn't he?"

She started to back away. "I have to go. I can't do this right now."

"And I can't let you do this to us. I can't let you do this to Danny. You send him back into that house and you may lose him for good."

"If I don't, I'll lose him. I have to go."

When she tried to leave, Chase caught her hand and reeled her into his arms.

She placed her palms against his chest and tried to push him away, but with only minimal pressure. "You have to let me go."

"I love you, Jess. I can't let you go. Not when it's taken so long to find you again."

As her tears began to stream down her face, he nudged her head against his chest and held her while she cried.

After a time, she raised her tear-stained face and gave him a soft kiss. "I love you, too. But I love my son, as well. I have to find a way to protect him, the same way I've been protecting him for the past week. You have to trust me when I say I'm doing this for him."

Then she wrested out of his grasp, sprinted down the steps and slid into the car. Before he could make it into the driveway to issue one last plea, she sped away.

He dropped down on the porch step and scraped his brain for some way to stop her from making the second biggest mistake of her life. The first had been marrying Dalton Wainwright to begin with.

He replayed the conversation over and over in his head. Then something suddenly occurred to him. Something she'd said about her son. A possible path to the truth.

I have to find a way to protect him, the same way I've been protecting him for the past week....

She'd been protecting Danny his entire life, not only the past week.

He'd been too stupid to see it, too worried about what she might have done to Dalton. But now it all made sense. She hadn't been lying to save herself. She'd been lying to save her child.

Going straight to the source would be the only way he'd know for sure. And he had no time to waste.

"MAY I HELP YOU, SIR?"

Chase didn't recognize the maid who evidently served as the first line of defense against intruders trying to breach Edwin's inner sanctum. She might be tall as a timber, and had a linebacker build a lot of men would envy, but at least she wasn't a three-hundred-pound armed guard. Still, this would have been a whole lot easier if Danny had gone home with Rachel and Matt after the holiday dinner, instead of staying behind with his no-good father at the Placid Palace.

He flipped open the folder containing his badge and held it up for her inspection. "I'm Deputy Reed with the sheriff's department. I need to speak with Danny Wainwright."

She perused his credentials but continued to block the entry. "Master Daniel is having his afternoon snack. He can't be disturbed at the moment."

Master Daniel? He felt like he'd taken a wrong turn and landed in some uppity estate in New England. Regardless, he didn't have time to wait until after snack time was over. He wouldn't wait, even if he had all day. "I need to speak to him now. It's important."

Before the hired help could level another protest, Danny ducked under her arm and ran onto the stone porch.

He threw his arms around Chase's waist and hugged him hard. "Did you come over to play catch with me?"

Too bad that wasn't the case. He ruffled Danny's hair

and set him back a bit. "Not today, bud. I came over to have a talk, man-to-man."

The maid finally stepped aside and gestured toward the entry. "You may come into the parlor to do that, sir."

Not a chance. If Dalton happened to be seated in said parlor, he'd lay him flat on his ass. Danny didn't need to witness another violent scene. "It's a nice day outside," he said. "I believe I'll just take a little walk with Master Danny."

"But, sir, I cannot allow—"

"You can, and you will, because I'm the law." He wasn't going to let any snobby mountain of a maid tell him what to do. "I don't know where you're from, but around here, that means something."

With her nose in the air, she turned around and closed the door behind her. He'd lay money that she was about to summon the real master of the house, Edwin Wainwright. Normally that would be okay. Old Ed didn't scare him, and he'd eventually have to deal with him anyway. He just didn't want to do it today. Not until he headed Dalton off at the pass, before he forced Jess to sign a devil's pact with the devil himself.

Chase circled the back of Danny's neck with his hand and walked him toward the corner of a lawn as massive as the city park. He almost laughed when the kid swiped a huge white flower from a perfectly-groomed bush. That ought to go over well with the landscapers. He just hoped the head gardener didn't come after him with a hedge clippers.

Before they'd traveled more than a few steps, Danny stopped and looked up at Chase. "Can I go get Bo? He's out back because Granddad won't let him in the house. He says he'll pee on the rugs."

Probably nothing Dalton hadn't done before in a drunken stupor.

He hated to disappoint Danny, but he needed his full attention. The dog would be too distracting. "Tell you what, kiddo. I'll come back tomorrow and we'll teach Bo how to catch a Frisbee. How does that sound?" If all went as planned, Danny wouldn't be there tomorrow. He'd be at Chase's house, with Jess, and they'd all be free to do as they pleased. Just like a regular family.

"That sounds okay, I guess."

So much for not disappointing him.

Chase spotted a stone table a few feet away, right beyond a row of low hedges that would provide some privacy. Maybe even afford them some time before Edwin called out the guard—or called the rest of the household staff—to have him extricated from the estate.

He sat Danny down on a chair and took the opposite seat. "Danny," he began, "the questions I'm about to ask you might be hard to hear, but you have to be honest with me. Okay?"

Danny began pulling petals off the flower and dropping them to the ground. "Okay."

He took some time to gather his thoughts and let Danny prepare for the next step. "The night your dad was hurt, did you see what happened?"

His eyes grew wide and he nodded.

Here came the tough part. "Can you tell me what you saw?"

Danny crushed the flower in his hand, but didn't respond.

"You can trust me," he said. "I'm not going to let anyone hurt you, no matter what you tell me."

Just when he was about to give up on getting answers, Danny blurted, "I didn't mean to do it. I swear I didn't."

He began to cry tears that shot straight to Chase's soul. "It's okay, kiddo. I know you didn't mean to hurt him. But you have to tell me exactly what happened."

Danny drew in a ragged breath and let it out slowly. "He kept saying mean things about me. He called Mom bad names. Then he grabbed her arm and I thought he was going to hit her. I ran at him and I pushed him as hard as I could." He sobbed then sniffed. "He hit his head on the fireplace. There was blood everywhere."

No wonder the kid was so messed up. "What did your mom do after that?"

"She told me it was an accident, and not to say anything to anyone. Then she told me to go upstairs. That's where I stayed until you came."

He understood all too well why the boy had been so traumatized. He didn't understand why Jess hadn't come clean in the first place. She was too smart to believe that anyone in their right mind would fault a nine-year-old boy for trying to protect his mother from a known tyrant. Even Edwin Wainwright, with all his connections and pious airs, wouldn't punish his own flesh and blood. He'd proven that by letting his son get away with murder for years. Maybe not murder literally, but Dalton had "borrowed" the preacher's car once to take a joy ride. And he'd painted graffiti on the outside of their rival high school's gym. Each time he'd come away without a fine or even a slap on the wrist.

He didn't have time to ponder Jess's motives now. He had to get to her before Dalton did.

After coming to his feet, Chase rounded the table and knelt eye-level with Danny. "You're going to be okay. As soon as we get this cleared up, you'll be with your mom again."

"I'm not going to jail?"

Chase grinned. "Not unless you want me to give you the grand tour."

Danny's expression brightened. "Cool."

"Daniel, come here to me now!"

Chase looked to his right to see Edwin quickly approaching, the guard-maid lumbering behind him. Trouble had arrived.

When Danny hopped up from chair, Chase stood behind him, hands on his shoulders. He'd be damned if he let Old Man Bag of Bucks intimidate the boy.

Edwin stopped short of the hedge, his normally neat silver hair flapping in the breeze like an aging heron's wings. "Deputy Reed," he said, his voice sounding winded and weary. "I'm going to have to ask you to unhand my grandson and leave immediately."

He made a show of looking behind Edwin to the maid. "If I don't, is she going to attack me with a ladle? If so, that'll earn her fifteen to twenty for assault on a police officer. Then who would wash your gold-studded shorts?"

After Danny giggled, Edwin grimaced like he'd eaten a jar of pickles. "I'm warning you, Deputy. If you're not out of here in sixty seconds, I'll call your father."

That was supposed to scare him? "Fine. He's at home watching the game. I'd call him for you, but I have to leave and take care of another problem." A problem old Ed had created. Literally.

"See that you do it immediately," Edwin said as he approached the table.

Chase turned Danny around and smiled. "Just hang in there for me, bud. I'll get you out of here as soon as I can."

Edwin hovered over Danny and tried unsuccessfully to look intimidating. "Go with Zelda, Daniel."

Zelda. That fit.

Danny obeyed, but when he looked back at Chase with a frightened expression, he gave him a thumbs-up to reassure him.

After Danny was out of earshot, he turned his ire on Edwin. "Before I do leave, there's just one thing I have to say to you, old man."

His face turned so red, Chase though his head might blow off his neck. "Do you know who you're talking to, Deputy?"

Yeah. King of the Bastards. "I'm talking to someone who doesn't have control over everyone, including me and your former daughter-in-law." He pointed a finger directly at his face. "I'll go now, but you can bet I'll be back. We have a score to settle." Beginning with convincing him to give Jess her job back.

Without waiting for Edwin's reply, he took off across the lawn, satisfied he now had the information that would finally stop Dalton Wainwright's reign of terror.

CHAPTER THIRTEEN

JESS HAD A PLAN TO STOP DALTON from forcing her back into his dysfunctional world. A plan that relied on a special device. A teaching tool that had saved her life on many occasions. She prayed that held true today.

Dalton had arrived on her doorstep a few minutes ago, looking every bit the pompous cat who'd dined on the canary. She didn't know what made her angrier— that he'd come an hour early, or that he didn't bother to bring her son.

As she reached up to retrieve dry goods from the cupboard, Dalton scowled at her from the seat that he'd taken at the dinette table to her right. "I thought you'd be through packing by now."

She'd purposely dragged her heels in that regard. "And I thought you were supposed to bring Danny."

"I told you he wanted to stay and play with the train set my father gave him. He wasn't nearly as enthusiastic about seeing you as you are about seeing him."

She'd bet her last nickel Dalton hadn't told Danny about the arrangement.

While she placed a package of pasta in a canvas bag, she glanced at the pen barely peeking out between two canisters on the counter. A silver pen that had recording capability—her secret weapon. Every time they spoke, a red light came on, indicating it was working. She'd strategically placed it where it would pick up the sounds, yet it was sufficiently concealed from Dalton. Or so she hoped.

"Leave the damn groceries, Jess, so we can get out of here."

She didn't miss a beat with the packing. "I don't like to waste food. Besides, there's not much at the house, and what's there is probably spoiled."

"You can go to the grocery store tomorrow."

He could go to hell for all she cared. "I deserve some patience. You didn't give me much time to get everything together." And of course, he hadn't offered to help. He just sat there, watching her every move like a hawk about to pounce on its prey.

He released an irritated sigh. "It shouldn't be taking you this long. Most everything you own is at our house."

She would prefer never to step foot in *his* house again. And that led to a question. "I haven't been allowed to go in there since the accident. If you can't clear up the charges against me until tomorrow, how do you plan to explain my presence if someone from the sheriff's department happens to stop by? Deputy Barkley seems to have made it his goal to guard the place."

"I've already taken care of Barkley. No one will be stopping by."

Jess suspected that meant he'd probably bought Barkley's cooperation. She took another covert look at the pen, and prepared to proceed with the plan. "I've been wondering about something. How are you going to get the charges dropped against me without revealing you have no recollection of the night's events?"

"Let me worry about that. You just worry about getting your stuff together."

Every time that red light illuminated, Jess felt one step closer to victory. "Tell me something else. Did you have anything to do with the missing fireplace iron?"

She glanced over her shoulder to see his self-satisfied smile. "I didn't take it," he said. "But I know who did, and I know where it is."

She put forth her best guess. "Buster Eustace?"

"Nah. I wouldn't trust that idiot with something as important as manufactured evidence. Barkley was more than happy to accommodate me with that, too."

Her suspicions had been confirmed. "How did you convince him to do your dirty work?"

"He's up to his eyeballs in debt at the bank, and he has a kid about to go to college. That made him an easy mark. And he didn't even cost me that much."

She almost laughed. Her dear ex-husband was confessing to the woman he'd accused of trying to murder him. Now who was the idiot? "I still don't know how you're going to explain the fireplace iron."

"Not a problem. It will magically show up in the corner, or it might work better if it rolled under the sofa. That's a less obvious place."

She was so close to the finish line, she could almost see the checkered flag. "You've thought this all out, haven't you?"

"Yeah, babe, I have."

She'd never minded Chase using that endearment. In fact, she loved hearing him say it to her. But coming from Dalton's mouth, it sounded totally patronizing.

"By the way," he said. "I want you to meet me tomorrow at the courthouse. We can apply for a marriage license and have a small ceremony at my father's estate next weekend. I thought it would be a good way to ring in the new year."

Right now, she'd love to ring his neck. "I don't see why we have to remarry when we could just live together."

"I want you to be legally bound to me."

Little did he know, by tomorrow, he could be entangled in his own legal issues. Of course, in all probability, Edwin would find a way to rescue his son from the system. Again.

Jess moved onto the cabinet housing the canned goods, satisfied that she had enough information to prove her innocence, as well as Dalton's own machinations. "I'm almost done here, so you can run along and I'll meet you at the house."

"That's a good one, Jess. I'll follow you there, just to make sure you don't decide to take off for parts unknown."

She frowned at his lack of insight. He truly didn't know her at all. "I've waited a long time to be with Danny again. Do you think I'd actually leave him behind?"

"I don't know what you'd do these days, Jessica. After what you did to the deputy, anything's possible."

She had a feeling he wasn't going to drop that topic for a long time. One more thing to use to her advantage. "I'm really surprised we didn't hear you sneaking around in the bushes while you were playing voyeur and taking pictures."

"You were too busy screwing your boyfriend to hear me." His tone hinted at barely-contained rage.

"You are going to destroy the pictures, aren't you?" she asked.

"I'll tear them up after I get what I want."

When he pushed away from the table, came up behind her and ran his hands underneath her shirt, Jess new exactly what he wanted. She couldn't stop the bone-deep shiver, and it wasn't because his touch turned her on. Just the opposite. "What are you doing?"

He formed his palms around her waist. "I'm trying to decide if you've lost a few pounds, and I believe you have. Try to keep it off. I don't like being seen with a fat wife."

She was trying to decide which weapon she should use to knock him over the head—creamed corn or beef consommé. To prevent landing back in jail on charges that would be justified this time, she side-stepped him and turned around, a can in each hand and sarcasm on her lips. "Why certainly I will do everything in my power to please my master."

He took on a look of determination, right before he moved in front of her and pinned her against the counter with his body. "You know, since you don't care for waste, and you've already wasted rent on this dump, we could just use that bed one last time. That way you'd get your money's worth."

She would most likely get deathly ill. "Good try, Dalton. But you don't get the goods until I get my son."

When he kissed her neck, she cringed. "Come on now, Jess. It used to be real good between us, before you turned into a frigid bitch."

And he'd turned into a cheating creep. "It might have been good for you, but not so much for me. You just climbed on, got off and went to sleep. Not my idea of a stellar time."

"That was before I knew you'd be interested in taking a walk on the wild side." Bile rose in Jess's throat when he rested his palm on her belly, right above the waistband on her jeans. "Don't think for a second Chase Reed can give you what you need."

He already has. He'd given her a son and his love, something Dalton would never understand. She wasn't even sure he was capable of loving anyone but himself.

When he took the cans from her grasp and set them on the counter, his eyes narrowed. "What in the hell is this?"

Her heart began to race as Dalton reached around her and held up the only thing that could earn her freedom. "It's an electronic pen," she said, clamoring for a believable explanation. "It records the time and temperature."

"Do you really think I'm that stupid?" He flung the pen to his right and it landed with a *thunk* against the back door. "You *bitch!*"

Seeing her one and only chance to escape, Jess grabbed a can, aimed for his temple, and hit him as hard as she could. She saw the stunned look on his face right before she shoved him backward, and then ran for the nearest exit. But her hands were shaking so badly, she fumbled with the lock that refused to give, wasting precious time.

Her head suddenly jerked back when Dalton grabbed a handful of hair. Then he twisted her arm behind her waist, sending an electric shock through her shoulder, as he spun her around.

He trapped her against the back door and sneered. "Where's your boyfriend now, Jessica?"

If only Chase were around. But he wasn't, because she'd sent him away. "Give up, Dalton. It's over."

"It will never be over, Jess. You're mine. You always will be."

She didn't dare let him see her fear. "I don't belong to anyone."

"Yes, you do. I sealed us together for life when I gave you that kid."

"He's not your son, Dalton," she said, without regard for her safety. "He's Chase's son, and I thank God every day that he is."

He slapped his palm against the door, right by her head. "You're lying!"

She should be quiet, but she couldn't think beyond all the hatred she'd been harboring for years. "I'm not lying. When you were busy issuing ultimatums to me ten years ago, I was making love with Chase. He gave me Danny, not you. And he can give me what you never could—his unconditional love."

She witnessed the minute Dalton went over the edge, felt it when he wrapped his hands around her neck. She clasped his wrists and tried to dislodge his fingers now pressing against her throat, but he was too strong.

The photo Chase had given Jess flashed in her mind, followed by a host of regrets. If she had told him Danny was his, she could die knowing that her son would be safe with his real father. But she hadn't. And she would die, if she didn't find a way to flee.

As she stared into the eyes of a madman, she experienced terror in its purest form. And then the fight-or-flight reaction kicked in. She used the only thing available to ensure she would live. Live to spend her life with her son and the man she loved.

Her trusty knee.

As Chase rounded the curve on his way to Jess's temporary house, a county cruiser sped past him, lights flashing. And when he heard the sound of another siren, he looked in his rearview mirror to see a fast-approaching ambulance.

He didn't have his radio turned on, so he had no idea what could be happening. But his gut told him he had to get to Jess.

Instead of pulling over, he punched the accelerator to the floor, relying on the turbo-charged engine for enough speed to go around the cruiser now in front of him. He might have hell to pay for failure to yield, but that was the least of his concerns at the moment.

He stopped the truck in the driveway, shoved it into Park and tore out of the cab, right before the cruiser turned in behind him. His heart pounded in his chest, and every worst-case scenario ran through his mind as he raced toward the porch at a dead run.

Relief washed over him when Jess came out the front door. Fury replaced the relief when he saw the angry welts on her neck.

After he took her by the arms, she flinched. "Are you okay?"

"I think he broke my shoulder, and aside from the fact he tried to choke me to death, I'm fine."

His need for revenge began to build to the boiling point. "Where is he?"

"In the house," she said. "Doubled over in the kitchen. His head's probably hurting, and his voice might be a little higher for a while, but he'll survive."

Under normal circumstances, he would appreciate her attempt at humor. At the moment, he only had one goal in mind—to find Dalton Wainwright and finally give him what he deserved.

Chase glanced to his right to see his father exit the car, which meant he had no time to spare. He turned back to Jess. "Wait here and tell Buck what happened."

Before she could respond, he yanked open the screen door and strode through the house to the kitchen. He found Dalton exactly as Jess had said he would, sitting in the kitchen floor, looking dazed.

He grabbed him by the collar, lifted him up and shoved him against the wall. "Give me one good reason why I shouldn't kill you with my bare hands right now."

Dalton tried to appear calm, but he couldn't mask the alarm in his eyes. "Hey, man. It was just a misunderstanding. No harm done."

"No harm done? She has the imprint of your fingers around her neck, you miserable son of a bitch."

"She started it," he said, sounding like the coward he was. "She whacked me up the side of the head with a can. I think she might have even given me a concussion. I had to defend myself."

Chase got right up in his face. "Let me tell you what we're going to do. I'm going to take you out back, and we're going to settle this, man-to-man. And while I'm beating the hell out of you, I want you to remember how Jess felt when you were *defending* yourself."

"Let him go, son."

He glanced at Buck in the doorway, but he didn't release Dalton. "I'm not on duty. I can do whatever I want with him."

"And you'll be doing it in front of a peace officer, because I'm not going to turn you loose on him. That means you'll end up behind the cage in the car, right next to him. You might want to keep in mind that Jess needs you."

Buck had said the magic words. He turned back to Dalton. "Today's your lucky day. But you never know what tomorrow's going to bring, so watch your back."

After Chase freed his hold from Dalton's collar, he took him by the arm to hand him over to Buck. But his father surprised him by holding up the cuffs. "I'll let you do the honors," he said. "I figure you deserve that much for not taking him out while you had the chance."

He grabbed the cuffs, yanked Dalton's arms behind his back with a little more force than necessary, and snapped the metal bracelets closed. "Dalton Wainwright, you are finally under arrest."

"I'll handle it from here," Buck said. "You go see about Jess. The paramedics are checking her out."

He would gladly relinquish his duty for that reason alone.

Chase found Jess seated at the back of the ambulance, a blue sling fashioned around her arm. He walked up to her, saw that bruises had begun to form around her neck and got mad all over again. "Is your arm broken?" he asked.

"Dislocated shoulder," she said. "I have to go to the hospital for X-rays before I know how bad it is. At least it's my left arm, not my right."

It was already bad enough. He suddenly remembered something he should have never forgotten. "Where's Danny?"

"Fortunately, still with Edwin. If Dalton would have brought him, this might not have happened."

"Or he might have seen it happen," he said.

She pinched the bridge of her nose. "You're right. That would have been horrible."

He should probably give her a break, but he needed to know exactly what had transpired to that point. He sat down beside her and rested a hand on her leg. "Can you tell me how this all went down?"

She sighed. "I decided to play along with Dalton's conditions that we remarry, and then defeat him at his own game. I used a digital pen to record the conversation, and got him to admit he didn't remember anything about that night. He'd concocted the entire story, and he paid Barkley to steal the fireplace iron."

He'd known all along something wasn't right with that sack of manure, Barkley. He'd deal with him later. "Go ahead."

"Anyway, Dalton saw the recorder," she continued, "and he went ballistic. I tried to get away, but he managed to catch me. If I hadn't kneed him in the jewels, he would have killed me."

"That's why you should never have tried this by yourself. Dalton's been heading toward this kind of violence for years."

"I realize that now," she said. "But I had to do something to clear my name. The pen's on the kitchen floor, near the back door. Hopefully he didn't break it and the confession is still there."

They might not even need the confession, now that he knew the real story. "I talked to Danny right before I drove over here. He told me he's the one who pushed Dalton, not you."

Her gaze shot to his. "I never wanted to keep that information from you, but I had my reasons for doing so."

"For the life of me, Jess, I don't know what they'd be. Danny's a beat-down kid who wanted to protect his mother from a worthless father. You should have realized he wouldn't be punished for that."

She folded the hem of her shirt, back and forth. "There's another reason I didn't say anything."

From the serious tone of her voice, he wasn't sure he could cope with the reason. But he still needed to know.

The sound of the slamming screen drew their attention to Buck leading Dalton down the porch steps. Since they'd have to pass by the ambulance on the way to the cruiser, Chase gently took Jess's right hand into his to give her support.

Dalton sent them both an evil glare as he approached. "Does he know what he's in for, Jess?" he asked.

Chase had learned to ignore the ramblings of a captured perp, but something in Jess's eyes sent up warning flags. "What's he talking about?"

When she didn't respond, Dalton started laughing. "You didn't even tell him the little bastard is his kid? That's great, Jess."

Buck yanked Dalton forward. "Move it, Wainwright,"

he said, without even showing one iota of shock over the revelation.

But Chase was shocked. And confused. "Is he saying that Danny is—"

"Your son," Jess said.

That sent Chase to his feet to face her. "Is it true?"

"Yes, it's true." She looked up at him, tears in her eyes. "I can explain."

Before she could begin, the EMT rounded the ambulance. "The ER's been notified we're coming, ma'am. We have to go now."

"I need another minute," she said. "I have to talk to Deputy Reed."

Filled with a sudden sense of resentment and anger, Chase backed away. "No, she doesn't need to talk to me. We're done. Go ahead and take her."

"Chase, please hear me out."

Ignoring her plea, he turned and started for the truck, a million thoughts racing through his mind, as well as the words Buck had said to him a few days ago.

She's been a Wainwright for a decade. She's bound to have learned something about lying....

His dad had been right. Chase had only seen what he'd wanted to see—the girl who'd been his best friend, the woman he'd always loved, couldn't be capable of something so damn cruel.

Betrayal, as sharp as shards of glass, cut him to the quick. If what she'd said about Danny was the truth, then she'd robbed of the chance to know his own child. She'd subjected her son—their son—to a contemptible man who didn't know the first thing about being a father.

He did have a lot of questions, and she did have a lot

of explaining to do. But he needed time to think, time away from her. Time to grieve everything he'd lost. Including her.

SHE'D LOST HIM.

After three days with no word from Chase, that reality had finally set in.

Jess had remained in the rental because she had nowhere else to go. With each passing moment, her hope for a normal life had begun to fade.

And the silence in the empty house...

That had been the worst part of all, and the reason she now sat at Rachel's kitchen table.

"What are your immediate plans?" Rachel asked as she set a glass of wine in front of Jess.

To get out of bed every morning. "I don't know. That depends on if and when they drop the charges."

"Savannah is certain they'll drop them," Rachel said. "With the nifty little pen confession, and Danny's statement, you'll be free and clear by the end of the week."

Maybe clear, but not necessarily free. "Buck said something about possible perjury charges."

Rachel's solemn expression didn't give Jess any substantial confidence. "Savannah mentioned you might have to deal with that in the future." She laid her hand on Jess's forearm, right below where the sling ended. "Look at it this way. Dalton will be rotting in jail a long, long time. That should give you cause to celebrate. Makes me want to jump for joy."

Jess was completely taken aback by the comment. "But he's your bother, Rachel."

Rachel shrugged. "I've never been one to believe in

the 'blood is thicker than water' thing. Dalton deserves to be locked up and I'll be glad to throw away the key. Then we can be assured he'll never be around you or his son again."

Jess realized she had to come clean with her former sister-in-law, before she heard it from someone else. But it was going to be tough, telling her that Danny—the nephew she'd been caring for in Jess's stead, was still caring for—wasn't her biological nephew at all. "How long do you think Danny will be at Matt's clinic?" she asked, just to be sure she could speak freely.

"I don't expect them for another hour."

"Good." Jess rimmed the wineglass with her fingertip. "I have something important to tell you. Something I don't want him to hear yet."

"You've been sleeping with Chase."

Her gaze zipped up from the glass. "How did you know that?"

"Matt told me he figured it out when he was helping with the roof that day. I personally think it's great. Even if neither of you realized it, the chemistry's been there since high school. I've always thought the two of you should have been together years ago."

"We were," Jess blurted. "Actually, only once."

Rachel raised a brow. "Really? When?"

"The night before Chase deployed to Afghanistan."

"Two weeks before you and Dalton married?"

Jess assumed that, like Savannah, Rachel had already taken out the mental calendar. "Yes, and before you ask, Danny could have been either Chase or Dalton's son." Now for the bittersweet truth. "As it turned out, he's Chase's."

She let Rachel digest the information before she spoke again. "This doesn't change anything. He'll always be your nephew, just not biologically."

"Of course it doesn't change anything between us." Rachel made a face and touched her belly. "Does Danny know?"

"Not yet, and are you okay?"

"Just a little twinge," she said as she shifted in her seat. "This baby boy loves to curl up in just the wrong spot. Now back to your baby boy. When are you going to tell him? After he goes to college?"

At the right time. In the right place. "After he's back with me, and I can convince Chase to tell him with me. That might be a problem since the good deputy is not speaking to me right now."

Rachel frowned. "Then Chase knows."

"Yes." She didn't have the energy to explain how he'd come by that information. "He's angry because I didn't tell him sooner."

"Well, he can just get un-mad," Rachel said. "He should be thrilled he has a son as great as Danny. I'm thrilled Danny won't be inheriting the Wainwright cut-throat gene."

Thank heaven for good friends. "Then you're not mad at me?"

"No, Jess, I'm not mad," she said. "I will be if you and Chase don't work this out. Danny deserves to have a real father. A good father. And you deserve to be with the man you love. You do love him, don't you?"

"Yes, I do." More than she could ever express.

Whether she loved Chase, or deserved to be with him,

didn't really matter. Not unless he decided to give her another chance. Or to forgive her.

And that possibility was beginning to look bleak.

CHAPTER FOURTEEN

FIVE DAYS HAD GONE BY since Chase had last seen Jess. Five long, terrible days.

He'd returned to work, spent his nights in seclusion, thinking nonstop. The nightmares involving the war had begun to subside, but two nights ago, they'd been replaced by another that had been equally as bad. He'd dreamed of Jess coming toward him, smiling in the way he'd always loved. But as he reached for her offered hand, she'd suddenly disappeared. When he'd awoken to find she wasn't there beside him, that had been the greatest torture of all.

And that was the first time he'd allowed himself to cry.

His emotions were still raw, and his mind still wrapped in confusion. He had a lot to consider, and decisions he had yet to make. He hadn't stopped loving her. He probably never would. But he wasn't sure if he had the strength to forgive her.

Right now, he just needed to keep moving forward, get on with his life, even if he couldn't imagine not having her in it.

Today, he decided to finish his business with Edwin Wainwright. At least he could ensure that Jess had a job waiting for her, enabling her to give Danny what he needed, even if he couldn't. He also wouldn't mind seeing how the old man had handled the news that his son had been remanded without bail. Maybe old Ed couldn't buy every judge in the county after all.

Chase had chosen the bank as the place for the confrontation for the sake of accessibility. He'd phoned ahead, so he knew Wainwright would be there until noon, before the place closed for the New Year's holiday.

He walked into the lobby and looked around. When he saw the gold nameplate on a nearby door, he started in that direction. He didn't even bother to check in with the receptionist. And she didn't bother to flag him down, proving some advantages did exist when you were the law.

He did rap on the door for his mother's sake. Missy Reed was a stickler when it came to politeness, and she wouldn't take too kindly to him not minding his manners. But that was the last courtesy he planned to show the rich man today.

After he heard, "Come in," Chase entered without hesitation. He'd expected to see Wainwright seated behind the massive mahogany desk, maybe smoking a pipe while he played with other people's futures, like they were pawns in his private game of chess. Instead, the man stood at the window, looking out on the downtown street.

He didn't intend to beat around the bush. "I promised I'd be back, Ed."

Wainwright dropped the curtain and turned around. He leveled a weary gaze on Chase, and didn't appear to be that surprised to see him. "Have a seat, Deputy," he said, indicating one of two nearby chairs.

He wasn't in the mood for small talk. "I don't plan to

stay long. I just wanted to stop by to say that when the school board meets next week, I expect you to reinstate Jess. It's the least you can do, considering the hell your son put her through."

"You may consider it done."

That was way too easy. "You'll convince the board to lift the suspension, just like that? No argument?"

"I give you my word." Edwin lowered himself into one of the chairs and folded his hands in his lap. "You don't have any children, do you, Deputy Reed?"

What a question to ask when the answer had so recently changed. But he still had no real proof Danny was his son, only Jess's claim. And even if it turned out to be true, Wainwright apparently hadn't heard the news. He wasn't about to enlighten him. "No. I don't have any kids." Not officially.

Edwin shifted slightly in the chair. "If you do decide to take that step, you'll eventually learn that you will go to great lengths to protect them. You believe their lies. You will lie for them. And no matter what you do, they will make their own mistakes. You only hope that those errors in judgment won't predict their future. And then you wake up one morning and realize that you're to blame for their failures."

The mogul before him wasn't only the callous business man everyone feared. He was a broken old man who'd just taken responsibility for his son's transgressions. Funny, Chase almost felt sorry for him. "I don't think you should carry all the blame for Dalton's actions. He's an adult in charge of his own fate."

"He's weak," Edwin said. "And I wanted him to be tough. I drove him to prove his strength. I didn't believe he would go this far. But now that he has, I've washed my hands of him. Still, there's no greater pain a father can experience than when he cuts a child out of his life."

That could explain why Dalton hadn't made bail, and why Edwin hadn't visited him. But unbeknownst to Wainwright, he'd solved one of Chase's dilemmas. If the past few days had taught him anything, he'd learned he had what it took to be a dad. And he couldn't desert Danny, whether he had a biological tie or not. "Do you think you'll ever forgive Dalton?" he asked out of curiosity.

"I already have, Deputy. His mother would have wanted it that way. She always said that if you rely on your heart to guide you, there is nothing that can't be forgiven."

Chase was immediately reminded of Jess's words on the night he'd told her about the war. Words everyone should learn to live by, including him. Especially him.

I believe if your heart is in the right place, anything can be forgiven....

And when he stopped to consider what Wainwright had been through after losing his wife, he had to respect the man on some level. "It must've been hard, raising two kids on your own."

He glimpsed unmistakable sadness in Edwin's expression before he composed himself again. "Yes, it was difficult. Ellen was a remarkable woman, and Rachel is a lot like her. That's why I know she'll make it through this latest crisis."

Chase wasn't aware of any crisis involving Rachel or Matt. "What do you mean?"

"I received a call right before you arrived," he said.

I've not only lost my son, I've lost a grandson. Rachel went into early labor, and the infant didn't survive."

This week could go down in history as one of the worst for the members of the six-pack. The thought of Matt and Rachel losing the baby they'd waited so long to have, made him sick. "I'm real sorry to hear that."

"So am I," Edwin said. "I'll be going by to see her at the hospital as soon as the bank closes."

He planned to do the same, only he wasn't going to let the job stand in the way of checking on his friends. Wainwright may have displayed some humanity, but he was still a hardnosed businessman, first and foremost.

And that reminded Chase he still had one more item of unfinished business. "Before I go, I have another request."

Edwin came to his feet. "And what would that be, Deputy?"

"Jess could be facing perjury charges for not revealing Danny's role in Dalton's injuries. You still wield a lot of influence around here, so I'd appreciate anything you could do to take care of that. As long as it doesn't involve money exchanging hands."

"I'll see what I can manage," Edwin said. "Jessica doesn't deserve to be punished more than she already has. And I'm living proof of what a parent will do to protect their child. That's all she's guilty of, protecting Daniel."

Wainwright was making perfect sense. He'd be damned if he ever saw that coming. "Thanks. I appreciate you taking the time to talk with me."

"One more thing," Edwin said. "I hope you continue

to take care of my former daughter-in-law. She's one of the few people who can make me smile."

Chase could absolutely relate to that.

After he left the bank, he started for the cruiser parked at the curb, then changed his mind and crossed the street to the city park. He planted himself on a bench and went over everything Wainwright had said to him about forgiveness and parents protecting their children. Every bit of it had hit home. Too close to home.

He had to remember that Jess had forgiven him when he'd told her about Safa. He couldn't forget that until he'd reconnected with Jess, he hadn't been able to forgive himself. If she'd been willing to grant him grace for his sins, didn't she deserve the same from him? And didn't Danny deserve a father who'd be there for him? The answer to all those questions was a resounding *yes*.

Now that he finally felt grounded enough to sit down and work things out with Jess, he couldn't wait to find her. And he knew exactly where she would be.

WHAT DID YOU SAY TO A WOMAN who'd just lost a child?

Jess had no idea. Even though she'd recently faced a similar situation, Danny had been returned to her yesterday, healthy and relatively content. They still had a long way to go to rebuild their relationship, and plenty of time to get there. Rachel, on the other hand, would never have the joy of watching her child grow, and that made Jess incredibly sad.

As she sought out her friend, she passed a few rooms filled with joyful family members, the sounds of crying babies echoing in the corridor. She could only imagine how torturous that must be for Rachel.

. She finally located the correct room, and when she came upon the slightly open door, she pushed it open and peeked inside. Rachel was lying on her back, her dark hair forming a halo on the pillow, her eyes tightly closed.

Since she was obviously sleeping, Jess wondered if she should leave and come back later. She opted to sit in the chair next to the narrow bed and wait. But she didn't have to wait long until her friend opened her eyes.

"Hey, Rachel," Jess said quietly. "How are you feeling?"

"Groggy." She rested her hand on her belly. "Empty."

She felt Rachel's pain as keenly as if it were her own. "I saw Matt walking across the parking lot when I pulled up, but I didn't have a chance to speak with him."

"I told him to go home."

Something in Rachel's tone disturbed Jess. "I'm sure he's exhausted, and he sounded so upset when he called me this morning. Of course, he has every right to be."

Rachel rolled slowly to her side and reached for Jess's hand. "We decided to call him Caleb. He was such a beautiful baby. He was so small, but he had these perfect little feet and hands and a lot of dark hair. They only let me see him for a little while before they took him away. And then he was gone. I asked to hold him, but Matt thought it would be too upsetting for me. No one cared how I felt about it."

Maybe that explained why Rachel had seemed almost angry with her husband. "Do they know why the baby came early? I hope it wasn't the stress of what happened with Dalton, and then you had to take care of Danny—"

"It's no one's fault, Jess. That's what they told me. But I can't help but think that I... Never mind."

Jess squeezed her hand. "If they said it's no one's fault, then I hope you believe that, too. You took good care of yourself during the pregnancy. You got plenty of rest. You ate well. Me, I practically ate everything in sight when I was pregnant with Danny."

"How is Danny?" Rachel asked. "I've been thinking about him since he left our place."

Jess marveled over her unselfishness. "He's doing okay. He's still quiet, but he's opening up more. I did talk to your counselor friend yesterday afternoon. She's going to see Danny next week. I gave her a brief history but we'll go more into depth then."

"That's good. And your arm?"

"It's going to heal on its own." She wished she could say the same for her broken heart. "I had a hard time getting used to the sling at first, but I'm learning to function with only one hand."

"Just one more thing we tend to take for granted, I guess."

When Rachel's eyes began to look heavy, Jess took that as her cue to leave. She came to her feet and released Rachel's hand. "I'm going to let you rest now. Do you know when you'll be going home?"

"Tomorrow," she said. "But I'm going to Dad's for a few days since Matt will be working."

That made little sense to Jess. "Surely he'll forget about work until you're feeling better."

Rachel shook her head. "Not Matt. When things go badly, he buries himself in work. He's a lot like my father in that respect."

Jess would never think to compare Matt Boyd to Edwin Wainwright. They were as different as midnight and morning. "I'll call you tomorrow to see how you're doing. If you're up to it, I can bring Danny by. I know he'd like to see his favorite aunt."

Rachel attempted a smile. "That would be nice. I'll let you know."

"Is there anything I can do for you before I go?"

"Yes, there is." Rachel punched a button on the remote and raised the head of the bed. "If you and Chase still haven't worked things out, then go find him and make him listen to reason. That's an order."

Jess was so happy to see Rachel smile, but she wasn't sure she had the courage for a confrontation. "I'll think about it."

"Don't think, Jess. Just do it. Life is too precious to waste, even for a minute."

She leaned and kissed Rachel's cheek. "You're absolutely right."

And she was. If Jess wanted to resolve her issues with Chase, she couldn't wait for him to come around. Otherwise, she could be waiting another ten years.

She left Rachel's room, bent on a mission. She would track Chase down and make him talk to her. Make him see they belonged together. How she was going to find him remained to be seen. Buy a police scanner? Put out an APB? Jaywalk in hopes that he would be the one to give her a ticket?

Making a trip down to the department seemed a much more logical course of action.

But as she pushed through the double doors and entered the lobby, she discovered she didn't have to look

far to find him. Chase stood right there, leaning over
the information desk, obviously flirting with the volunteer, if the silver-haired lady's schoolgirl smile was any
indication. The bad boy had returned. But he was still
her bad boy. Or that's what she hoped.

He wore his uniform, and he wore it well. Khaki shirt,
dark jeans, brown rough-out boots and the cowboy hat
Buck insisted his men donned during duty. A throwback
to the Old West, even if Placid was much farther east.

As he moved away from the desk, he sent a glance
her direction, then did a double-take. She couldn't escape now, even if she wanted to.

They crossed the waiting room at the same time and
met in the middle.

"I thought I'd find you here," he said.

And he hadn't avoided her. A good sign. "I just left
Rachel's room."

"How is she?" He looked and sounded seriously concerned.

"As well as can be expected," she said. "She was
about to drift off when I left her."

"Then I guess I'll wait until later to see her."

Okay. Now what? Time to get with the program. "If
you have a few moments to spare in the next couple of
days, I'd like to talk to you. Of course, feel free to wait
until Monday, after the holiday."

"I have time now," he said. "Maybe we could find a
place around here."

Jess couldn't imagine where. The county hospital
was small, basically an emergency room, a maternity
ward—which seemed to be the most popular place—and
two other medical floors. They did have a small lounge

with vending machines, but people would be going in and out. As far as the lobby went, she surveyed the area and saw only two available chairs, each located on opposite sides of the room.

"Do you have any suggestions?" she asked him after exhausting all possibilities.

"There's a courtyard not far from the front door, with tables and chairs. We could sit there. I'd offer my place, but I only have about an hour before I have to get back to work."

She'd vote for his place, but she understood he had a job to do. Besides, any setting would work, as long as she had the opportunity to speak to him. "I have to pick up Danny at a friend's house in a while, so the courtyard it is."

They left out the sliding glass doors and claimed a table and chairs in the corner of the small patio.

Once they were settled in across from each other, Chase took off his hat and set it on the table, brim up. He slicked his hand through his blond hair that glinted in the sunlight, just like Danny's hair. "It's warm today," he said. "Especially for December."

"It's almost January."

"Yeah, you're right."

For two people who used to talk about everything, it seemed strange that they could only discuss the weather. Back to square one.

After a time, Chase finally broke the uncomfortable silence. "How's the kid?"

She was pleased he was interested in Danny. "He came home yesterday, and he's doing all right. He starts counseling next week."

"That's good."

"He asked about you several times."

That brought about his dimpled smile. "Oh, yeah?"

"Yeah. He mentioned something about you teaching Bo how to catch a Frisbee."

"I forgot about that. Maybe I'll have a chance to do that soon."

She decided to put him to the test. "I spoke with Mom yesterday and filled her in on what's happened. Needless to say, she's shocked. She also suggested that Danny and I move close to her and Dad."

His expression went somber. "Are you going to do it?"

That depended on how this conversation went. "I've thought about it. Danny doesn't want to leave, even after everything that's happened. But I think he'll eventually warm up to the idea."

"What about you, Jess? Do you want to leave?"

Not really. Not at all. "I don't have much reason to stay. I don't have a job and—"

"That's been resolved. You should be reinstated next week."

She could only gape for a few moments. "How do you know that?"

"Because I just came from Wainwright's office to plead your case, and he's agreed to convince the board that it's the right thing to do. It's his way of making up for what Dalton did to you."

He could have gone all year without bringing up her ex. "Thank you for going to bat for me. The question is, why did you?"

"I care about what happens to you and Danny."

"Because I'm the mother of your son?"

When he didn't immediately respond, Jess feared she already had her answer.

"That brings me an important question," he finally said. "How do you know Danny is my son when you've never asked me for a paternity test?"

She launched into a brief explanation about the blood type issue, and finished by saying, "But if you're not convinced, you are welcome to request a DNA test."

He released a rough sigh. "I don't have to. I know he's mine."

An acknowledgment she'd waited a long time to hear. "In my opinion, the dimples are a dead giveaway."

"That, and he's a switch-hitter, just like me when I played ball."

They shared a smile until Chase grew solemn again. "Why didn't you tell me about him sooner, Jess? If I'd known about him, I would've left the Army earlier. I sure as hell wouldn't have signed on for three tours."

Yet he wouldn't have afforded her the same consideration. "And I spent all those years in denial. I wouldn't let myself believe you were his father because I was so afraid you would never come home alive. You just kept going back, and every time you'd write and tell me that, I'd cry for days."

"Why? You had Dalton."

"Yes, and I loved you. I realized it the night in my dorm. But then you said it was a mistake, so I settled." And that was the first time she'd truly admitted it to herself.

"It would have been a mistake back then," he said. "I wasn't ready to settle down and have a family. It hasn't been all that long ago that I figured out I would never be ready for it."

Well, that was that. He'd all but said that their futures were heading in opposite directions.

Before she broke down and bawled, Jess scooted the chair back and stood. "Now that I know where you stand, I need to go. Call me if you want to see Danny. If you don't, then let me know that, too. I'll try to explain it to him as gently as possible."

As she turned to leave, Chase caught her wrist. "Don't go, Jess. I still have a lot to say to you."

"I believe you've already said it all. I had every intention of trying to convince you that we should be together. That what we have is so rare, we'd never find it with anyone else. But you obviously don't feel the same."

"You're wrong. That's exactly how I feel. You just didn't give me a chance to say it."

Jess dropped back into the chair for fear her legs might betray her. "Then you still love me?"

He took her right hand and brought it to his lips for a soft kiss. "I couldn't stop loving you, even if I tried. I just had to have time to sort out all my feelings. Then Wainwright said a few things that helped me understand why you did what you did. You were only trying to protect Danny. And I'm willing to forgive you for withholding the fact that I'm his father, if you'll forgive me for not giving you the benefit of the doubt."

She'd never understood what it meant to have your heart soar, until now. "I forgive you for everything you've ever done wrong in your life. Except for maybe those hideous slippers you bought me on my sixteenth birthday."

The sun had nothing on that beautiful smile. "I think the reindeer underwear more than makes up for that."

"Agreed." She felt it was time to put all teasing aside and consider her son. Their son. "When do you think we should tell Danny that you're his father?"

"We should probably ask the counselor her advice about that. In the meantime, I want you and Danny to move in with me."

This was all happening so fast, it made her head spin. "And leave my lovely abode with the questionable plumbing and dilapidated roof? Of course, you never did install that shower. Do you know what it's like to lower yourself into a tub with only one arm?"

The sexy devil shone through his dark eyes. "Believe me, babe, when you're at my house, I'll be glad to help you bathe."

She had another serious consideration. "As much as I want to move in with you, I'm not sure that's a good idea right now. Some people around here still don't approve of cohabitation before marriage. Danny's been exposed to enough scandal already."

"Actually, I thought about that." He fished through his pocket, pulled out a gorgeous diamond solitaire and held it up. "I saw this in the window of the jewelry store next to the bank. I just walked right in and bought it."

The moment was so surreal. Unbelievable. Wonderful. "Is it for me, or were you going to give it to the lady at the information desk?"

He grinned. "It's for you." He moved into the chair beside her and lifted her left hand without moving her bum arm. "Jessica Keller, would you do me the honor of being my wife?"

A tear slid down her cheek, and the words she'd never thought she would have the chance to say, flowed out of her mouth with ease. "Yes, Deputy Reed, I will marry you."

He leaned over and kissed her like he meant it, without any regard to the people milling about the area. Finally, she could make others uncomfortable with a serious public display of affection.

"I've been thinking," Chase said after he broke the kiss. "It would be great to ring in the new year with a wedding."

Jess laughed. She couldn't help it.

And Chase clearly didn't see the humor in the situation. "What's so funny?"

"It's just that I've been proposed to twice in the span of six days, and both of you said almost the same thing."

Chase sent her sour look. "Who else proposed to you?"

"Dalton."

His features relaxed. "I'm glad you turned him down."

"So am I." She rested her bent elbow on the table and propped her cheek on her palm. "Now you were saying?"

"Let's get married on New Year's Day. I happen to know a man who has the power to get the marriage license rushed, as long as we go apply for it now."

"What man is that?"

"Edwin Wainwright."

She couldn't imagine what had transpired between Chase and her ex-father-in-law, but she didn't care, as long as it had brought the love of her life back to her. "I don't know, Chase. Today's Friday, and that means we only have two days to get ready. I have to call my parents to see if they can fly in. I have to find a dress and—"

He stopped her protests with another kiss. "You've always been a jumper first, and a thinker later. It's time for us both to jump."

A leap of faith worth taking. "Okay. But we do need to tell Danny together. And it might be nice to decide on a place to have the ceremony, although I have no idea where that would be."

He cracked a crooked grin. "I happen to know a man who can take care of that, too."

"DON'T YOU THINK IT'S kind of weird, getting married at your soon-to-be wife's ex-father-in-law's house?"

Chase glared at his best man, Sam McBriar. "Look who's talking," he muttered. "You're about to get married on an old bridge."

He returned his attention to the small crowd that had gathered for the hurry-up wedding, held in the Wainwright estate's massive living room. It had all come together without a hitch. Jess's parents were in the first row, still looking somewhat shell-shocked. His parents were on the opposite side, and seated behind them, Edwin Wainwright and his maid, Zelda. The woman had starting sobbing the minute the string quartet had begun to play.

Sam's fiancée, Savannah, serving as Jess's maid of honor, started down the makeshift aisle, and when she reached the flowered arch, she winked at her future husband. Jess had planned to include Rachel as an attendant, but she hadn't felt like coming downstairs for the wedding. And Matt had declined to be a groomsman if his wife couldn't take part in the ceremony. That was the only glitch they'd encountered so far. A disappointing glitch.

When the music began to build, and Jess appeared on Danny's arm, Chase found it pretty hard to breathe. She was dressed in an off-white gown, with matching sling, and held a bouquet of white flowers from the garden. She looked as beautiful as he'd ever seen her look, and in a matter of moments, he'd willingly agree to see only her for the rest of his life.

After she reached his side, Jess handed the bouquet to Savannah and took Chase's hand, while Danny stood by Sam.

"Friends and family," the justice of the peace began. "We're gathered here today to join this man and this woman in holy matrimony. And at their request, they'll take it from here."

Chase had felt a little self-conscious about reciting his own vows, until Jess had called him the night before and they composed them together. He cleared his throat and focused into Jess's eyes, the place where he'd always found strength. "Jess, I promise to be faithful to you and to trust you for the rest of my life. I promise to take care of you and Danny, and to make sure you always have a solid roof over your head, as well as an appropriate shower. And I'll never ask you to iron my shirts." He waited for the chuckles to die down before he continued. "I also promise to always be your best friend, and to give you a part of myself that I've never given to anyone else. My heart. I love you, babe, and I always will."

He noticed Jess's lips quivered a little, but she didn't

cry. Not yet. "Chase," she began, "I promise to be faithful to you for the rest of my life. To give you another child, but no more than three. And I will try to deliver the occasional back flip, as soon as I'm out of this blasted sling." The chuckles turned to laughter that quickly subsided as Jess continued. "I promise to hold you when bad dreams disturb your sleep, and to be completely honest with you from this day forward. I accept you for better or worse, knowing that our worst times have already passed. And as the day comes when I draw my last breath, your love will be the one true thing I take with me."

Chase realized she hadn't mentioned the last vow, but that made it all the sweeter.

They stood there smiling at each other, until the justice of the peace interrupted the moment with the exchanging of the rings. By the time the kiss came around, Chase was more than ready to seal the deal. And he did, maybe for a bit longer than some would deem appropriate. That was just too bad.

"Ladies and gentlemen," the JP announced, "I present to you Chase and Jessica Reed, and their son, Daniel."

Chase took Danny's left hand, Jess took his right, and they walked back down the aisle, this time as a real family. The family Chase never knew he wanted, until he met the son he never knew he had. And his life had finally come together through the love of one sassy, spontaneous and determined woman—his very best friend.

When the crowd began to gather to offer congratulations, Jess turned and smiled, then let go of Chase's hand. But that was okay with him, because he knew he wasn't really letting her go.

And he never would again.

* * * * *

HEART & HOME

Heartwarming romances where love can
happen right when you least expect it.

COMING NEXT MONTH
AVAILABLE DECEMBER 6, 2011

#1746 THE COST OF SILENCE
Hometown U.S.A.
Kathleen O'Brien

#1747 THE TEXAN'S CHRISTMAS
The Hardin Boys
Linda Warren

#1748 BECAUSE OF THE LIST
Make Me a Match
Amy Knupp

#1749 THE BABY TRUCE
Too Many Cooks?
Jeannie Watt

#1750 A SOUTHERN REUNION
Going Back
Lenora Worth

#1751 A DELIBERATE FATHER
Suddenly a Parent
Kate Kelly

You can find more information on upcoming Harlequin® titles,
free excerpts and more at www.HarlequinInsideRomance.com.

HSRCNM1111

REQUEST YOUR FREE BOOKS!
2 FREE NOVELS PLUS 2 FREE GIFTS!

♦ Harlequin®

Super Romance®

Exciting, emotional, unexpected!

YES! Please send me 2 FREE Harlequin® Superromance® novels and my 2 FREE gifts (gifts are worth about $10). After receiving them, if I don't wish to receive any more books, I can return the shipping statement marked "cancel." If I don't cancel, I will receive 6 brand-new novels every month and be billed just $4.69 per book in the U.S. or $5.24 per book in Canada. That's a saving of at least 15% off the cover price! It's quite a bargain! Shipping and handling is just 50¢ per book in the U.S. and 75¢ per book in Canada.* I understand that accepting the 2 free books and gifts places me under no obligation to buy anything. I can always return a shipment and cancel at any time. Even if I never buy another book, the two free books and gifts are mine to keep forever.

135/336 HDN FC6T

Name	(PLEASE PRINT)	
Address		Apt. #
City	State/Prov.	Zip/Postal Code

Signature (if under 18, a parent or guardian must sign)

Mail to the Reader Service:
IN U.S.A.: P.O. Box 1867, Buffalo, NY 14240-1867
IN CANADA: P.O. Box 609, Fort Erie, Ontario L2A 5X3

Not valid for current subscribers to Harlequin Superromance books.

**Are you a current subscriber to Harlequin Superromance books
and want to receive the larger-print edition?
Call 1-800-873-8635 or visit www.ReaderService.com.**

* Terms and prices subject to change without notice. Prices do not include applicable taxes. Sales tax applicable in N.Y. Canadian residents will be charged applicable taxes. Offer not valid in Quebec. This offer is limited to one order per household. All orders subject to credit approval. Credit or debit balances in a customer's account(s) may be offset by any other outstanding balance owed by or to the customer. Please allow 4 to 6 weeks for delivery. Offer available while quantities last.

Your Privacy—The Reader Service is committed to protecting your privacy. Our Privacy Policy is available online at www.ReaderService.com or upon request from the Reader Service.

We make a portion of our mailing list available to reputable third parties that offer products we believe may interest you. If you prefer that we not exchange your name with third parties, or if you wish to clarify or modify your communication preferences, please visit us at www.ReaderService.com/consumerschoice or write to us at Reader Service Preference Service, P.O. Box 9062, Buffalo, NY 14269. Include your complete name and address.

HSR11

Lucy Flemming and Ross Mitchell shared a magical,
sexy Christmas weekend together six years ago.
This Christmas, history may repeat itself when they find
themselves stranded in a major snowstorm...
and alone at last.

Read on for a sneak peek from
IT HAPPENED ONE CHRISTMAS
by Leslie Kelly.

Available December 2011, only from Harlequin® Blaze™.

EYEING THE GRAY, THICK SKY through the expansive wall of
windows, Lucy began to pack up her photography gear.
The Christmas party was winding down, only a dozen or so
people remaining on this floor, which had been transformed
from cubicles and meeting rooms to a holiday funland. She
smiled at those nearest to her, then, seeing the glances at her
silly elf hat, she reached up to tug it off her head.

Before she could do it, however, she heard a voice. A
deep, male voice—smooth and sexy, and so not Santa's.

"I appreciate you filling in on such short notice. I've
heard you do a terrific job."

Lucy didn't turn around, letting her brain process what
she was hearing. Her whole body had stiffened, the hairs on
the back of her neck standing up, her skin tightening into
tiny goose bumps. Because that voice sounded so familiar.
Impossibly familiar.

It can't be.

"It sounds like the kids had a great time."

Unable to stop herself, Lucy began to turn around,
wondering if her ears—and all her other senses—were
deceiving her. After all, six years was a long time, the mind

could play tricks. What were the odds that she'd bump into *him,* here? And today of all days. December 23.

Six years exactly. Was that really possible?

One look—and the accompanying frantic thudding of her heart—and she knew her ears and brain were working just fine. Because it was *him.*

"Oh, my God," he whispered, shocked, frozen, staring as thoroughly as she was. "Lucy?"

She nodded slowly, not taking her eyes off him, wondering why the years had made him even more attractive than ever. It didn't seem fair. Not when she'd spent the past six years thinking he must have started losing that thick, golden-brown hair, or added a spare tire to that trim, muscular form.

No.

The man was gorgeous. Truly, without-a-doubt, mouthwateringly handsome, every bit as hot as he'd been the first time she'd laid eyes on him. She'd been twenty-two, he one year older.

They'd shared an amazing holiday season.

And had never seen one another again.

Until now.

Find out what happens in
IT HAPPENED ONE CHRISTMAS
by Leslie Kelly.
Available December 2011, only from Harlequin® Blaze™

Copyright © 2011 by Leslie Kelly.

HBEXP1211

LAURA MARIE ALTOM

brings you
another touching tale from

When family tragedy forces Wyatt Buckhorn to pair up
with his longtime secret crush, Natalie Poole, and care
for the Buckhorn clan's seven children, Wyatt worries
he's in over his head. Fearing his shameful secret will
be exposed, Wyatt tries to fight his growing attraction
to Natalie. As Natalie begins to open up to Wyatt,
he starts yearning for a family of his own—a family
with Natalie. But can Wyatt trust his heart enough
to reveal his secret?

A Baby in His Stocking

Available December
wherever books are sold!

www.Harlequin.com

HAR75387

Harlequin® *Romance*

SUSAN MEIER

*Experience the thrill of falling in love
this holiday season with*

Kisses on Her Christmas List

When Shannon Raleigh saw Rory Wallace staring at her
across her family's department store, she knew he would
be trouble…for her heart. Guarded, but unable to fight
her attraction, Shannon is drawn to Rory and his inquisitive
daughter. Now with only seven days to convince this
straitlaced businessman that what they feel for each other
is real, Shannon hopes for a Christmas miracle.

**Will the magic of Christmas be enough
to melt his heart?**

Available December 6, 2011.

Snowflake Bride

JILLIAN HART

Grateful when she is hired as a maid, Ruby Ballard vows to use her wages
to save her family's farm. But the boss's son, Lorenzo, is entranced by this
quiet beauty. He knows Ruby is the only woman he could marry, yet she
refuses his courtship. As the holidays approach, he is determined to win
her affections and make her his snowflake bride.

Available November 2011
wherever books are sold.

www.LoveInspiredBooks.com

LIH82891R